Previously published Worldwide titles by
WENDY ROBERTS

A GRAVE CALLING
A GRAVE SEARCH
A GRAVE PERIL
A GRAVE END

BURNING HOPE

WENDY ROBERTS

WORLDWIDE

TORONTO • NEW YORK • LONDON
AMSTERDAM • PARIS • SYDNEY • HAMBURG
STOCKHOLM • ATHENS • TOKYO • MILAN
MADRID • WARSAW • BUDAPEST • AUCKLAND

W(RLDWIDE™

ISBN-13: 978-1-335-45357-0

Burning Hope

First published in 2022 by Carina Press.
This edition published in 2022 with revised text.

Recycling programs for this product may not exist in your area.

Harlequin Enterprises ULC
22 Adelaide St. West, 41st Floor
Toronto, Ontario M5H 4E3, Canada
www.ReaderService.com

Printed in U.S.A.

BURNING HOPE

For my not so little ones.
You are my heart.

ONE

WHEN I PARKED my camper van at the dollar store where I worked, all I wanted was coffee. Murder wasn't on my mind.

It was predawn and my day off. Pincher's Dollarama wouldn't open for hours, but I arrived hoping to fill my to-go mug from the staff coffeepot in the storeroom. My plan was to get my caffeine, then hit the road and enjoy the day. My cupboards were bare, and my boss told me when I started that I could help myself to coffee whenever I pleased.

I didn't bother to turn on the lights, and yawned as I made my way down the dimly lit aisles. My foot connected with a box on the floor and I cursed loudly as I stumbled, nearly colliding with a pen display.

Then I entered the storeroom and flicked on the fluorescent lights. Immediately my nerves began to ping. Something wasn't right. The back door slapped against the frame, and a breeze cut through the room. I shifted my travel mug from one hand to the other just as a gust caught the door, swung it wide and then slammed it shut. I rolled my eyes.

"Dammit, Penny, I've been telling you to fix that door for weeks."

Papers swirled like autumn leaves around my feet as I made my way across the room to secure the door. I berated myself for my unease but there was something spooky about being alone in a store before the sun came up. The stockroom wasn't big but it was crammed. Half a dozen rows of floor-to-ceiling shelves with each ledge jammed tight with boxes. Even more containers were stacked on the floor so it was like walking through an obstacle course. I stepped over one box to get to that back door and, as I did, I was hit with the unmistakable coppery scent of blood.

I peered down the aisle to my right and saw my co-worker, Murray, facedown on the floor; his normally greasy snow-white hair was stained crimson. Fresh blood oozed from his wound and pooled on the floor around him.

A shocked whimper escaped my throat and I dropped my mug. It clattered to the floor and I snatched it up as I took a step back.

"This just happened," I murmured. "The blood isn't even dry yet."

I spun in a frantic pirouette, but I was alone.

Except for Murray.

My breath was coming in fast jagged breaths as I stared at my gruesome coworker. His hands were up and out to the side as if to break his fall. There was a yellow slip of paper in the creeping red pool next to his right hand. Murray's bulldog face was turned to the side and held a look of twisted surprise.

Once again, a gust of wind whacked the door against the frame with a loud crack, and my heart pounded against my ribs. My head said GO but my feet were frozen to the spot.

Suddenly I heard tires squealing on pavement. I ran to the rear door and stuck my head out. I stared up and down the alley but whoever had been there was gone.

My whole body trembled as I yanked the door closed and bolted it behind me.

The hair on the back of my neck stood up as I sprinted from the storeroom and out through the front of the store. Once outside I pressed myself into the shadows of the storefront and stifled a panicked scream as I fumbled for my phone. With sweaty hands I called the police. My words tumbled from my mouth in a frantic and urgent jumble that the operator had me repeat over and over again.

"A body! At Pincher's!" I cried.

Finally I was assured that police were being dispatched.

As I paced, waiting for the local law, I looked all the way up one side of Main Street and then down the other. The killer was out there. Whoever did this could be watching me right now. Suddenly I felt like an easy target.

I decided to wait inside my camper van parked only feet away. Hurriedly I climbed inside and locked the doors. I jammed the keys in the ignition and my foot itched to stomp the accelerator at the first sign of anyone other than cops, but the town was eerily quiet. It was still a couple hours before the dollar store was due to open. Even the town coffee shop, diner and grocery store were still dark. My hands were white knuckled as I clutched my empty coffee mug in two hands and waited.

"Where the hell is the marshal?" I muttered as I nervously cut my gaze left and right.

It was supposed to be my day off. My boss ordered me to take a rest day since I'd worked without a break for two weeks. But money was tight, I was low on groceries, and I wanted coffee. Now while the town of

Hope Harbor slept and dawn had yet to break, I'd stumbled on a murder.

Again.

It felt like an hour but was probably only a few minutes before Marshal Joel Cobb's car raced up beside my camper and screeched to a stop.

As the marshal approached my van, I rolled down my window and waved my hands frantically in the direction of the store entrance, shouting, "Someone killed Murray!"

He frowned and raised his eyebrows in a confused question, as if my words could have another meaning, but then he disappeared inside the store. I tapped my fingers impatiently on my dash, waiting for his return. When he came out, he removed his hat, dragged his hands through his short-cropped hair. His eyes were frantic even as he tried to appear all business.

"Stay put," he told me through my rolled-up window.

I nodded and watched him make a call. The marshal was probably in his early thirties, five foot ten, fit, and sported a neatly trimmed mustache. He usually had a toothpick bobbing in his mouth, but it was absent at the moment. Cobb was known to be friendly to most everyone in town, but he and I weren't exactly besties.

While he was on the phone I went further into my van and put my kettle on for tea, then used my washroom. I stared at my reflection in the mirror as I washed my hands. My hair was still uncombed and the jagged short layers of my red hair stuck out comically. I splashed cold water on my freckled face that looked even more pale than usual with the shock.

While my tea brewed, I ran a brush through my hair, aware of the bristles as they scratched at the long scar that snaked across my scalp beneath my shoulder-length hair. As I filled my travel mug with a tea bag and hot water, I glanced at the picture of my grandmother taped to the wall above the sink.

"It's another murder, Nan," I whispered. "Why does this keep happening to me?" Her gentle smile frozen forever in the photograph had no reply. I kissed the tip of a finger and pressed it to her face, then returned to the driver's seat to wait.

"You got this," I assured myself with a whisper of encouragement.

But still my hands shook, and my stomach churned as Marshal Cobb approached my window.

"Okay, Sheriff Duthroyd is on his way. Tell me everything, Red," he ordered. "And don't leave out a damn thing."

After a deep breath I described every detail. I told him that I unlocked the front door of Pincher's Dollarama and made my way to the back storage room that was also the store's office and staff room. I informed him the purpose of my visit was only to get some coffee to go and I held up my travel mug as if that proved it.

"Did you hear anything? See anything different when you walked in the front door?"

"No, but I hadn't turned on the lights in the storefront and I tripped on a box of school supplies in the aisle." I frowned. "That's probably what did it." I nodded and blew out a jagged breath. "The killer heard me make that sound and took off because—"

"Leave the investigating to me, okay. Just tell me facts."

"Fine. When I entered the storage room, the back door that opens onto the alley was slamming in the wind. The door frame has some rot and needs replacing. I mentioned that to Penny before, but she always just shrugged and said she'd tell Murray to put it on his list."

I rubbed the back of my neck. When my boss told me she'd get Murray to do it I thought at the time that the doughy old stock boy, who moved at the pace of a snail, would never get around to fixing anything. Now I realized that if Murray hadn't been so lazy, he might've saved his own life. "All I wanted was coffee."

I thought about the oozing hole in the back of Murray's head, and nausea washed over me.

"Go on," the marshal snapped.

I described what I saw: the papers scattered all over the floor and, otherwise, nothing unusual. Except poor dead Murray.

"The staff coffeepot and artificial creamer are in the back corner next to Penny's desk." I pinched the bridge of my nose and continued. "So many boxes around. School supplies, and now the Halloween decorations have arrived. The room is jammed so I didn't see him at first." I swallowed thickly. "When I rounded the corner and stepped over a box, well, that's when I saw him."

"Think carefully." Marshal Cobb wagged a finger at me. "Did you hear or see *anyone*? Did you look out the back door and check to see if anyone was running away from the scene?"

"I heard a car squealing away." I briefly closed my eyes before I added, "But when I looked outside, I didn't see anyone at all. They were gone."

"You're absolutely sure?" Cobb's eyes were hard marbles, and I could tell he was trying to look in charge as he took down everything I said, but this had to be way above his pay grade in this tiny town.

"I'm positive."

An hour later I was still sitting in my van but there was now crime scene tape across the door of Pincher's Dollarama, and Marshal Cobb was standing on the sidewalk talking to my boss, Penny. I sat frozen to my seat with a front row view as the small crowd of locals continued to grow. Wouldn't be long before all 534 residents of Hope Harbor were standing out front with eyes wide and mouths tsking and tittering. Previously the locals I encountered seemed polite and kind, but now I looked at each and every one of them like a person who could've shot Murray in the back of the head.

The sunrise had the onlookers casting long, ghoulish shadows. I trembled and retreated to the back of my van.

From my bed in the back, I could still view spectators between a part in the drapes. Whenever a new person joined the group, there was a collective turning of heads and nodding of chins in the direction of my van. My rear window was open slightly and I could hear snippets of conversation. The discussions were about poor Murray being killed and that odd new girl who lived in a van covered in bubble decals who found his body.

I had news for them. This odd new girl couldn't wait to burn rubber out of their creepy little town.

When I moved back up to the driver's seat I saw Penny standing in front of the store looking lost as the marshal talked to her. Abruptly she began sobbing and Marshal Cobb just turned away with his phone pressed to his ear. I couldn't stand to see my elderly boss in such distress, so I climbed out of the van and went to her. Penny pushed past the marshal and fell into my arms, pressing her rosy and puffy face against my shoulder.

"Oh, Red," she sobbed. "It's Murray! They say

he's dead. Shot in the back of the head." She lifted her tearstained face to look into mine. "Joel said you found him. Oh, no, poor you." She pressed against my shoulder again, shaking with renewed sobs.

Penny was in her midseventies with a soft round face and a head of gravity-defying teased and lacquered silver hair that added a few inches to her original five feet. I patted my boss's back and made "There, there" noises while I strained to look around her to watch the crowd for anyone suspicious. Suddenly a sheriff's department vehicle pulled up and the marshal fast walked toward it as the sheriff and two investigators climbed out.

Penny peeled herself off my shoulder to look and, as she stepped away, was surrounded by a gaggle of local women who took turns hugging her while trying to pry her for details. Information was currency in Hope Harbor and these women wanted to be supportive but also get any gruesome tidbits. I could hear Penny tell them that I'd been the one to find Murray.

Whenever one of the locals attempted to walk toward me, I held up a hand to stop them. I felt too sick about what I'd seen and wasn't participating in this next level gossip. My name would already be on the lips of everyone at all the stitch-and-bitch coffee klatches. I only wanted to give my statement and, hopefully, point my bubble van far away from Hope Harbor.

Marshal Cobb brought the investigators inside Pincher's. Before the door closed behind them, he narrowed his eyes at me and mouthed *Stay*. I couldn't help but sigh. I'd been in town less than a month and the marshal didn't like me or my van and treated us like a blight on his picturesque town.

It wasn't long before Cobb was back on the sidewalk, leaving the investigators inside the store.

"Who could've done such a thing?" Penny asked the dozens of onlookers. She pulled a wad of tissue from her ample cleavage and blew her nose.

"Let's get someone to give you a ride home, Penny." Marshal Cobb put a gentle hand on her arm. "You don't need to stick around. Go home and rest and I'll be in touch later."

"I'll give you a ride," I offered Penny. "You're too upset to be driving yourself. One of the others here can take your car back to your place."

"No, you need to talk to the sheriff next." Cobb pulled a toothpick from his pocket and wagged it in my direction before putting it in his mouth. "Someone else can drive her."

Half a dozen ladies wrangled for the privilege of driving Penny home, and once that was settled Cobb told the remaining crowd they needed to get off the street and let the police do their work.

"Go home. Or go to work." He made shooing motions with his hands. "Let the police do our jobs."

After a bit of hesitancy, most of the crowd dispersed. The diner and coffee shop were now open down the road. Some groups went together to huddle over their mugs and still keep an eye on Main Street. Others only moved to the other side of the street, and some locals defied the marshal entirely by only taking a couple steps backward. I told the marshal I'd be in my van until I was needed.

"Fine. But don't you even think of putting your key in the ignition," he warned.

"I won't," I protested and hated that those words slid out with a tiny bit of a whine.

Inside, I made myself another cup of tea just to keep my hands busy. Once seated at my small kitchen table, I could watch things unfold in front of Pincher's Dollarama. The medical examiner showed up from a neighboring, much larger town. The few remaining chatty townsfolk grew so quiet you could hear the wheels of the gurney on the pavement. A lump formed in my throat a few minutes later when the body bag got wheeled out.

Eventually Marshal Cobb came knocking with another man at his side. I opened the sliding door and allowed them inside. The investigator introduced himself as Sheriff Duthroyd. He had a stocky build, was in his fifties with deep grooves around his pale blue eyes that seemed to say he'd seen worse than a dead guy in a dollar store.

"You're Scarlet Hooper, is that right?"

I nodded. "People just call me Red."

"Okay. Red." He smiled kindly.

The sliding door to the van remained open, and the crowd that had crossed to the other side of the street now inched closer and did not hide their curiosity. Some brazenly stepped forward toward my door, hoping to hear what was said.

"We need you to tell us everything from the beginning," Cobb announced with a puff of his chest.

Sheriff Duthroyd shot him a warning glance and Cobb's mouth snapped shut into a tight, thin line. He stepped around the table and lowered himself onto the passenger seat of the van while Duthroyd took the seat at the table across from me. It was obviously time to let the big boy handle things and I could tell Cobb didn't like that one bit.

"There's not much for me to tell." I cleared my throat and gave a nervous shrug. "I just found him there." My voice shook as I added, "There was lots of blood and I knew…" This was not my first time seeing a body, but it never got easier. I swallowed thickly. "He was dead and it looked like it had just happened."

"I talked to the owner of the store and she mentioned you weren't expected to work today."

"I, um…" I felt color creep up from my T-shirt and flood my face. "I came in to use the coffee maker. I was out of coffee and—" I hastily added, "Penny doesn't mind. She told me I could help myself whenever I wanted so I was just going to make some coffee and take it to go." I lifted my travel mug that was filled with tea.

"Okay." The sheriff smiled sympathetically. "Describe the scene to me."

I told him everything I saw and he interrupted to ask questions along the way.

"The back door was open? Did you hear footsteps leaving?"

I shook my head but told him about the sound of screeching tires on pavement.

"Do you think someone broke into the store through that back door?"

"Well, the door frame is rotten and it needs a good shove to close properly, so it could've been left open by Murray, or even Penny…"

"Or you?"

"No." I shook my head. "I never use the back door and I always make sure it's locked before I close up."

"Okay, and did you notice anything strange? Was anything amiss?"

"No, except there were papers blowing everywhere. The back door let the wind inside so all the papers on Penny's desk were scattered around." I put a hand to my forehead. I felt feverish and sick to my stomach. "A yellow piece of paper was under Murray's hand."

Sheriff Duthroyd looked at Marshal Cobb. "Was that put in evidence?"

Marshal Cobb shrugged. "Yes. There were a lot of papers around the body, like she said, probably blown off Penny's desk. Any of them around the body or with blood were labeled as evidence."

"Good." Sheriff Duthroyd turned back to me. "Let's start with how long you've been working at Pincher's Dollarama?"

"About a month. Penny offered me a job shortly after I came to town."

A crack of thunder caused me to flinch. It began to rain, and the clutch of locals giving me the hairy eyeball from a few feet away still did not make any motion to leave.

"Could we close the door?"

Duthroyd reached for the handle and slammed the door shut. Bubbles shook with the force, and a tense sudden quiet settled over us like a damp blanket.

"So you've lived and worked in Hope Harbor a month?"

"She just rolled up one day in her bubble mobile," Cobb added with a snort of derision that made me want to punch him in the throat.

"You live in the van?" Duthroyd waved a hand to encompass our surroundings. "Cozy."

He glanced around and my gaze cut to the pile of dirty clothes on my bed in the back. Poised on the top of the pile was a pink thong. I blushed.

"I was planning to go to the laundromat today since I had the day off." I drummed my fingers on the table. "Can I get you tea? I'm out of coffee and I don't have milk because my fridge isn't working but I have sugar somewhere and—"

"I'm fine." He nodded to my kitchen area. "Huh. No propane stove?"

I knew he was just trying to make small talk to put me at ease, but that casual observation caused my stomach to tighten.

"The van was my grandmother's before she passed. She preferred an induction cooktop instead of gas." I tried, and failed, to keep my tone even. There was a hitch in my voice at the end which, thankfully, the sheriff took for my emotion regarding my grandmother's passing.

"Sorry for your loss."

He pulled out a notebook from his pocket and flipped to a fresh page. His voice was as calm as a gentle breeze. "Could we start with your full name and date of birth?"

"Scarlet Joan Hooper. September 16, 1993." I laced my fingers on the table in front of me.

"Happy birthday in a few days."

"Thanks."

"I need to get some background information about you since you were the person who found the body." He smiled. "Have you made a lot of friends since you've been here?"

"Um… I've just been working and keeping to myself. Lots of people come into the store so, sure, I get to know people. Hope Harbor has a population of five hundred thirty-four people so I'm pretty sure that when I added my name to the ranks everything about me spread far and wide before Marshal Cobb here could even issue my first ticket."

"You've had a few of those, haven't you?" Cobb chuckled from the front seat, and I scowled in his direction as he used his toothpick to clean under his fingernails and then stuffed it back between his lips.

"Not my fault," I grumped.

The town of Hope Harbor didn't allow overnight camping within city limits, and it had taken me some expensive tickets before I learned exactly where those limits were. Marshal Cobb seemed to get a kick out of tracking me down to give me a citation.

Duthroyd stated, "This is the first murder this town has seen in twenty years."

"Did they catch that first murderer? Maybe this is a serial killer who likes to wait a couple decades between." I said it as a dumb joke but Duthroyd looked at me flatly.

"It was one of my first cases and long before Marshal Cobb's day, but twenty years ago Mr. Daily tossed his wife in the wood chipper. He confessed and died in prison a few years ago. Tell me more about yourself and your reason for coming to Hope Harbor."

Jesus, a wood chipper? My stomach soured.

"I've been on the road living in my camper van since my nan died." I cleared my throat. "I started having vehicle troubles…battery and the fridge…and when I arrived in Hope Harbor I thought it would be good to work awhile to save up the money I needed. Pincher's had a Help Wanted sign in the window." I shrugged.

Eventually someone might run my name and see

that this wasn't the first murder associated with Scarlet Hooper. Fingers crossed I'd be long gone by then.

"I guess your official address is…" He glanced around the van. "Wherever you park it?"

"Basically." I hooked my thumb to indicate north. "Farmer Miller is letting me park on his property."

"And where were you parking before Hope Harbor?"

I tap-tapped my fingers quicker on the table between us and gave him the names of a few other towns I'd resided in the last year; listing them quickly and casually as if the exact names had no connection to me. Or dead people. Making sure to include the names of towns where a quick Google search would trace back to me anyway. I intentionally left out a few areas where I anonymously helped an investigation and slipped away in the night.

"After Nan passed, I just went on the road. Camping in parks mostly, then coming into a town and working as a dishwasher or store clerk when I needed money."

And trying to figure out the frightening and bewildering visions I'd begun to have that were triggered by fire. Attempting to make the fire-seeing talent work for me instead of against me.

"So you've been here, there and everywhere." The sheriff smiled as he added, "The store doesn't open until ten but you showed up before dawn on your day off just to get a cup of coffee?"

"My van sometimes is finicky about starting. Like I said, it needs some work. Farmer Miller happened to be going past me real early, and I got him to give me a boost. I thought I might as well drive straight into town then." I cleared my throat and admitted shyly, "Plus, I didn't want to be in Penny's way when she opened at ten. Honestly, she doesn't mind if I help myself to as much coffee as I want. She told me so herself."

"So you have keys for the store and you've opened for her before?"

"Yes." I nodded and the sheriff scratched that down in his notepad. "Penny doesn't come in to work every day, and a lot of people have keys to the store. There seems to be a pretty relaxed type of security around here."

"Is that so?"

"Sometimes when I open in the morning, there'll be a few bucks on the counter and a note from the lady who runs the diner or Noah from the hardware store or God knows who else." I nibbled a cuticle. "They just help themselves to what they need and leave a note and a few bucks on the counter."

The sheriff glanced over at Marshal Cobb, who smiled and nodded.

"Small-town living. People trust each other." He frowned. "I guess until now."

"Also, even if people don't have keys, that back door lock is wiggly."

"Yes, you mentioned the door." The sheriff's eyebrows went up in question. "So if it wasn't closed quite right, anyone could've just pushed that back door open?"

I nodded and he wrote a couple more lines.

"How well did you know the victim?"

"As a person, I didn't really know him at all." I shrugged. "He'd pick up supplies for Penny, do repairs and stock shelves in the store a few days a week. Yesterday he replaced one of the fluorescent light bulbs that burned out. We didn't associate at all beyond work."

But I knew Murray well enough to despise the very sight of him.

"Marshal Cobb tells me that Murray had a reputation around town for being a little handsy with the ladies," the sheriff mentioned coolly, his gaze leveling mine. "He ever place his hands on you?"

"No."

"You sure? Not a pat on the rump, or an unwanted breast grab?"

Murray was a slovenly older guy who wore his jeans below his beer gut and his thinning hair slicked back. I thought about the time he came up behind the cash counter, put his hands on my hips and proceeded to grind himself up against me. It wasn't the first time, but it was the last. Lightning quick I'd grabbed a letter opener from the drawer under the register and pressed it to his cheekbone, saying, "Ever do that again and I'll pluck your eyeballs from your head and make you eat them. Got it?"

Murray seemed to take my threat seriously because he learned not to mess with the new girl in town. Due to the fact that I'd threatened him, there was no way I was sharing this tidbit with the sheriff or Marshal Cobb.

"Never." I looked him in the eyes as I said it and folded my arms across my chest.

He wrote that down and then underlined it.

I didn't want to be the main suspect just because I found the body, so I raked my thoughts to find something good to say about Murray. "I know he had a reputation for being a little grabby but when I think of Murray I smile thinking of the times there were little kids in the store and he'd make them laugh by making goofy faces or telling silly jokes." I smiled. "Someone that good with kids has to have a kind heart."

It was a bit of a stretch, but the sheriff nodded as if he bought it even if the marshal looked skeptical. The next question was whether I'd seen anyone or anything unusual around the store.

"No. Same people come in day in and day out. Nothing strange."

"Was it unusual for Murray to be at work late at night or early in the morning?" His pen was poised over his notepad as he added, "It looks like he was only dead a very short while before you found him so that meant he was here even earlier than you. That's an odd time to work, isn't it?"

My heart thudded painfully against my chest. "I—I'd have no way of knowing if he had a habit of working really late or super early. If he came in the store when I wasn't here, how'd I know?" Then I thought about it. "But, sure, sometimes I'd come into work in the morning and there'd be new stock on the shelves or new boxes in the storeroom, and that would be Murray because Penny only pops in an hour here and there and she doesn't do any of the heavy lifting."

"Where were you last night?" The sheriff had an easy smile on his face as if we were talking about the weather and not my alibi.

"Up until nine o'clock I was parked behind the diner using their Wi-Fi to watch a movie," I admitted. "After that I was stopped for the night in Farmer Miller's field right up until he gave me a boost this morning." It wasn't much of an alibi and we both knew it.

"Do you own a gun, Red?"

"No." The lie tripped easily off my tongue and I resisted the urge to glance at the location where I kept it hidden.

"Grab me a GSR kit," Duthroyd told Cobb.

Marshal Cobb hopped out of the van to grab the gunshot residue kit and returned a minute later.

"Just standard procedure," Duthroyd said as he opened the kit and retrieved the two dabbers labeled left and right hand.

"I know," I replied and then added quickly, "I know you have to be sure I didn't fire a gun."

"Have you washed your hands since you found the body?" Duthroyd asked as he used one sticky dabber and pressed it to my right hand and then did the same with my left.

"Um." I cringed. "I used my bathroom and so, yeah, I washed my hands."

"Of course you did," Cobb retorted sarcastically. "Conveniently washing away evidence!"

"Now, Marshal, we can't blame a girl for needing to pee," Duthroyd said with an easy smile but then slowly added, "When you said 'I know' about the GSR test, is that because you've had this done before?" He placed the dabbers back in the evidence envelope and pressed a sticky dabber to the cuff of my long-sleeve T-shirt and wrote my name on it.

"I just watch a lot of crime shows." I let out a forced laugh.

"Everyone's a crime scene expert these days," he chuckled in return. "Do we have your permission to search your, um, home?" He waved a hand to indicate all of Bubbles.

With a dry swallow I gave a quick nod and waited outside. While I heard the cupboards in my van open and close I stood staring at my feet while the locals stared at me. Fat droplets of rain ran down the back of my neck and chilled my spine. I was wondering how I was going to explain the gun I had tucked next to my mattress. The gun I'd just told them I didn't own.

It wasn't long before Duthroyd slid the van door open and invited me back inside. As I slid the door closed behind me I glanced around but didn't see my gun. They'd gone through the pile of my dirty laundry and lifted up a front corner of my mattress, which still sat cockeyed. Could they actually have missed it? A warm flood of relief spread through my gut.

The sheriff asked for my cell phone number. As he wrote it down, he told me he'd be checking with Farmer Miller to confirm what I'd told him about giving me a boost this morning and whether or not I was parked on his land all night. I didn't even think Miller could see my van from his farmhouse, but I didn't add that. He flipped his notebook shut.

"Marshal Cobb will be the primary on this case," the sheriff said, giving a nod to the marshal, who straightened proudly. "I have a big case I'm working on in another town, but he'll keep me up to speed." With that, the sheriff tossed his business card on my table.

Cobb rooted through his own pockets, pulled out a card and did the same. "If you remember anything else that could help be sure you let one of us know."

"Oh, and we're obligated to tell you not to leave town," Duthroyd said. "You'll need to stay in Hope Harbor until this is sorted."

Cobb nodded in agreement, the toothpick in his mouth bobbing to the side as he spoke. "Yup, no leaving town until the killer is locked up."

"There's a problem with that because town ordinance says I can't park Bubbles in town overnight, so I have to leave town every night. I park at Farmer Miller's field, outside town limits, so that Marshal Cobb won't ticket me."

"Just stay in the vicinity then, okay?" Cobb said, rolling his eyes.

Sheriff Duthroyd put his hand on the door to the van and then turned with a smile. "What's with the bubbles? Your grandmother buy this thing off a clown or something?"

Even though it was a lighthearted question, it still stung.

"My nan loved bubbles. Thought they were whimsical and fun so we put the decals on the van and she christened the thing Bubbles. She left it to me in her will, and I just don't feel right about changing it."

He gave a slow nod. "Again, I'm sorry for your loss." He seemed to think about it and then asked, "Also, out of curiosity, is there a reason why the nails on your right hand are a different color from the ones on your left?"

"Well…" I glanced at my hands as if only noticing now that five fingers were painted bright pink and the others were blue. "I didn't have enough of one color to do them all. I'm trying to quit biting my nails and I thought painting them might help."

"Is it working?"

I drew my thumb from my mouth where I was already nibbling on the corner of a nail.

"No," I admitted.

When he pulled the door to the van open, we found the rain had stopped and the crowd outside had grown. People were crowded in the road and sidewalk discussing the excitement of the first murder in town in twenty years. Sheriff Duthroyd and Marshal Cobb hopped out of my van. The crowd parted for the sheriff as he made his way back to his vehicle but then closed in again, staring blatantly at Cobb who just stood in front of my open door scowling and looking unsure about what he should do next.

Noah Adams, who ran the hardware store down the street, was standing only a few feet away with an unlit cigarette dangling from his lips. I watched as he pulled a chrome Zippo lighter from his pocket. My heart began to pound in anticipation and, in one smooth motion, he flipped the hinged lid of the lighter open and slid his thumb downward against the metal wheel to bring the wick to blaze. Part of me wanted to look away, but it was too late. My gaze was locked onto the amber flame and I could feel the heat as if it was held an inch from my face instead of a couple yards away.

My fingers went to the large scar on my scalp hidden by my hair and pressed it as if doing so would keep thoughts away. A sudden breeze kicked up, and it took a while for Noah to encourage his cigarette to catch. The small fire lasted only a few seconds while the end of Noah's smoke became a bright cherry.

In a distant memory I heard the tinkle of wind chimes and smelled the heavy scent of something burning within me. Someone called my name and, abruptly, I was back from my trance.

"Are you okay?" Cobb asked, with a tilt of his head. "You look like you're going to be sick."

I squeezed my eyes shut, steadied myself with a grip on the door frame, and gave my head a quick shake.

Then I cleared my throat and announced, "Marshal

Cobb, you need to speak to Noah Adams." My hand quivered as I pointed a finger in Noah's direction. "He hated Murray and he's really glad he's dead."

My voice was much louder than I intended. Noah's gray eyes pierced mine and his lips turned down in a scowl. He, along with most of the crowd, heard my accusation. I slid my door shut, hopped into the driver's seat and backed out of my spot, leaving Marshal Cobb, Noah Adams and dozens of townies staring after me with judgment in their eyes.

TWO

I DIDN'T END up doing my laundry. If I had to stay near town that would've meant using the local laundromat that doubled as the coffee shop and bakery. I would've had to spend a couple hours under the disapproving scrutiny of people attempting to appear nonchalant as they slid glances my way, whispering to each other about the first murder in twenty years happening once the new girl showed up. I knew I was a suspect. In a town this size nobody wanted to believe someone they'd known all their life was a murderer. It was much easier to think the girl in a clown car was a killer.

Between town and Farmer Miller's field there was a highway rest stop. I visited there to use the sani dump and refill Bubbles's fresh water tank. And to check on my gun, which had slid under the farthest corner of my mattress and been pinned between the frame of the bed and the van walls, most likely when they'd tossed my dirty clothes into the rear corner and flipped up the front of the mattress. I wrapped it in a T-shirt and slid it back into the cubby next to the bed with a relieved sigh.

I really wanted to stomp the accelerator and launch my camper van down I-5 as far away from this tiny ocean town in the Pacific Northwest as possible. Maybe I could get to Mexico before they even noticed I was gone. And maybe I'd end up caught and cooling my

heels in a jail cell instead of in my van. Guess I was
stuck in Hope Harbor until they identified the killer.

Thinking of Murray brought to mind the sight of him
sprawled on the storeroom floor, his white hair painted
a gruesome red. I didn't like the guy, but he didn't deserve to be shot in the back of the head. Nobody did.
My stomach turned.

"Looks like I've got myself into another mess, Nan."
My dead grandmother did not reply but I could visualize
her kind smile and almost feel her arms wrap around me
in a comforting hug. I missed her like a phantom limb.

With a sigh I headed back to my camping spot and
backed Bubbles onto the gravel pad that Farmer Miller
used to access his fields. The last of his raspberries had
been harvested months ago, and my white van with the
pink and purple bubble decals stuck out like a neon sign
that said Weirdo Inside.

The marshal did a slow drive by my van to check
that I was where I needed to be. I offered him a wave
that he didn't return. He wasn't the only one who took
it upon themselves to drive by. A gaggle of teens in the
back of a silver truck tossed empty beer cans in my direction, littering the nearby ditch. I went for my phone
to take their picture and they screamed "Murderer!" as
they left a patch of rubber on the pavement and then
laughed as they peeled away.

This town had gone from being my charming escape
to feeling like a sinister prison.

The hours dragged by slowly without the benefit of
the dollar store job I desperately needed. I was painfully aware of the diminishing data on my phone plan,
so I rearranged my cupboards and swept out my tiny
floor space. For dinner I feasted on grilled cheese sand-

wiches. Life in a camper van was simple and I liked it that way. But I didn't enjoy the way my life in the last couple years seemed to attract murder.

The photo I had of my nan was taken on the day we took Bubbles out on the road for the first time. She was wearing her huge sunglasses with the pink frames and a floppy straw hat and was blowing bubbles through a soapy wand to commemorate our journey.

"Damn, I miss you." I choked back tears and touched the picture tenderly.

When the sun slid down the horizon, I dug out an old favorite paperback and a bottle of wine. I was into my third glass when I heard the sound of a car slowing and then parking on the gravel shoulder a few feet away.

Earlier I'd drawn the drapes around my windows and locked my doors but now I hit the button on my key fob that armed the alarm and turned out the single light I was using to read. I peered out between my drapes at a dark pickup. I silently prayed the teens from earlier hadn't returned full of booze and false courage.

My heart pounded against my ribs when I saw hardware store guy, Noah Adams, hop out of his truck. Even in the dim evening light I could see the firm set to his jaw. His purposeful stride did not look like he was paying a friendly social call.

"Shit."

He rapped his knuckles three times on my sliding door, and I sat there frozen to my seat.

"I know you're in there, Red!" Noah shouted and punctuated his voice with a couple more knocks. "Just want to talk to you about what you said to Joel about me hating Murray."

I held my breath and listened to the sound of his

boots crunching on the gravel outside my door. He marched back and forth and cursed under his breath.

"I would've called, but I don't have your number," he shouted at my van, his tone irritated. Then he lowered his voice. "Look, we can have this conversation through the door if we have to."

"Go away or I'm calling the cops!"

"Jesus, I just want to talk!"

But his voice held a level of heat that said the conversation might result in him ripping my door off its hinges and punching me in the face.

My gaze skipped to the cubby between my mattress and the wall where I stashed Nan's old gun. She bought it for our protection on the road and made sure I knew how to use it. I started to walk to the back of the van and snagged my phone from my pocket, preparing to call 9-1-1.

Just then I heard another vehicle pull up outside. I chanced another look and a whoosh of relief left my lungs when I saw it was Marshal Joel Cobb.

Noah met him on the road and they exchanged a few words before Noah stormed back to his truck. A moment later the pickup revved to life, made a U-turn and headed back toward Hope Harbor.

"Hey, Red, open up," Marshal Cobb said.

"How did you know he was here? I was just about to call 9-1-1." I slid the side door open wide.

"Coincidence. I was coming by to chat with you."

"Oh." I shooed a swarm of bugs away from the gaping door. "I guess you'd better come in before every mosquito in the county does."

The marshal took a seat at my dinette and, after I

slammed the door shut, I picked up my flyswatter and took out a couple of sneaky pests.

"Told you and the sheriff everything I knew earlier." I poised my weapon over a mosquito on the kitchen table. *Thwack!*

"Gotcha, you vampire bastard," I hissed triumphantly, then took a seat opposite Cobb. "You should know some of the town's teens have been driving by and harassing me."

He frowned. "In what way?"

"Screaming at me. Throwing beer cans at my van. It was a silver pickup."

He nodded. "Sounds like the Johnson boys. They're pretty harmless."

"That's how you handle harassment? With a boys-will-be-boys attitude?" I glowered.

"I'll pay them a visit."

"Okay. What else do you need?"

His voice was low and gruff. "Sheriff Duthroyd sent me a file. It's time you told me about Aberdeen and Seattle."

The names of two places where I'd also been embroiled in murder cases slid between his lips and dropped on the table between us.

The flyswatter slipped from my hand onto the floor and, suddenly, the three glasses of wine I had earlier swirled in my head. I drew in a steadying breath before I answered.

There was no way this was going to end well.

"I don't know what to say." That was the honest truth.

"Well, Red, how about you start by filling me in on how a twenty-eight-year-old transient girl has murder follow her everywhere?" He wagged a finger so close to my face, I had to resist the urge to bite it off. Then he folded his arms across his chest and leveled me with a hard stare.

"Look, I have done nothing wrong. Not here. Not in Seattle. Not in Aberdeen." I clutched my hands together on the table between us and straightened my spine. "Just a few coincidences. That's all."

"I don't believe that." He rolled his eyes. "There's something you're not telling me."

There was a lot I wasn't going to tell him.

"There's nothing to tell," I lied with a shrug and forced a casual nonplussed look on my face.

"Then I'll be the one to talk and you can fill in the blanks. You were just twelve when you were in a wreck and your mom died and your grandmother took you in." His voice softened as he added, "Sorry for your loss."

Just the mention of the car wreck was a blow to my sternum that caused me to suck in air through my teeth, but the marshal just cleared his throat and plowed on through.

"You began having headaches when you were twenty and had to drop out of college. Turned out to be some rare brain tumor that required surgery. Took you a few years to get back on your feet but then your grandmother had cancer so it was your turn to be the caregiver. When she found out the cancer had returned, she sold her thrift store and the two of you bought this van and hit the road. She died, what? Two or three years ago now? Again—" he leaned in and gently said, "my sympathies."

"Thank you." My gaze skipped over to the picture of Nan and then back to him.

He rubbed his neck and leaned back in his seat. His

lips twisted into an amused grin. "And this is where things get weird because, according to my source, you have some kind of psychic talent. Apparently you can—" he drew air quotes "—see things."

There is only one person who could've given him any of that information and it turned my gaze to steel.

"I don't know how you found her, but it sounds like you've been talking to Brandy." I narrowed my eyes. "She is not the world's most reliable source about anything and especially not me." I punctuated the last word by thumping my chest.

"She said she did a long stint in rehab since she last saw you. Honestly, she sounded pretty clearheaded."

"Well..." My voice faltered. I didn't know Brandy had gone to rehab. Last time I saw her she was frantically going through our dead grandmother's storage unit trying to get her hands on anything she could hock for a fix. I told her I never wanted to see or hear from her again. The guilt of that still stung. I knew it was an illness, not a choice. Still, her actions had made it necessary for me to walk away. "No matter what she told you, my sister and I aren't exactly on good terms. The only thing she's an expert on is heroin and how to use it to destroy everyone around her." I drummed my fingers on the table. "Also, she loves nothing more than to spin a good story and it sounds like she sold you a whopper."

"Are you telling me it's all lies? Not that I believe in psychic weird stuff. It's a bunch of bs, as far as I'm concerned." He guffawed and then tilted his head and regarded me coolly. "But you should know I've got calls in to the detectives who handled those other murders... the one in Seattle and the one in Aberdeen. One way or another, I'm getting the truth."

I blew out a long breath between my lips and it came out like a childish raspberry.

"I'm not psychic." I forced a laugh. "I just happened to be in the wrong place at the wrong time in Seattle and Aberdeen, and you can ask around all you want. That's all they'll tell you. Sure, I was able to give the police some information that happened to be helpful." My fingers went to the long scar under my hair and then I quickly readjusted my posture. "Honestly, Marshal, I wish you luck on finding whoever killed Murray. And, like I said before, maybe you should have a chat with Noah Adams about that because looking at me is a waste of time and Noah, well, you saw how pissed off he was..." I waved my hand in the direction of the road. "If he'd gotten his hands on me, maybe you'd even have another murder on your hands!"

I got to my feet and took two steps to the door, but the marshal did not take the hint and get to his feet.

"I've known Noah Adams my whole life. I've never seen him hurt a fly."

I retrieved my flyswatter from the floor and punished another pesky mosquito. "Well, some of us aren't partial to flies."

"Last night Noah was visiting his dad in his care home in Bellingham like he does a couple evenings a week."

"All night?" I challenged.

"No," he conceded.

"Also, didn't the sheriff say that Murray was probably killed real soon before I found him? Like this morning? I mean the blood was still pulsing from his frigg'n' head when I found him and—" I squeezed my eyes shut and swallowed the sour taste in my mouth. "Who's to say Noah Adams didn't just head back to his hardware store after taking out Murray just before I arrived?" I shook my head. "I don't mean to tell you how to do your job, but you need to check security cameras and find out who was skulking around Pincher's before dawn."

"This is Hope Harbor. We have one gas station, a coffee shop, a diner, a hardware store, a grocery store and Pincher's. Not a single one of those has a security camera. People here don't even lock their doors at night."

"Well, maybe they'd better start because there's a killer on the loose." I put my palms up in front of him. "Obviously, I'm not the powerful psychic my sister portrayed to you. Just an ordinary gal, living out of her van and working at a dollar store."

He harrumphed and got to his feet. "You found the body." He folded his arms and then lowered his voice to an angry whisper. "And you washed evidence off your hands before we could test for GSR."

"There was nothing to wash off." I spoke to him between clenched teeth.

"Don't be leaving town," he said seriously.

"Technically I'm already outside of town." I smirked. "We both are."

"You know what I mean!" he roared.

I flinched at his anger. "Kind of hard to hide when your house is a camper van with bubble decals."

His lips flickered into a smile before his face turned to stone.

When he left, I vented my frustrations on another bug. I knew that he was going to speak to the cops in Aberdeen and Seattle. He wasn't going to find out anything about my so-called talent, but he would still be suspicious. Most people go their entire lives without having their names tied to a murder. I'd chalked up half a dozen in a couple years. All I wanted to do was burn rubber out of this piss-pot town but now I was stuck here. There'd be no getting free of Hope Harbor until the murder was solved.

At the back of the cupboard where I kept my towels was a three-wick candle. It was in a large glass jar of creamy soy wax that smelled of vanilla. With a house on wheels there's always the danger that things are going to slam around in the cupboards so all my dishes and glasses were plastic. Almost nothing I owned was glass, except for this candle.

Grabbing my barbecue lighter and candle, I got comfortable at my table before lighting the three wicks. Unfortunately, divination was hit or miss for me. Even when I got clues like Noah Adams hated Murray, they were often obscure details and, sadly, never a blinking neon sign that said So-and-So Is the Killer.

It may not be a perfect science, but I first realized fire scrying was a thing after Nan passed. I guessed that removal of my brain tumor had something to do with it. All I knew was that if seeing visions in fire was my new normal, I was determined to make it work for me.

Cracking my neck and rolling my shoulders I settled in my seat. After a deep breath that I exhaled slowly, I looked into the flames; not directly at the fire, but more through it. I tried to relax my thoughts and draw in slow, even breaths.

The first thing that came to my mind was, once again, that Noah Adams hated Murray. However, that feeling dissipated and was replaced with a close-up image of a mass of bright blond hair. The vision morphed from the curly blond hair to Murray's silvery locks matted with blood, and then returned to thick golden curls. I tried to think of who in town had curly blond hair. Closing my eyes tight and then again gazing into the flames, I tried to hit reset on that image but, repeatedly, what came before me was a vivid mass of light-colored locks.

My head began to ache and then a numbing tingle traveled along my scalp, itching across the long scar and down my neck. I gave up, blew out the candle, and exhaled as the sound of distant wind chimes and a burning scent wafted through me.

"So frustrating," I grumped.

The candle needed to cool before I put it away. I left it on the counter and grabbed the wine. I decided I needed the rest of the bottle while I thought through this horrible day. Abruptly the wind picked up and rocked the van with an enraged force.

When I crawled under my covers that night, I tried to block out images of Murray's shattered skull and the threatening hard eyes of Noah Adams. I opened the drapes and peered out into the ebony night. A lightning bolt cracked the sky and lit up the muddy rows in the fields around me. The bare bushes of this year's raspberry crop shuddered in the wind and rattled their branches like sabers.

For the first time since I'd been traveling on my own, I didn't feel safe.

I WOKE UP the next morning with the sun angled through the edges of the curtains and stabbing me in the eyes. Struggling upright, I snagged my sunglasses from the counter and tore open my sliding door to get some fresh air into the van. In robotic fashion, I filled my kettle and cursed the fact that it would be another morning of tea instead of coffee. That made me think of Murray and his head oozing from a bullet hole. I moaned as that terrifying reality washed over me again.

I assumed that Pincher's Dollarama would be closed after what happened yesterday. But I should really check on Penny. I snagged my phone and punched in my boss's number. If I couldn't work at the dollar store today, maybe she needed me to do something else to help out. My call went to voicemail so I tried the store.

"You've reached Pincher's Dollarama, we're gonna be closed for a few days." Penny's voice broke a little before the message continued, *"This machine does not take messages."*

After my tea was made, I poured it into a travel mug and crossed my fingers when I put my key in the ignition. It took a couple of tries and I was cursing the battery and my depleted bank account when it finally started. With a loud "Hurray!" and a sigh of relief, I hit the road.

Minutes later I angle parked Bubbles on Main Street in front of the grocery store just down the road and across the street from Pincher's. Hope Harbor's Main Street was cutesy quaint in the way that towns with only one commercial street could be. In my mirrors I could see the yellow crime tape marring the faded white trim of the dollar store. In twenty-four hours the town had gone from charming to unsettling.

There were some lookie-loos holding court outside the dollar store. They stood, many with coffee in hand, heads tilted and jaws wagging. No doubt boasting about their assumptions and playing detective. When I climbed out of the van, the group spun in an eerie synchronized turn toward me.

Ignoring them, I made my way inside the small grocery store, where I was the subject of sidelong stares and whispers as I filled my basket. I grabbed a bag of ice, two apples, milk, some ground beef, burger buns and the least droopy bouquet of flowers available.

Out of the corner of my eye I saw Marshal Cobb looking intently at magazines by the checkout. I lingered in the back of the canned goods section and hoped the marshal would just buy a magazine and leave but he seemed to be biding his time. Eventually I hustled by him and unloaded my items.

The young woman manning the register was about my age. She had a pierced nose and a mass of curly blond hair tumbling from a messy bun, and she gave me the only smile I'd probably get today. I couldn't stop staring at her hair. It reminded me of what I'd seen in my vision. The clerk's lips quickly turned from a smile into a sympathetic frown when my purchases didn't go through on my debit card.

"You want to try again?" Her badge said her name was Melody.

"Ummm…" Heat rose up from the collar of my shirt and flooded my face. Marshal Cobb was behind me now and I could feel his stare and the glare of other patrons burning holes in my back.

"Can we try without these?" I handed her the apples and milk.

Melody rang it through again and this time my card worked.

"Have a nice day," she said, saccharine sweet.

As I made my way out the door, I glanced back to see Marshal Cobb grinning like a smitten teenager at Melody. Nice to know I wasn't his only focus of the day, but I sure hoped he was actively working Murray's murder and not just fishing for a date. Hurriedly, I took my purchases back to the van.

I stopped short when I got to my vehicle and saw someone had scribbled a message on the window using a black Sharpie: MURDERER!

I spun around searching the street but nobody was nearby holding a marker.

"Damn," I muttered with a shaky voice as I climbed inside.

I stuffed the bag of ice into my small fridge that didn't work a damn. The ice would keep the hamburger meat from going bad until I could eat it tonight. The bouquet of daisies and carnations rested on the passenger seat as I made my way through town. Every person I drove past glanced my way with anger and judgment in their eyes.

I'd only been to Penny's home once and that was to drop off something she'd forgotten at the store. Her house was a small older bungalow with green siding and yellow trim. The yard was uncluttered, and it looked exactly how you'd imagine an older woman's house might look, with colorful windmills in the tidy garden and a dried flower wreath at the door.

Penny's small blue Honda was in the driveway, and parked behind it was a red four-door sedan. If she had company, I didn't want to interrupt so I'd just give her the flowers and leave. She had a bright straw mat that said Welcome Friends and one of those melodic doorbells that greeted me and my hangover with the Westminster chime. I could hear footsteps approach the door and then sensed someone peering through the peephole.

"Oh my goodness, Red!" Penny smiled when she opened the door.

Immediately I was pulled into a tight hug. She was still in her bathrobe and I'd never seen her without her sky-high teased hair or full makeup. She looked older and fragile without her face on.

"I—I'm so sorry to intrude." I extricated myself from her grip and thrust the flowers at her. "I just wanted to stop by to see if there's anything you needed me to do and give you these. How are you doing? I tried calling but—"

"My phone's been ringing off the hook so I just turned it off," she explained, taking the flowers and breathing in their scent. "Come in and join me for some coffee."

"I don't want to bother you," I said quickly, remembering the red car in the driveway. "Especially if you have company."

"Please come in. I insist."

When I stepped inside, I removed my shoes and became immediately aware of hundreds of eyes on me.

"Wow." I blinked rapidly. "You have quite the doll collection."

"Those are my girls." She chuckled. "Been collecting them my whole life."

"They sure are…" I searched for a different word than *terrifying* "…colorful. Yes, they're sure colorful."

"Thank you."

I followed Penny to the back of the house into the kitchen, where there were even more shelves holding dolls in every size imaginable. As I took a seat at the kitchen table, Penny put my flowers in a vase that was in the shape of a doll and then brought over two mugs of coffee. The mugs, thankfully, weren't doll heads but the sugar and creamer on the table were. The figurine decor was a little unsettling and a lot disturbing.

The ceramic creamer doll head had a ponytail as a handle. It looked delicate, so I used two hands to pick it up and added a dollop of cream to my cup. I took a long dreamy sip. I'd taken to drinking coffee black or with powdered artificial creamer since my fridge died but, man, I sure appreciated the luxury of dairy to smooth the bitterness.

"I just want to say that I don't believe you had anything at all to do with Murray's death," Penny said as she ladled three spoons of sugar into her mug and stirred vigorously. "No matter what everyone else is saying."

"Everyone's saying I killed Murray?" I choked on my next mouthful of coffee.

"It's a small town, dear. You're new and we haven't had a murder here since Johnny Daily tossed his wife in the wood chipper twenty years ago."

"But that doesn't mean I'm the one who killed him," I explained, tapping my chest and speaking more loudly and forcefully than necessary.

"Of course not!" Penny went to the counter and came back with a plate of muffins. "Help yourself. You're much too skinny and I can't eat them anyway."

My stomach growled noisily.

"Thank you." I took a bite of a blueberry muffin but my throat was dry with worry and I needed to wash it down with the rest of my coffee.

Penny was quick to refill my mug.

"I don't know what to do." I fought to keep the concern from my voice, but it snuck in anyway.

"Red, you don't have to do anything. The police will figure this whole thing out."

"That Marshal Cobb probably doesn't have a lot of experience with murder," I murmured into my coffee.

"Well, no," Penny admitted but then added brightly, "But he's very good at what he does. Once the diner had a break-in and someone stole a bunch of steaks from their freezer, and the marshal tracked down those rotten Cooper boys and had the meat back in the diner before it was even fully unthawed."

"That's great, Penny, but murder isn't quite the same thing."

"It's still investigating, isn't it?" She reached across the table and patted my hand. "In the meantime, you just keep to yourself and don't be bad-mouthing Noah, because Lord knows he's a town favorite."

I cringed. "So, everyone in Hope Harbor knows I told Marshal Cobb that Noah hated Murray?"

"Yes, a few people heard you make that accusation." She clucked her tongue and shook her head. "Now don't get me wrong, it's not like it's untrue. Noah *did* hate Murray. But then most people did. I may have been the only person in town who cared for him even in the slightest." Her eyes brightened with unshed tears.

"Everyone in town's been giving me the stink eye. Someone even wrote *murderer* on my window."

"Well, that's not right." She sighed. "Unfortunately, people are gonna talk. After all, this is the biggest thing to happen to this town since—"

"The wood chipper thing. I know. Did you know Murray a long time?" I asked around a mouthful of muffin. "I know he worked for you but—"

"They met at my wedding," someone said, and I

turned to see a thirtyish woman wearing a pale pink nightgown. She was petite and pretty except for her face being pinched with annoyance. Her short blond hair jutted out in every direction, and she ran a well-manicured hand through as if to tame it.

"Red, this is my daughter, Tess."

"Nice to meet you." I struggled to remember if Penny had ever mentioned she had a daughter.

"She's been staying with me the last few days." Penny leaned in and loudly whispered, "Her husband left her."

"Gawd, Mom, I'm standing right here," Tess complained, but her voice was without venom. She went to the cupboard and got down a massive doll head coffee cup, filled it to the rim with coffee and then leaned against the counter instead of joining us at the table. "It was a huge wedding and I didn't know half the people there. I believe Murray was a friend of my ex's family. Mom and Murray met and it seemed to be love at first sight."

"Love?" I tried to keep the surprise from my voice. "Really?" My eyes grew big and I had to snap my mouth shut. I thought about Murray with the bulldog face, beer belly and greasy hair and couldn't imagine him with anyone. Least of all Penny, who was impeccable in appearance and had a demeanor that was candy-sprinkle sweet. I tried to keep the shock from my voice. "I didn't know you two were together."

"That was a lo-o-ong time ago." She waved it away with a wrinkled hand.

"I couldn't imagine working with an ex," I admitted.

"Me either." Tess snorted.

"The romance didn't last but the friendship did. Plus,

he was a hard worker so I hired him to keep stock, and he tended to mind his own business except for grabbing the occasional tush."

I blushed as if she'd read my mind.

"Yeah, he was a real catch." Tess smirked, then lowered her face into the bouquet on the counter. "You brought flowers?"

"Yes."

"That was nice of you." But the way she said it, with her voice going up at the end like it was a question and her mouth in a frown, suggested I had an ulterior motive. She raised her mug in my direction. "Mom has told me nothing but good things about you. Nice to finally meet you, but too bad it's because of Murray's death." Tess yawned into her mug, then placed it onto the counter. "If you two don't mind, I'm going back to bed."

As soon as Tess was gone Penny leaned in.

"I think she's depressed. All she does is sleep all day." She made tsking sounds and shook her head. "Maybe I'll get her to help out at the store when we reopen. Even Murray's death didn't get much of a rise out of her." Penny sipped her coffee thoughtfully. "But then she always despised him."

Hmm. Enough to kill him? "Why do you think she disliked him so much?"

"Tess just always thought Murray was out to take advantage of me." Penny laughed at the thought, then added defiantly, "I might be older but I'm not senile and I can sure as heckadoodle look out for myself."

"Penny, is there anyone in town who you think hated Murray enough to kill him?"

She slowly shook her head and shrugged. "He wasn't everyone's favorite but he'd been here for years and peo-

ple were kind of used to him. People disliked him…"
Her face took on a vague, distant look before she returned to the moment. "But to actually kill him? I truly
have no idea."

"Do you have any idea what he was doing in the
storeroom so early in the morning?"

"I imagine he was just finishing up what he should've
done the day before." She sighed. "He had a fondness
for beer and fishing so sometimes he was called to finish a few bottles in the middle of the day instead of putting a shipment away. Just the other day I was giving
him hell for not unloading our new shipment of statio-
nery. With it being back-to-school time there have been
people looking for those things, but he was taking his
sweet-ass time getting it done. The boxes were on the
floor just waiting to be brought out front. Those boxes
are heavy which is why he was handy to have around.
Not to mention all the Halloween stock that arrived."
She paused with her coffee cup halfway to her lips. "I
don't know who'll do all that stuff now."

"I will," I said immediately and not just because I
could really use the cash. Penny had given me a job
when she didn't know me at all. I owed her. "I can come
in early and stay late to make sure it gets done."

At least until Murray's killer was gone. Then I was
out of here.

"Thank you, dear. That would be most helpful." She
ran a trembling hand through her white curls. "I wonder who'll be cleaning Murray's apartment? He had
no family to speak of…" Her voice trailed off. "I guess
that'll be me too."

"If you need help with that, just let me know." But I

was pretty sure the cops were going to be all over his place until this was solved. "Did he live in town?"

"Oh yes, just next door in Barb's basement apartment." She waved an absent hand in the direction of the next house.

"Did he have any family that need to be notified?"

"No, he was an only child and his parents passed long before we met."

"Well, there's no need for you to worry about cleaning his apartment or how the store will make out. I'm here for you." I finished my coffee and got up to rinse out my mug. I asked if there was anything at all she needed me to do.

"Not until we can reopen the store. Oh, but you can take those muffins off my hands." Penny got to her feet, snagged a bag from a drawer and began dropping the muffins inside. "Barb brought these over this morning. Every single morning she drives into town to meet the other old biddies for coffee at the diner and brings back baked goods. Today she decided to grab those for me but they're blueberry, even though she knows I have a serious blueberry allergy. I swear she's just trying to kill me."

"Are you sure Tess wouldn't like them?"

"She's trying to cut out carbs." Penny rolled her eyes.

"Okay. Thank you then." I was more than happy to take them off her hands.

She was walking me through the living room when she suddenly clapped her hands. "I almost forgot!" She went to a credenza in the corner of the living room and moved the flamboyant skirt of a particularly elaborate doll sporting a large peach parasol. Waving a piece of paper in the air, she returned and handed me my pay-check. "Today's payday."

I could've kissed the old lady on the lips right then and there. "Thank you so-o-o much."

"You earned every dime." She waved her hands. "Marshal Cobb said we should be able to open up in two days. Guess I'll see you bright and early Saturday."

"I'll be there," I promised, then added, "Penny, you don't need to come in on Saturday. If you need to take more time off, you just leave the store to me. I won't let you down."

She thanked me again for the flowers as I walked out the door. Then, as I was making my way down her sidewalk, she called out, "Oh and, Red?"

"Yes?"

"Don't be worrying your little head about what folks say. You sure don't look like a killer to me."

"Um. Thanks."

Barb was pruning shrubs in her front yard a few feet away. She didn't hide her stare and narrowed her eyes at me as I rushed by swinging my bag of muffins and clutching my paycheck. Penny might not think I looked like a murderer but it was pretty clear that others in this town didn't feel the same way.

As soon as I was behind the wheel, I did a U-turn and noticed Marshal Cobb climbing out of his vehicle, which was parked in the neighbor's driveway. He must be looking through Murray's apartment. Cobb turned to face me and I could see his scowl out of the corner of my eye as I exited the street. The hard glare he gave me caused me to sweat.

As I drove down Main Street then cornered at the service station heads turned. In case word spread that

I was seen fleeing from town, I figured I'd better make a call. I dialed the marshal and it went to voicemail.

"It's Red. Don't want you to think I'm skipping town. I'm just headed to Bellingham to do laundry and some banking." I paused. "My phone will be on and I'll be back at Farmer Miller's field for the night."

As soon as I could step on the gas, I nosed my van toward I-5. Even though the marshal had told me to stick close to the area I'm sure he wouldn't mind if I went to the next town. Bellingham was less than a half hour away and I wanted to deposit my check and go to the laundromat away from the prying eyes and judgmental stares of the Hope Harbor busybodies.

As I drove outside town limits it felt like the weight of the world had lifted from my shoulders. Except for the fact that I had the visual of Murray's blood-soaked head playing on repeat in my mind like a B horror flick.

Once in town I quickly found a bank machine to deposit my check and then a laundromat that had good Wi-Fi. I stuffed my dirty clothes and bedding into garbage bags and hauled them inside along with my laptop. While my first loads washed, I downloaded movies onto my laptop and a fresh playlist onto my phone.

I also scoured the internet for any information on Murray's killing. All the local headlines mentioned it and there were pictures of Pincher's and even an unflattering photo of me talking to the marshal. In the picture I looked like a deer in the headlights: my eyes were wide and my hands raised as if I were going to strike the marshal, when all I'd been doing was talking animatedly about what I'd seen inside the store.

An article in the local rag stated that Scarlet Hooper, who'd only been a resident of Hope Harbor for four weeks, was the person to find the body. They may as well have painted a *K* for killer on my back. I dreaded going back to town. At least Penny said I wouldn't need to be at work for two days. I could certainly avoid people until then and, who knows, maybe Marshal Cobb and the sheriff would even find the killer in the meantime. Perhaps someone would walk into the station and confess. Apparently, doing laundry and having more than a dollar in my bank account made me unrealistically optimistic.

With my headphones in I was humming along to my new playlist and folding my clothes while I scrolled through social media pages for Hope Harbor hoping someone, anyone, was pointing a finger at who could've killed Murray. Abruptly, I caught movement out of the corner of my eye. I startled when I realized it was none other than hardware store owner and possible murderer, Noah Adams.

My jaw dropped along with the pink panties I'd been holding.

"What are you doing here?" I demanded, plucking the earbuds from my ears.

"I'm guessing the same as you—pondering the mysteries of the world and trying to figure out world peace." He walked over to a dryer, yanked open the door and then unloaded his warm clothing onto the folding counter directly in front of me.

"Why wouldn't you use the laundromat in town? The one that's also the bakery and coffee shop? It's three businesses in one. Can't beat that," I grumbled with exasperation.

"I could ask you the same question."

"Be straight with me." I snapped a towel and then

folded it quickly. "Did you follow me here because I wouldn't open my door to you last night?"

"Follow you?" His eyebrows went up in bemused enjoyment. "My washing machine is broken and the part is on order. Since I was coming into town to visit my dad at his care home across the street—" he hooked his thumb in the direction of a brick building across the way "—I thought I'd kill two birds with one stone."

Noah Adams had thick dark hair that curled around his ears and a day's beard growth that somehow made him look even more attractive than he had a right to. His gray eyes were hard and unnerving. His gaze never left me as he folded a T-shirt.

"Who's running the hardware store?" I began folding the rest of my clothes at lightning speed.

"My nephew." He tilted his head. "You ask a lot of questions for someone who basically accused me of murder yesterday and then wouldn't answer her door last night. I should be the one interrogating you. Let's start with why you told Joel Cobb I killed Murray?"

"I didn't say that." I huffed. "I told him that you *hated* Murray."

He rolled his eyes and dragged a hand through his dark unruly hair.

"Darling, *everyone* hated Murray." He tapped his chin and looked up at the ceiling in a look of concentration. "As a matter of fact, I'm probably the only one who hid it so well that nobody knew how much I despised the man. That's why I was curious and I—"

"Decided to scare me and come banging on my door at night while I'm camped in the middle of nowhere?"

"You're on Miller's farm. Everyone knows that and it's hardly in the middle of nowhere. Plus, it was barely after sunset. I would've called first, but I didn't have the number for the Bubble Mobile hotline."

My lips pinched into a line at his mocking tone.

"Well, no need to worry." I picked up stacks of my folded clothes and placed them into trash bags. "Everyone in town lo-o-oves you and thinks you're some sort of god and just as innocent as a newborn baby."

He tossed back his head and laughed, and the emotion entirely changed his appearance; his gray eyes softened as they crinkled at the corners and his entire body appeared to relax. I was tempted to laugh along but then I admonished myself.

Remember, Red, many serial killers are attractive and charming.

"Being the young widower in town has its advantages. Everyone sees me as a little fragile."

A widower? I inwardly squirmed until I remembered my gaze into his cigarette lighter flame and the ferocious hatred for Murray that flowed from Noah in that moment. I glanced at the breast pocket of his plaid shirt and saw the bulge of a lighter and pack of cigarettes. Maybe he'd light one up outside and I'd get another chance at reading a flame.

"Sorry for your loss," I mumbled. "But don't you worry, your fragile reputation wasn't tarnished at all. I'm the suspect since I'm new to town and found the body."

"If you didn't do it, I'm sure even young Joel Cobb will figure that out. This isn't the first murder in Hope Harbor. Twenty years ago—"

"Daily put his wife in a wood chipper. I know. What a colorful history for such a wee little town." Then I scowled. "You said 'if' I killed Murray. Let me set this straight. I didn't kill him. I had no reason to kill him. I'd like to think if I planned to take someone out I'd certainly not do it in the place where I worked and then announce to the world I found his body."

"Like you said, you're the new girl in town. It's hard for people to imagine their next-door neighbor is a killer. Much easier to think it came from an outsider."

"Small-town narrow-minded thinking," I huffed.

"Yeah, well, we're pretty protective of our own in Hope Harbor. Which isn't a bad thing. You can't blame folks for not trusting the person they know the least. Especially since there hasn't been a murder—"

"Since Daily stuffed his wife in a wood chipper," I finished. "You sure got to Pincher's pretty quick after I found Murray's body. Why is that?"

"Are you asking me if I have an alibi?" His smile just irked the hell out of me.

"Well, do you?"

"Not really." He shrugged. "I make it a habit to get to the store early to restock the shelves before opening, and by the time I arrived word had already spread about Murray. You might remember there was quite the crowd standing with me outside the store."

I harrumphed and snagged my bags off the counter.

"Are you leaving? Can I buy you a coffee or something?"

"Marshal Cobb would most likely lose his shit if he thought for one second I was out of town even a minute longer than necessary," I said hastily. There was no way I was giving in to Mr. Dimples. "Honestly, I can't wait until this is all over and I can permanently put Hope Harbor in my rearview mirror."

"Really?" He frowned. "I, for one, would be sad to see you go."

Wait a second, was he flirting with me? It flustered me so much I tripped over my own two feet as I headed for the door.

"Hey, Red," he called out to me as I reached the door.

I turned to find him holding up the pink thong I'd dropped.

Blushing the same color as those undies, I strode over and snatched them out of his hand and stormed out the door. Once back inside Bubbles I thought about hanging around and seeing if he'd step outside for a smoke but there was no way to discreetly hide with Bubbles and, honestly, I was too bothered by his flirtatious comments to stick around.

All the way back to Farmer Miller's field I was replaying the brief conversation I'd had with Noah Adams in the laundromat. I'd been so sure he was the murderer but one look into those eyes and I could feel my resolve weaken. He was right about one thing: just because he hated Murray didn't mean he killed him. But he did admit to hating Murray and he did admit to being around at the time Murray died.

Noah Adams might be good-looking but that sure doesn't make him innocent, I reminded myself. *People thought Ted Bundy was charismatic too and he killed thirty-six women.*

I pulled into the parking lot of a store a block away and used their Wi-Fi to do more online research on Murray's murder. Hope Harbor had its own social media page, which I'd joined at Penny's request. I'd only ever posted store sales on her behalf but now I found myself receiving dozens of notifications from the group.

I'd been tagged in a post stating that I should be locked up before I hurt anyone else. Dozens of commenters agreed. Some guy I'd never met even came right out and stated he was carrying a gun and if I did anything remotely suspicious he'd shoot me dead before even calling the marshal.

I took a screenshot of the threat and sent it to Cobb. Then, with trembling hands, I removed myself from the online group. My head was spinning as I drove back toward Hope Harbor. When I turned onto the quiet stretch of road that wound its way toward Farmer Miller's fields, I saw a yellow Corvette pulled off to the side of the pavement near the field pullout where I camped. It was not exactly the kind of car that was common in Hope Harbor.

"Now what?"

I slowed down and angled the van so I could back in, all the while keeping an eye on the yellow sports car. As soon as I turned off the ignition, the driver's door of the Corvette opened. My heart dropped when I saw the driver.

Oh no-o-o!

Flipping her long, jet hair over her shoulder as she walked toward me was my sister, Brandy.

THREE

"Hello, Scarlet!"

Brandy was wearing five-inch spike heels and a miniskirt. As one does when walking a gravel shoulder in the country.

I slid the van door open and regarded her coolly. "How did you find me?"

"Some cop found me in Seattle and asked me a bunch of questions about you. He found *me* because I'm listed and not living out of a van like some kind of vagrant hobo. I'm reachable by any kind of an online search just in case someone, like my baby sister, ever wanted to reach out." She sniffed indignantly. Lowering her dark sunglasses to the end of her nose she added coolly, "When I asked where you were he said he couldn't say, but since he'd already told me he was calling from some teeny tinker town called Hope Harbor, it only took Google and a couple hours' drive to get here."

"And then what? You just drove around every road in the vicinity until you found me?"

"Nope." She smiled brightly. "When I stopped for gas in town they told me *exactly* where you and the granny bubble wagon were parked."

"The joys of small-town living." I frowned.

"Well…" She looked the van over with a slow shake of her head. "Aren't you going to invite me in?"

With a long exhale I stepped aside and allowed her to climb inside.

"Marshal Cobb mentioned you were in rehab and that you're clean. How long has it been? A week? A month?" I asked.

Brandy kicked off her heels and fell backward, sprawling out on my freshly made bed. Her waist-length black hair fanned out around her pale face and she stretched, arching her back like a cat. "I dumped the junk a few years ago and became my rehabbed-beauteous self. My veins are clean and so is my head." She sat up on her elbows and wiggled her eyebrows at me. "Are you surprised?"

"Shocked," I admitted. "So pretty much right after I saw you last?"

"Yes. I wish I could say that you were the cata-lyst. But, honestly, after our big blowup in Nan's stor-age locker when you told me I could pawn whatever I wanted as long as I never spoke to you again, I didn't even flinch. A few days later, out celebrating my thirty-third birthday, I went on a bender and overdosed on Mexican Mud. When I came to in the hospital, I real-ized I just might have used up the eighth of my nine lives. Figured I was too old to play and decided to ditch it for good."

"That must've been hard. Good for you." I could feel myself becoming hopeful. She was the only family I had in this world.

Still, I knew I had to take her words with a large dose of skepticism. Brandy had a long history of bend-ing the truth. Also, even though I knew her addiction issues were a serious sickness, I struggled not to be pissed about the horrible way she'd treated all of us while she was using.

I took a seat and began drumming my fingers on the table. "And you're here because…?"

"You need me, that's why." She got up from the bed, walked over and patted me on the head like a puppy before digging coral lipstick from her purse and applying a fresh layer of color. "I know we've never been close, but since Mom and Nan are both gone, it's up to me to show you the ropes."

"What ropes? How to tie my own noose?" I snorted.

"How to train your psychic abilities."

"My what?" I played dumb and frowned as my heart skipped a beat. "Hey, I have zero interest in learning whatever scamming racket you've got going on."

Brandy didn't deny it. Instead, she spun around, eyed the van with interest and changed the topic.

"You're really living in this rolling tin can? I figured you would've sold it and moved on with your life." She opened the bathroom door. "You could literally sit on the toilet and spit in the sink. You're tiny but how do you shower without turning yourself into a pretzel?" She closed the door and began opening cupboards and drawers.

I could feel my fury rising, and when she went to open a side cupboard in the back, I yelled, "Stop!" I shook my head. "Leave that one alone."

"Why?" Brandy's hand was paused on the latch and her eyes brightened with amusement. "What's in here? Sex toys? A hoard of secret cash? The bones of your enemies, or…" She smiled sadly then rolled her eyes. "Oh no-o-o, this was Nan's cupboard, wasn't it?"

"Yes."

"Scarlet Hooper, are you telling me you've been living in this bubbleicious joke for two years without her and haven't gotten rid of her old lady dresses and wrinkle cream?"

"I donated most of it," I blurted defensively. "I keep Nan's ashes in there and a few of her personal things. Besides, it's not like I need that cupboard. I'll—I'll do it when I'm ready."

"Fine." She lifted her hand off the cupboard and I exhaled. "Jeez, Scarlet, if this is your home, make it *yours*." She pointed to the picture of our grandmother on the wall. "Don't keep it a mausoleum to Nan."

"I have made it mine." I pointed to the back mattress. "I no longer have it set up with two single beds, it's a large queen now, and I switched out some of the dishes and…" My voice trailed off because really that was all I'd done. "I go by Red now. Not Scarlet. You'd know that if I ever heard from you. How long do you plan on staying with me?"

"Oh God, I'm not staying *here*." She shuddered with revulsion and pushed her sunglasses up her head. "I'll grab a hotel in Bellingham. I have some business there anyway."

I wanted to ask what kind of business but thought it might be better if I didn't know.

"I'll hang around until I'm confident you've learned what I can teach you and that you're not going to wind up in jail for killing that guy." Brandy walked over, slumped into the chair across from me and waggled a finger in my direction. "*Did* you kill him?"

"Of course not!"

Brandy shrugged. "Goddess knows you've always

had an angry streak." She chuckled and then abruptly clapped her hands. "Shall we start lesson one?"

"Lessons in what?" I rubbed the back of my neck and when she didn't reply, I blew out a long breath. "You're really not leaving town until you've taught me some life lessons to ease your guilt for treating us all like crap? Fine then. Let's do this." I was more than a little curious now. "Tell me everything I supposedly need to know from my big sister."

"Well, I have a business to run so I can't possibly tell you everything or even a fraction of that in one sitting. And I'm sure not going to babysit you, but I'll keep coming back until this is done."

"Whatever." I waved a hand in her direction.

"First lesson is don't cheap out on a good manicure. Two different color polishes?" She clucked her tongue. "Your hands are a mess. Stop biting your nails like an infant."

I stuck my hands under my thighs and thrust my chin out defiantly. "Thanks for the sisterly love. You can leave."

"Oh my God, stop being so sensitive! I was joking about that being lesson one." With a smirk she added, "Kind of joking. Anyway, what I really need is to find out what you already know about your talent. Without Mom and Nan around to wrap you in bubble wrap, you must've figured out some stuff. Last I knew you hadn't even tried anything with fire, and Nan was still trying to pretend you were the normal one." She spat out the world *normal* like it tasted putrid.

Brandy was my sister but that didn't mean I trusted her with that most personal part of me. I frowned, wondering how she knew about my abilities when I'd only recently discovered them myself.

When all I did was stare at her, she tapped the table between us.

"C'mon, Scarlet…and, no, I will not be calling you Red." She sneered. "How do you summon your energy and abilities? I know fire is your thing but—"

"How do you know anything about me and fire?"

"Wow. Have you not figured out anything about our family?"

"What do you mean?"

"I mean, our freaky psychic heritage and inheritance!"

"Inheritance?" I chewed the corner of my lip. "How? From who?"

"Jesus." Brandy tucked her hair behind her ears and looked at me incredulously. "Nan did water scrying. Mom did the boring tea leaves thing. I use mirrors and you—well, the way you freaked out every time there was a birthday candle within a mile radius of us growing up, I always knew your thing must be fire."

My jaw dropped and when I shut it, I squeezed my eyes shut and tried to absorb this revelation. "So… Mom and Nan knew about…"

"You and fire?" She gave me a sympathetic smile. "Of course they knew."

"And your mirror thing… Did Mom and Nan show you how to do your mirror thing?"

"Nope. Self-taught."

"And Mom and Nan were psychics? I don't remember them ever—"

"Oh they were very good at hiding it from their sweet

innocent angel." Brandy smirked and used her thumb to turn a ruby ring on her pointer finger.

"Hold on." I grabbed her hand. "That's Nan's ring."

"She gave it to me." Brandy yanked her hand back.

"No way! I looked all over for that ring when Nan died."

She'd removed it when she lost too much weight at the end of her illness but, before that, I'd never seen her take it off. It had belonged to her mother, and her mother's mother before that. Seeing it on Brandy's finger stung.

"How could she give you the ring when you hadn't seen her for months or a year before she died, and she wore it up until just a few weeks before she was gone? I was with her every second. I hardly left her bedside and I certainly never saw you there."

"Nan gave it to Mom first, remember? Well, after Mom died Nan took the ring back and told me that the ring would go to me when she was gone. She put it in a coffee can in the storage unit a few weeks before she died and messaged me to tell me where it was. It was always handed down to the oldest girl. I'm the oldest girl, shrimp. After I heard she died, that's when I met you at the storage unit."

"Wait, she messaged you telling where she was putting the ring because she was dying? And you still didn't come see her? Or come to the funeral?"

"I'm not proud of that." Brandy examined her manicure instead of looking me in the eye. "Truthfully, I was far down the rabbit hole and I was so messed up I don't think her words even sank in."

Seeing that ruby ring on Brandy's finger infuriated

me but if it was what Nan wanted, then I'd let it go. What difference did it make all this time later?

"Hey, you got the van," Brandy pointed out. "And I got the ring. Are we going to fight about what Nan left us? Is that really what she'd want?"

"No." I closed my eyes and took a deep breath before I changed the subject. "So you really taught yourself how to do psychic stuff?"

"Yup. Oh, Mom always said she'd show me eventually when I got clean but then you killed her and—"

"I did *not* kill our mother!" I roared, my throat burning with the force of my fury. "Get out. Get the hell out of my home!"

"Whoa. Fine. Another driver T-boned Mom's car and she died instantly but if you hadn't insisted on taking her out that night…"

"It was *her* idea. She wanted to go to the exhibit and—"

"And why do you think she wanted to go to that particular exhibit, Scarlet? Huh? Do you remember what it was called?"

"It was an art exhibit called Playing with Fire," I mumbled. "She said it would be inspiring."

"Inspiring?" Brandy snorted. "She was trying to finally tell you about your talent, and she thought bringing you to an art exhibit showing you the beauty of fire might be a gentle way to start that conversation. She told me all about her plan."

My head was swirling. Could that be true? Were we only on the road that night because of me? I had only been twelve. My memory of that time was a blur of tears and heart-wrenching pain. "Even if that's the truth, it was a drunk driver who blew the red light and killed her and—"

"Yes, and I dealt with him because you sure as hell didn't." Brandy slammed her palms on the table between us.

"What do you mean, you dealt with him?" My eyes grew big with horror. "He was killed in a hit-and-run accident. Someone drove into him at a crosswalk on a rainy night…" My breath caught in my throat and I gasped. "Jesus, Brandy, tell me that wasn't you."

"Does it matter? Justice was served." She yawned. "I'm just saying that our own mother wanted you to take charge of that area of your life. I thought Nan might do it during the years you lived with her but, since she didn't, it falls on me."

My head was swirling. I put my hands on either side of my face as if to stop my world from spinning. Nan had raised me through my teen years. Brandy would skip back into our lives periodically when she needed money.

"Nan had to nurse me back to health after my brain surgery." I was twenty and away at college when debilitating migraines caused me to drop out. That was when they found the tumor.

I shook my head and gathered strength to point a finger in Brandy's face. "You were certainly nowhere to be found at that time, were you? You're here to play big sister now, but where were you during the years I was recovering? While I was relearning how to walk and talk, and Nan was struggling to help me, you were too busy sticking a needle in your arm to even see if I was alive or dead. Then, at twenty-three when I was finally strong enough to get a job and help around the house,

Nan found that lump. All her surgeries, the chemo, the recoveries and then just when it looked like remission, the cancer struck again. Back and forth for years and it was all on *me*. I was the one that helped sell her thrift store and the house to pay her medical bills. You didn't even show up until after the funeral to loot through her stuff!"

As I brushed an angry tear from my face I saw a brief flicker of emotion in Brandy's eyes. Then she cleared her throat and resumed a look of cool boredom.

"Enough rehashing the past," Brandy said, then added with a wink, "The doctors excised our only other sibling from your head so you're all I've got for family."

"Whaaat?" I grew still. "Who told you that?"

"Who told me that your brain tumor was a rare intracranial teratoma containing the hair, teeth and bone of your twin?" She comically wiggled her brows at me. "Oh, sis, sometimes these psychic abilities of ours are handy for finding stuff out. Haven't you discovered that yet?" She pinched a piece of lint from her blouse and dropped it onto the floor. "Or maybe I just slept with your doctor." She shrugged. "Either way, I was checking up on you all along and, yes, even during the time I was living with a needle in my arm."

"I think you should go." I got to my feet and opened the sliding door for her.

"Sit down. I know this is a lot to absorb but you're a grown-ass woman and it's time you learned this stuff. Besides, you're not getting rid of me that easy."

"Then let's talk tomorrow." I got out my cell phone. "Give me your number and I'll send you a text so we know how to reach each other."

She closed her eyes and rattled off some digits. "Is that your number?" she asked.

"No." Eerily she was only one digit off.

"This skill is far from perfect." She sighed. "I've been trying to see your phone number in a mirror." When she gave me her number, I sent her a text that just said, It's Me.

"Ha!" She smiled at her phone. "I was sure close, wasn't I?"

I nodded.

"Before I head out, tell me about this murder."

I told her everything that had happened and everything I knew so far.

"You discovered the body and you're new in town. Neither of those things work in your favor. Even if he was the town perv, people will be looking for justice." She pulled out her car keys. "Hopefully the gunshot residue test comes back negative."

"It will. I didn't kill him and I didn't touch a gun."

"There's such a thing as transfer though. A doorknob, items in the room, a light switch…anything else with GSR that you touched could've transferred onto you."

I didn't want to think about that.

"I'm going to leave you with one piece of advice before I go." She cleared her throat and leveled her amber eyes at mine. "Don't be a victim. Fight. A small town like this would love to pin this murder on the new girl in town, and if you don't stand up for yourself, they might just succeed."

She drew me into a tight hug. I closed my eyes and squeezed her back.

After Brandy was gone, I made a burger patty and

fried it, while complaining to Nan about Brandy and all the revelations of the evening.

"I wish you'd told me about fire, Nan." I kissed a fingertip and pressed it to her picture. "I started to figure out this stuff once you were gone. My reactions to seeing fire. The visions that came with it. It would've been helpful to have someone I trust teach me these things." I sighed. "I don't know if I can trust Brandy enough to learn from her."

I opened my sliding doors and sat in the entrance, dangling my feet off the ground as I ate. There was enough of a breeze to keep the mosquitos away. I thought about all the bombshells Brandy had dropped in my lap and realized that even though I didn't trust her, she was right about that last piece of advice. I needed to stand up for myself.

And I needed to find out more information about Murray's murder before the cops tried to pin it on me.

I stuffed the last of my burger in my mouth, hopped out of the van and stretched. A few yards away a murder of crows was making a helluva racket as they swooped at something in the nearby grass.

Probably a big fat rat. I shuddered. "Go get 'em, boys." I dusted my hands on my jeans and made to climb back in the van when I heard a pitiful squeak. Turning toward the sound I saw a brown ball of fluff trying to cross the road while the crows surrounded and pecked at it.

"Oh my God!" It was a kitten.

I ran toward the road and the crows reluctantly took flight onto the nearest phone wires and watched me.

"Hey, little buddy." I scooped the cat up and the little guy hissed pathetically at me. "It's okay." I nuzzled him against my chest and brought him quickly into the van. I checked him over for injuries but, when I didn't see any, I put him on the ground and got him a bowl of water. He promptly stuck his face in it, dumped most of it onto the floor, then lapped up what spilled.

"I bet you're hungry." I flung cupboard doors open but, sadly, no food fairy had delivered groceries. Then I remembered the muffins from Penny this morning. I broke up some muffin pieces. "Can cats have blueberries?" I wasn't sure and made certain to remove any berry pieces from the crumbs before I tossed the bits to the floor.

While the little guy devoured the bits of muffin, I dialed up Farmer Miller and asked if he was missing a kitten. He said his feral barn cat had kittens a few weeks ago. He'd caught the mom and had her fixed and thought he'd rounded up and given away all the kittens but must've missed one.

"Guess you're a mom now," the old man joked.

"I live in a space barely meant for one person." I frowned. "Are you sure you don't need another barn cat?"

He said if I set the kitten free outside his barn then it would survive just fine.

As I watched the tiny guy pounce and attack a wayward piece of muffin, my heart began to swell and I knew that was never going to happen. I stared at the brown ball of fur trying to decide what to do. When he squatted on my floor and left a mess for me to clean, I made a decision.

"Guess you live here now, at least temporarily, and that means we're going to have to go to the store."

As I headed for town the little guy clawed up my pant

leg, attacked a fly on the dash and then disappeared into the back. When I pulled up to the grocery store I found him hanging from the curtains by my bed. I was rethinking my decision to foster this kitten but then he let out the tiniest meow and my heart melted.

"Try not to destroy the place while I'm inside."

The grocery store had cat food and litter but no litter-box. I added a pound of coffee to my basket and headed for the checkout.

Melody, the blonde who'd served me earlier, eyed my purchases. "You got a cat!"

I explained what happened with the crows and she placed her hand over her breast.

"Awww. Bless your heart, you rescued him!" She put my stuff in a bag and gushed, "I have cats and I just love them to bits. They are my everything. Have you ever had a cat before?"

"Never," I admitted.

She put a hand on my arm and looked me seriously in the eyes. "It'll change your life. In a good way."

That felt like a high expectation for a tiny kitten. I asked about the other things I needed.

"The hardware store will have litterboxes, bowls and all that stuff. Noah has an entire pet section." Melody rang up my order with a smile. "If you ever need any cat advice, give me a call." She wrote out her cell number on my receipt and stuffed it in the sack.

I was thankful for Penny's paycheck or I wouldn't be able to pay for any of this, but I was supposed to be saving for a new battery for the van. Also, I wasn't looking forward to seeing Noah at the hardware store. Maybe I'd get lucky and he'd still be in Bellingham.

My phone chimed before I started the van. It was a

social media message from someone I didn't recognize:
DIE! KILLER! DIE!

I replied: Who is this?

I searched the profile associated with the message but
it was blank. My heart pounded as I took a screenshot of
the message and sent it to the marshal. I looked up and
down Main Street, eyeing the people going about their
everyday lives, milling around in front of Pincher's and
chatting in small groups. The message could've come
from any one of these people. A week ago I thought that
this sleepy town was a perfect retreat while I earned
some money. Now it felt dangerous to even drive down
Main Street.

Quickly I pulled up to the hardware store and made
my way inside. Noah Adams was standing a few feet
away helping a woman make a decision about some gar-
dening tools. He eyed me curiously, but I made my way
directly to the pet section at the back of the store, where
a middle-aged woman offered me a look of angry dis-
gust and grumbled something unflattering about murder and new people in town before she stomped away.

A gangly teen with bad acne asked me if I needed
help. When I explained about the new kitten he began
filling my arms with everything I needed and stuff I
didn't.

A few minutes later I stumbled to the counter with
my arms loaded with supplies. I had a small crate, litterbox, leash, harness, food bowls and cat toys. I dumped
the works noisily onto the counter.

"Let me guess." Noah picked up a toy mouse. "You
got yourself a goldfish."

"Feral kitten was being attacked by crows next to
my van, so what could I do?"

"You could've just left it at Miller's barn and it would've had a long, happy and productive life as a mouser."

"If it didn't get torn apart by birds first. Besides." I cleared my throat. "This is just temporary. I'm just going to foster him until he's like, you know, old enough to stand up for himself."

"Right." He chuckled as he rang up my purchases. "Did my nephew help you with all this stuff?" He held up a ball with a bell inside. "He has a way of, um, encouraging people to buy more than they probably need."

"He did help but I'm okay with it."

"In that case, you might as well accept that you are now owned by a cat, and by the time you're done with checking it for fleas and getting those first shots, it's gonna be yours for life."

"Fleas? Shots?" I swallowed. "Guess I'll have to find a vet."

He told me how much I owed and I cringed as I dug out my bank card.

"You're in luck." He yelled over my head. "Hey, Shell, can you come here for a second?"

An older woman in filthy overalls came to the front counter.

"Shell, this is Red. She's decided to adopt a feral kitten." He turned to me. "Shelby here is our local vet."

"I guess I need to make an appointment to bring him in to your office."

"You're the gal that lives in that bubble camper that's parked out front?"

I nodded.

"I'll come take a look at him after you're done paying."

I thanked her and then balanced my purchases in my arms and somehow managed to maneuver my van door open without the cat escaping. Seconds later the vet was at my door. I gathered up the kitten and received a few scratches for my trouble.

"He looks a little skinny," I said. "Is he going to be okay?"

"First of all, he is a she. Second, once you start feeding her she's going to be fine. No sign of fleas but she's about nine or ten weeks so is going to need some shots, a deworming and to get some regular flea treatment. My office is just by the gas station and I could do it now, if that suits you. I'll be heading out of town to deal with a sick horse in a few minutes but need to stop by and get some supplies at my office anyway."

She handed the kitten back to me and I snuggled her against my chest.

"Any idea how much all that is going to cost?" I shuffled uneasily from one foot to another.

She sighed. "I'll do it all for twenty bucks if you promise to get her spayed in a few months."

"Deal."

"You got a name for her?" Shelby asked.

I snagged a muffin crumb from the cat's fur. "Her name is Muffin."

She nodded. "I'll see you and Muffin in a few."

The checkup didn't take long, and I felt tears well up in my eyes when Muffin got her shots even though the cat didn't seem to mind at all. Once we left the vet I spent some time setting up Muffin's litterbox and finding a place I could stash it where I wouldn't trip over it, which wasn't easy in such a cramped space.

Muffin quickly gobbled up the stinky canned food

I gave her. And when I plopped her into the litter, she only played with it a few minutes but then actually used it. She was a genius!

I put an old towel in the crate and then I stuffed her inside because it wasn't safe to have her leaping and pouncing all over me while I drove. Even though she protested by hissing and clawing at me through the vent holes, she was fast asleep in seconds.

I'd parked on Main Street next to the service station where it appeared everyone in Hope Harbor pulled up to get gas. The stares, glares and mouth-dropping curious gawks Bubbles received in a short period of time was ridiculous.

A few days ago I'd broken my only pair of cheap sunglasses, and I decided to brave the leers of the locals by walking into the service station for a replacement pair. Inside the few customers simultaneously stopped talking and watched me. I snagged the first pair of sunglasses on the rack. They had a thick white frame and really dark lenses and probably would look too big for my face.

Someone in the back of the store mockingly coughed and spat, "Murderer." And a few others in the store chuckled.

I paid for the glasses and got out of there, feeling the weight of angry eyes on me. Slipping the large glasses on my face, I wasn't even surprised to see Marshal Cobb had pulled up alongside Bubbles and was peering inside my driver's window.

With a muttered curse and remembering all the unpaid tickets in my glove box, I called out to him as I got close.

"Before you say anything, you can put your ticket

book away. I am *not* camping here in the middle of Main Street. I was just at the vet's and now I'm heading back to Miller's farm."

"I had a few people send me messages that you seemed to be just hanging out in town. People watching." He moved his toothpick from one corner of his mouth to the other. "It's making people nervous."

"Is that so." I rolled my eyes and felt anger boil in my gut. "All five foot three of me is a threat to people filling their pickup trucks with gas?"

"Yeah, I think it would be best if you just stayed in your clown car on Miller's farm and didn't come into town."

"Did you see the screenshots I've sent you? The threats? It would be helpful if you did something about those," I hissed. "I feel like I have a target on my back!"

When he didn't reply I pushed by him to open the driver's door, and the marshal put a hand on my arm and whispered in my ear.

"The lab came back with the gunshot residue test. It was positive." His eyes were hard and his hand on my biceps was tight.

I pulled out of his grip and took half a step back. "That's impossible!" I shook my head frantically. "How could I have gunshot residue on my hands when I didn't fire a gun? I didn't even touch one!"

"Guess that's the magic question then," the marshal drawled.

I remembered what Brandy said and hastily added, "But there's such a thing as transfer. I could've gotten the GSR on my skin just by touching something that the killer touched, so that doesn't prove anything."

"It's not enough to lock you up, but it's a black mark

next to your name, Red. Don't go far. When I need to talk to you, I want to know where to find you and—" Cobb was interrupted by a tap on the shoulder by Noah Adams.

"Hi there, Marshal, how are you this evening?" To me he said, "Are you ready to go for that cup of coffee now?"

"You two going for coffee?" Cobb looked skeptical.

"Yes. Yes, we are." I nodded vigorously. "But don't you worry, I'll be back parked on Miller's farm in just a bit."

The marshal gave a sharp nod, then walked away.

"Thanks," I told Noah.

"I was just getting gas and the look on your face said that you might just run the marshal over with your van if you got the chance."

"I was seriously thinking about it," I laughed. He leaned against the side of my vehicle as I opened the door.

"Hold on, what about my coffee?" Noah asked.

"Oh. You were serious?" I inwardly recoiled, thinking of our conversation at the laundromat. "How about another time?" I put my key in the ignition and turned it to start up the van but all I got was a click. I tried again but Bubbles's battery wasn't giving me any juice. "Damn."

"I'll give you a boost."

"I'd appreciate that."

"After you have coffee with me."

I sighed. "Deal."

The coffee shop across the street that doubled as a bakery and tripled as the laundromat was closed.

"The diner's still open and I'm starved," he said.

I slow nodded. "Okay. Give me a second."

I checked on Muffin, who was fast asleep in her carrier, grabbed my purse and hopped out of the van. A dozen pairs of eyes witnessed the two of us cross the road and make our way down the street to the diner. No doubt the Hope Harbor gossip grapevine was heating up. The entire town should be apprised of our coffee date before I even got a sip of caffeine in me.

As if to ensure the rumor mill had extra fodder, Noah opened the door for me and placed his hand tenderly on the small of my back as I stepped inside the restaurant. It was a warm and familiar gesture that didn't go unnoticed by anyone in the restaurant, or by my lower back, which felt the heat long after his hand was gone.

We slipped into a corner booth and I shyly met Noah's gaze across the table. He had his usual look going on: hair mussed, five o'clock shadow across his jaw, and a permanent half smile.

The waitress arrived for our order. She was all of sixteen and had an obvious crush on Noah because she smiled sweetly at him, then touched his arm as she handed him a menu while mine was tossed onto the table in front of me.

"We got the prime rib on special, Noah. I know that's your favorite."

When we arrived I told him I'd only be having coffee because I had a burger not that long ago, but the menu had me craving something sweet. Noah ordered the prime rib special and I asked for a vanilla shake with extra whipped cream.

When the waitress left I explained, "My fridge isn't working in Bubbles so I get my calcium on the road."

"No need to explain yourself to me. I love a milk-

shake myself." He paused. "How long you been without a working fridge?"

"Too long."

"Trouble with your battery and no fridge, huh? I'm
guessing living out of a camper van hasn't been easy."

"Sometimes it's amazing. There are times I disappear into the forest for days and it's pretty magical.
I've seen a lot of the beautiful views on the road." And
some bodies, but I wasn't going to tell him that. "The
only reason I've stayed in Hope Harbor this long was
because Penny offered me a job and I'm saving to get
the battery and fridge fixed."

We made small talk between noisy slurps of my
shake and Noah shoveling large quantities of meat and
potatoes into his mouth. I brought up Murray's murder
by leaning across the table and speaking quietly.

"You don't gotta whisper, Red. Everyone in town
knows Murray got shot. Hell, I doubt anyone here is
talking about anything else." Noah waved his hand to
indicate a number of townsfolk tucked into booths and
tables.

"If all the sidelong glances are any indication, they're
also talking about us," I said, keeping my voice low.

"Which is exactly why I suggested we go out and
be public so everyone can see you're not a murderer."
He shrugged and offered a smug smile. "Like you said,
I'm well-liked in town so maybe if people see that I like
you, they'll cut you a break."

I caught the angry stare of an old man who'd just
entered the diner.

"I admire your optimism, but I don't think this'll
change anything." I blew out a breath and lowered my
voice to just over a whisper. "The gunshot residue test

they did on my hands came back positive." I blinked back tears. "The marshal is loving that evidence against me."

Noah scrolled through his phone, then looked up at me. "Every site I visited on the matter says that GSR won't prove anything. Even the marshal knows it sure doesn't say you killed Murray."

I closed my eyes and sighed. "Thank you."

Noah reached across the table and gave my hand a squeeze. "Everything's going to be fine. You'll see."

"You don't know that."

"Guess I'm an optimist." He polished off the rest of his food, pushed his plate aside and then excused himself to use the restroom.

The waitress swooped to our table to gather the plates. "You need to leave Noah Adams alone," she hissed under her breath. "We don't need another murder around here."

I just blinked up at her in surprise. "Excuse me?" I reached for the last of my milkshake but she snatched the glass off the table and balanced it on the tray with the rest of the dirty dishes.

"You heard me." She sneered. "Everyone knows you killed Murray and it's just a matter of time before they put your ass in jail."

As Noah returned, she slid the bill onto the table and offered him a saccharine smile.

"You okay?" he asked. "You look a little pale."

What Brandy told me earlier jumped into my head: *Don't be a victim. Fight. A small town like this would love to pin this murder on the new girl in town.*

I didn't want to be railroaded by this hick town. I

needed to take things into my own hands. "Know what I'd like now? A good old-fashioned bonfire."

"I have a firepit in my backyard. I suppose we could—"

I got to my feet and placed my hands on my hips. "Let's do it."

FOUR

MUFFIN AND I followed Noah in his pickup after he boosted my van. The cat meowed pathetically, obviously tired of being in the crate. The entire way I kept telling myself that this might be the oddest thing I've ever done. Especially because if Noah *was* involved, I was about to be alone with him. In the dark. With a fire bringing God knows what out of my subconscious.

He lived about a mile outside of town. His house was an older brick two-story on a couple acres with a long tree-lined drive and beautiful gardens. It was the kind of place a stable family man would call home and fill with children. As soon as I pulled into his driveway, I took advantage of the one remaining bar of cell service to text the address to Brandy just so someone would know where I was going to be.

I followed up the address text with: Just being safe & letting you know where I am. Noah Adams's place. Going to have a fire here. Hoping to get info.

She replied with: Message me every 30 minutes so I know you're okay. Also I hope he's cute.

And followed that with a winky emoji.

"Cute? I'm looking at a possible murder charge down the line and Brandy is hoping I'm with a cute guy," I grumbled to myself as I hopped out of the van. "Guess I can expect her to be my Rock of Gibraltar, like usual."

"What's that?" Noah asked.

"Nothing." I hesitated. "I should grab Muffin, right? Put her on a harness and let her get some fresh air."

"Muffin?"

"The kitten."

Muffin let out a loud meow turned howl to make herself known. I climbed back inside the van, found the leash and harness for Muffin, and it took me multiple attempts and a few hand lacerations to get her secured. When we got out of the van and I put her on the ground, she rolled on the grass trying to get the harness off. Eventually I scooped her up and followed Noah to his door. He opened it wide and I hesitated.

"I'm guessing your firepit is out back? How about I just meet you there."

He gave me an odd look. "You realize if I'm going to kill you it's just as likely to happen in my dark backyard as inside my house."

I took a step back and clutched Muffin to my chest. The look on my face must've caused him to realize that I was a split second from burning rubber.

"Kidding!" He chuckled and shook his head. "If you're so convinced I'm a killer, why are you here?" When I didn't answer he pointed to the side of the house. "You can get to the yard just through that gate."

Walking in the direction he pointed, I followed a path lit by solar garden lights. At the gate, I glanced at my phone and saw that last bar of service had disappeared altogether. Stuffing my phone in my pocket, I kept walking with a wriggly kitten in my arms. At the back he had a large deck illuminated by strings of white lights and, honestly, it looked like the least homicidal fiend domain I could imagine.

Ted Bundy was good-looking and charming, I reminded myself. "Ouch!" Muffin bit my finger and I put her down on the ground.

Just off the deck was a circle of logs around a fancy stone and iron firepit that looked expensive and custom-made. I'd been visualizing a pile of wood in a hole in the ground. This looked like it was arranged by some-one with a Pinterest obsession. I walked slowly toward the firepit area because Muffin needed to attack every blade of grass along the way. Abruptly, the patio doors slid open and I jumped.

"Beer? Wine? Iced tea?" Noah called out.

"Beer, please," I replied and immediately regretted it. What if he planned on slipping a roofie in my drink? I'd made up my mind not to even take a sip but when Noah arrived he handed me a bottle that hadn't been opened.

"You have a beautiful property." I unscrewed the lid to my beer and took a sip.

"Thanks." He opened a beer for himself and put it down next to a log on the opposite side of the firepit. "Pull up a log and I'll do the manly stuff."

"Building a fire is manly stuff?" I rolled my eyes and took a seat on a log near the grass edge so Muffin could pounce in the lawn.

Noah busied himself making the fire. It took him only a couple minutes before it was raging.

"Impressive," I said but I was trying not to look di-rectly at it and, instead, focused on Muffin so as not to be drawn in too soon.

"Me. Man. Make. Fire." Noah thumped his chest dramatically. "Dryer lint is my secret. It's awesome fire starter." He winked and took a long swallow from his beer.

"Good to know."

I made a mental note to use dryer lint as kindling in the future. I'd shortened Muffin's leash so she couldn't get anywhere close to the fire. She was doing somersaults in the grass beside my seat and biting the leash as if it was her mortal enemy. I realized Noah was staring at me and when I glanced up he quickly looked away.

"You can smoke if you want. Don't worry about me." I pointed to his shirt pocket bulging with a pack of smokes and lighter.

"Trying to quit." He patted the pocket. "Just carry them around as a reminder. I hadn't had one in a few months until yesterday when I heard about Murray."

"I tried smoking once in my teens, but I never got the hang of it," I admitted. "It's hard to look cool when you're choking and coughing until you vomit." Also, now that I looked back, it reminded me that when the match was struck I'd felt so dizzy looking at it, I thought I'd pass out before I even took a puff.

He laughed. "Guess it turned out to be a good thing."

"Guess it did." I took another drink and angled in my seat to look directly at Noah. "Speaking of Murray, who do you think killed him?" The glow of the fire played in his eyes, and I looked down and gave Muffin's head a scratch.

"I think it could've been just about anyone in this town."

"Anyone?" I pulled my face into a frown.

"Sure." He shrugged. "I doubt it was a planned thing. I can't imagine anyone was lying in wait in Penny's storeroom waiting to take him out. If someone was planning to kill him, they'd do it somewhere other than Main Street, right? Everyone knew Murray liked to go fishing at the crack of dawn. Seems like if it was a planned thing, they would've snuck up on him at his fishing hole. It's in the middle of nowhere and it probably would've taken a while to find his body." He held up a hand. "Before you think I'm a suspect because I know his favorite fishing spot, I was one of the few people he ever asked to come along. I thought a day of fishing might make me like him more. It didn't."

"I didn't even know he liked to fish."

"Which is probably why the entire town thinks you're the most likely suspect."

I felt my eyes sting and before I could stop it, a fat tear slid down my face.

"Oh he-e-ey, don't cry." He had a note of panic in his voice. "I mean, I *personally* don't think you killed Murray. If I did, I wouldn't've invited you back to my place, now would I?"

"Thanks." I sniffed and wiped my face with my shirt sleeve. "How long ago did your wife die?"

"Oh now we're going to talk about her? You trying to make me cry too?"

"No!" I blurted and then realized he was joking. "You don't have to answer if you don't want to."

"It's not a secret and she was no longer my wife when she passed." He finished off his beer and placed the bottle at his feet. "We married pretty quick after college and I caught her cheating before our first anniversary."

"Ugh. I'm so sorry."

"Don't be. I'm just glad it was then and not a dozen years later with a handful of kids, right?"

"Right."

"Anyway, she shacked up with a boyfriend but when she found out she had cancer he ditched her pretty quick. Since she had no family to speak of and she needed care

I suggested she move back. It wasn't as a husband and wife thing. I took care of her until she died."

"Wow." I shook my head slowly in amazement. "That's not something most people would do." I sighed and closed my eyes briefly. "Good lord, I can understand why people in town are pretty protective of you. You're like the town saint or something."

"I wouldn't go that far but, yeah, people around here are a little overprotective of me." He chuckled. "I think I've had no fewer than a dozen marriage proposals since she passed away. I've stopped accepting dinner invites because it's always a setup. Even Penny tried to fix me up with her daughter."

"Tess? She's very pretty and I hear her husband left her so she's free for the taking."

"Oh gee thanks. Have you met her? I doubt a more depressed person exists on the planet." He took a swig from his beer. "She wasn't even separated at the time Penny tried to fix me up. Penny said she just wanted Tess to know there were better options."

"It must suck to be so popular." I laughed but then thought of my own lonely existence and it was hard not to feel sorry for myself. Noah Adams had an entire town looking out for him. I had nobody. Unless you counted Brandy and I sure as hell didn't. "You've lived in Hope Harbor your entire life?"

"Yup."

"So when Murray came to town and he and Penny became an item, that must've been big news."

"Kind of but not really. Everyone loves Penny so they were just happy for her."

"How did everyone feel when they split? Anybody

love Penny so much they carried a grudge against Murray?"

"Nah, we're talking years ago. She was the one who broke it off but since she was always friendly to him and never had a bad word to say, nobody cared that much one way or another. Things may have been different if she'd been bad-mouthing him all over town but she never did."

He took a long stick and poked at the fire, creating sparks. I physically turned my body away from the flames.

"I know you're trying to make sense of his murder," Noah said. "But you're best just leaving that to the law."

"Easy for you to say, you're not the new person in town who everyone suspects." And the one receiving threats online.

"You know what we need?" he asked, getting to his feet. "Marshmallows. I'm sure I've got some around the house somewhere."

"That sounds good." I smiled.

As he walked toward the back door I could hear a landline ringing inside. I heard his voice answer and a conversation begin but was too far away to hear specific words. This might be the perfect time to do what I came to do.

Gathering Muffin into my arms, I closed my eyes and took in a few slow, deep breaths, then focused on the flames in front of me. Distant wind chimes echoed in my head, and the swirling scent of smoke filled my senses. I reached to touch the long scar under my hair and gradually entered my trance. A log made a loud crack, and sparks flew a few inches beyond the pit, but

I ignored all that. I was feeling intensely dizzy and extremely nauseated.

The next thing I knew, I woke up flat on my back to the sound of yelling. With a moan I grabbed my head and sat up to find Brandy standing over me, holding a gun pointed at Noah.

She screamed, "What did you do to her?"

He replied, "Nothing! She must've fainted."

"I'm good!" I patted her leg so she'd move, then scrambled to my feet and steadied myself. "Seriously, I'm fine. He didn't do anything to me. I felt woozy and next thing I knew you're here playing Annie Oakley." I blew out a breath. "Why are you here and where is my cat?"

Brandy put her hands on my shoulders and looked me in the eyes. "Obviously you've been drugged, Scarlet. You don't have a cat."

"Muffin is here," Noah called out. He bent and picked up the kitten and walked her over.

Brandy looked from the kitten to Noah and to me.

"A kitten adopted me this morning." I shrugged. "Put the gun away before someone gets hurt."

"You're really okay?"

"Yes." I had the corner of my thumb in my mouth as I nervously nibbled a hangnail.

"Stop biting your frigg'n' nails," she barked, slapping my hand out of my mouth. Then she tucked the weapon into a holster at her ankle. "I sent you half a dozen messages to see if you were okay and you didn't reply. Last text I got was you telling me this address so of course I rushed over."

"There's no service out here," Noah remarked. He was eyeing Brandy and me with amusement.

Brandy looked at her phone to confirm the lack of cell service.

"Ugh." She rolled her eyes. "I don't know how you live out here." She straightened and looked from Noah to me. "If you're here under duress you just need to tell me the code word."

"What code word?" I blinked.

"The one we had when we were kids. The word Mom told us to use if we were ever in trouble but couldn't say over the phone."

"Pineapple?" Then I slapped my forehead. "Oops. Guess we'll need a new code word."

"I don't know what I'm going to do with you. I left a meeting for this. Text me when you leave and don't forget, lesson two tomorrow. I'll send you a message first in case you...you know...have a late night." Brandy combed her long hair with her fingers and regarded us both coolly before she disappeared.

"So, you have a sister..." Noah chuckled and rubbed the back of his neck.

"I am so-o-o-o sorry." Muffin was biting at the buttons of my shirt so I lowered her to the ground. "I'll just get going."

"Really? You think I'm letting you get behind the wheel? Nope, you just fainted so you'll sit your ass down for a minute. You look pale as hell."

I lowered myself onto the log where I'd been sitting before. "Sorry to freak you out."

"No worries but I'd like some kind of an explanation. Have you been sick?" He pressed his hand to my forehead. "You're a bit warm but that could be from the fire."

"Um..." How do I even begin to explain what happened without sounding like I'm hallucinating? I rubbed the back of my neck. "I guess I just fainted because of the heat from the fire, or maybe because of the stress and—"

"You should definitely see a doctor about that." He had his hands on his hips and a hard glint in his eyes. "Also, tell me about your sister showing up here and almost blowing my head off."

My mind was still fuzzy, but I knew I'd seen something in the fire that made me tense. I debated what to tell him and decided that since he'd shared about his wife the least I could do is talk about Brandy.

"I hadn't seen Brandy since just after my grandmother's funeral a couple years ago. She was a hardcore heroin addict and I told her I never wanted to see her again. Then the police found her to ask questions about me because of Murray. Next thing I know she shows up in town playing big sister. She's staying in Bellingham and determined to, um, reconnect now that she's clean." I winced. "I don't have any local friends so when I pulled up in your driveway it occurred to me that nobody knew I was here, and it wasn't really a safe or smart thing to go to a man's house without at least telling one other person so I texted her your address and just said this was where I would be."

"And then when she didn't hear from you, she went into big sister executioner mode."

"Apparently."

"Okay." He stuffed his hands into the front pockets of his jeans. "But you're wrong about one thing." He cleared his throat and looked at me with soft eyes. "You said you don't have any friends in town, but you've got me. I'm your friend, got it?"

He went back inside and returned with marshmallows and a big glass of water.

"Sugar and hydration is what you need."

A smile played on my lips as I nodded. I drank the water and played with Muffin as he expertly toasted a couple of marshmallows on a stick and then handed them over to me. They were gooey and sickening sweet but he was right.

I felt immediately better but I desperately needed to leave and sort my head. It was coming back to me that I'd seen in his fire the same mass of blond curls that were in my earlier vision and nothing about that described Noah. I got up to leave and Noah walked Muffin and me around to the front of the house, and I thanked him for the fire and the beer.

"Next time we'll do s'mores," he promised with a goodbye wave.

When I turned the key in my ignition, all I got was a click in reply. Noah had started to walk back to his house but now he turned around.

"Dammit." I tried again and the response was the same.

"Another boost?"

I nodded and with a sigh I popped the hood.

Noah brought his truck out of his garage and turned it around so our vehicles were hood to hood while I got out and retrieved my jumper cables from the back compartment.

Bubbles roared to life immediately.

"Did you leave an interior light on?" Noah asked while disconnecting the cables and handing them to me.

"No, I just need a new battery."

"I have some on sale at the store." He slammed Bubbles's hood shut and then turned and shut his own. "And I could throw in the friends-with-the-owner discount."

"I appreciate that. I've been saving some money from my paycheck to get that done and also get a new fridge but I'm still a long way off from either. Especially after dropping money on a cat." I opened my door.

"What do you do about groceries without a fridge?" He looked concerned.

"Sometimes I buy a bag of ice. Honestly, it's not that big a deal. I'm only one person so…" I shrugged. "But as soon as I have enough in the bank, I'm going to take you up on that discount for a battery. Thanks for the boost." I smiled. "And the milkshake, the beer, the marshmallows and putting up with my stupid sister."

"Anytime." He grinned. "Except your sister." He shook his head. "She scares the hell out of me."

"You and me both." I laughed and began backing out of the driveway. Just before I pulled away, I used that one bar of service and sent Brandy a text saying I was heading back to my parking spot and all was good. She replied with a thumbs-up.

The drive started out with Muffin squeaking and hissing angrily from inside her crate but by the time I'd pulled onto Miller's field, she was quiet. I had a pounding headache either from hitting my head when I fell off the log, or because of the overall psychic experience. Headaches were common after I attempted any kind of fire-seeing, along with the strange smell of burning and the sound of wind chimes. All those things together made me concerned about one big thing.

Maybe my tumor wasn't entirely gone.

Or maybe it was coming back.

Would fire-seeing somehow trigger it? Make it grow fast and furious until I was debilitated?

Those thoughts were always in the back of my mind but, for now, I pushed them aside. I was anxious to pop a couple ibuprofen and climb into bed.

After I yanked the parking brake, I reached to pull the drapes closed. They wrapped around from the driver's side window, across the windshield and snapped into place at the passenger window. I had them halfway closed when headlights appeared up the road.

"Keep going…just keep going," I pleaded but the vehicle slowed and then pulled to the shoulder a few yards away. It was a marked police car and when Cobb climbed out, my heart sank.

Before he could knock I slid the door open.

"Something I can help you with, Marshal?"

"Your sister in there with you?" He stuck his head inside and took a look for himself.

"No, she's not," I said, unnecessarily because he could obviously see my entire domain from the door.

"I heard there was a yellow Corvette ripping through town." He sniffed. "You and her joyriding tonight?"

Joyriding? We're not sixteen!

"I was at Noah's place having a bonfire. Brandy visited briefly. She's staying in a hotel in Bellingham. Not sure which one but I'm sure you could use your investigative skills to figure that out and ask about her driving skills yourself."

"How long is she planning on sticking around?"

"I'm not sure. She doesn't exactly listen to me." Which was putting it mildly.

"We don't need her kind around our town."

"Her *kind*?" I narrowed my eyes and straightened

my spine. "What *kind* is that, Marshal? The kind who comes to keep an eye on her sister to make sure she's not being bullied for something she didn't do? That kind?"

My anger seemed to amuse him and I could see him fight to keep his face serious.

"No, ma'am, I'm talking about the kind of person who's a known shyster, a scammer. A woman who likes to bilk hardworking people and screw them out of their money by pretending to read their future."

"I don't know what on earth you're talking about." But I had a sick feeling in the pit of my stomach. "If this is about Brandy, she might be my sister, but I've had nothing to do with her for years. She wouldn't even have known where I was if you or Sheriff Duthroyd hadn't given her a call to check up on me."

He offered a quick shrug. "Right. When you talk to her, you can tell her to crawl back under whatever rock she crawled out from under."

"Unless she's committed some kind of crime, I'll ask you to watch your mouth about my sister." I folded my arms and steadied myself for the response.

"Oh you know what she is…" he spat back. "The less you have to do with her, the easier things will go for you. Just remember to stick close to Hope Harbor until this thing is cleared, got me?" He touched the brim of his hat. "Have a good evening."

I pulled all my drapes and blinds then hit the lock fob twice and the alarm button to be absolutely sure I was locked up tight. After stripping down to a T-shirt, I opened the crate for Muffin, who remained snoring softly in the back corner. I brushed my teeth and climbed into my bed exhausted and riled up at the same time. The corner of my fitted sheet had come up and I scooted over to tuck it securely back under the corner of the foam mattress. Instinctively, my hand checked the cubbyhole beside my bed. It was meant for magazines but behind an old issue of *Vogue* I kept Nan's 9 mm Glock. Loaded. Just in case.

When I saw Brandy tomorrow, I needed to ask her more questions about what sketchy schemes she'd been up to. Closing my eyes, I thought back to a mass of golden hair that had appeared in my visions along with a sickening feeling of unease. Noah had seemed kind and genuinely friendly; not to mention he was easy on the eyes. Still, there was something about the original vision I had and the man's pure hatred for Murray that had worked its way under my skin like an uncomfortable itch. Just before I drifted off, I thought about Noah and his comment about us being friends.

Was it possible to consider someone both a friend and a murder suspect?

FIVE

In my dreams I was fighting ninja warriors all night. I woke up to find the ninja's name was Muffin and my forearms were covered in tiny scratches. There was also a distinct but disturbing image of Noah in my dreams with his face twisted in rage. The visual was so clear and foreboding that I shuddered. After I removed the cat from my face, I filled her food and water dishes before making coffee.

I used a tissue to dab at some of the tiny cuts on my forearms. "You realize that if you kill me in my sleep it's going to end badly for both of us."

Muffin's response was to wind between my feet, climb my leg like it was a scratching post, and then purr loudly in my arms.

"Damn, why do you have to be so cute?" It was official. I had fallen head over heels in love with a furball with deadly murder mittens intent on reducing me to one big scab.

I kept the cat cuddled in my arms while I drank my coffee and ate the last of Penny's muffins. My mind kept hitting Replay on Noah's soft gaze as he was telling me he was my friend, and then that vision morphing to become the Noah in my dream whose face was lit with fury. When I pushed those thoughts from my head, I thought of Marshal Cobb calling Brandy a con man, and the golden curls that had already come to me in vision twice.

I fired off a text to Brandy asking when she was coming over. She texted back: Sleep now. Talk later.

She'd never been a morning person growing up and I guess that hadn't changed. My next message went out to Melody from the grocery store. She was the only one I knew that had hair even close to what I'd seen in my vision.

Hi it's Red. Do you have time to meet for coffee to talk about cat stuff?

A split second later she replied:

Always! I don't work til noon. How about my place?

She sent me her address and I replied that I'd be there within the hour as long as my van started.

Having a shower in my small camper took a bit of acrobatics and timing because the hot water tank was small and the bathroom was minuscule, but I had it down to a fine art. As long as I put a foot in the sink and grabbed the toilet behind me, I could even shave my legs. It was a skill. The tiny cat cuts all over my arms and legs stung when touched by my body wash but the warm water still felt great.

I wrapped my body in one towel and my hair in the other and almost tripped over Muffin when I stepped out of the bathroom. The little puffball was hissing while looking at the sliding door and her hair was standing up. I let out a squeak of surprise when I looked at my door and saw the outline of someone through my drapes.

A quick knock was followed by, "Hey, Red, it's me."

"Noah?"

"Yeah." He cleared his throat. "I've got something for you."

"Just a sec."

I dropped the towels, scrambled onto my unmade bed to reach my clothes cabinet and snagged a sundress to slip into. My thoughts crept to the scary Noah in my dream and I took a sharp knife from my cutlery drawer and placed it on my counter just within reach. Then I scooped up Muffin, pressed Unlock on the fob and slid the door open a crack. "Hi."

He held up a car battery. "Surprise!"

"A battery? Is that for me?" I blinked rapidly. "Noah, I really can't afford—"

"It's a present."

"A present?" I parroted skeptically as I opened the door wider. "But why..."

"I thought of flowers but you seemed more like the car battery kind of gal."

"I am. Definitely, but I don't feel good about such an expensive gift and—"

"Look, you can't have unreliable transportation, especially when that vehicle is also your home. It just isn't right." He pointed to the front of the van and I scrambled over to the driver's seat to reach for the lever to pop the hood. I stuffed a reluctant Muffin into her crate and then slipped my feet into flip-flops before joining Noah at the front of the vehicle.

"How can I help?" I peered into the engine.

"Just give me a bit of space and I'll get it all done in a few minutes."

"But—"

"It's really not a two-person job but you can make me a cup of that coffee I can smell from here."

"That I can do." I hopped back in the van and quickly made my bed, hung up my wet towels in the bathroom, then got down one of my stainless enameled coffee mugs.

It wasn't long before Noah slammed the hood down and then stepped inside, closing the door behind him.

"I really don't know how to thank you."

He pointed to the mug on the counter. "I'll take that as payment."

"Do you take sugar? I don't have cream because of the fridge situation but I have lots of sugar and—"

"Black is fine."

"Please, have a seat." I placed the coffee on my table and refilled my own cup. "I'm… I'm a bit overwhelmed by your generosity," I admitted, and I suddenly felt close to tears.

Muffin was howling from her crate so I turned away from Noah and brushed a tear away from my cheek as I opened the cat's door. The kitten hopped out and leaped to the counter and then to my bed.

"She's making herself right at home, I see."

"Yeah." I began to nibble my thumbnail and caught myself. "Just gotta get her to stop using me as a scratching post."

Noah moved to sit down, nonchalantly picked up the butcher knife resting on the table and wordlessly handed it to me. I blushed as I slipped it back into the cutlery drawer without explanation.

"I'm going to pay you back," I promised as I brought my coffee over and slid into the seat across from him. "It might take me a couple months but—"

"Stop." He smiled over the rim of his mug. "I said it was a gift. It's old stock that I'd already marked down and hadn't sold."

I didn't know if I believed him, but I thanked him again as he took a sip of his coffee.

"Hmmm. This is really good."

It had taken me weeks to learn how to make half-decent coffee using the pour-over pot I had instead of a coffee maker.

"I confess the battery isn't the only reason I stopped by." He put the mug down on the table and I felt nerves itch beneath my skin when his gaze met mine. "I also wanted to see how you were doing. It occurred to me after you left you might've had a concussion from falling off the log. I didn't see how you landed but maybe you hit your head or something." He frowned. "I should've insisted you stay so I could keep an eye on you."

Oh, that never would've happened. "No concussion." I smiled and rubbed my head, my fingers toying briefly with the long scar hidden by my hair. "Not so much as a bump."

"It's none of my business but I heard you had brain surgery so…"

"You heard that, huh?" I chuckled wryly as I shook my head. "There really is no such thing as privacy in a small town, is there?"

"Nope. If you're looking for privacy, you've definitely come to the wrong spot of heaven."

"It was a benign tumor and I'm fine. Really."

"Good to know." He took another sip from his mug, and Muffin climbed up the legs of his jeans and curled up to sleep in his lap.

"You're like a cat whisperer."

"Animals like me." He laughed and shrugged. "So, what are you up to today?" He put up one hand in a stopping gesture. "Just asking casually as a friend and not because I need ammunition for the Hope Harbor grapevine."

I smiled and told him I was going to go visit Melody.

"I take it she's going to fill you in on all things cat?" He smirked and gently stroked Muffin's back.

"That's the plan," I admitted.

Hopefully, she'd also give me some kind of insight as to whether she was the person showing up in my visions. I left that last part out.

"Just don't catch cat fever from her." He chuckled.

"Fever?"

"You'll see." He smiled mischievously.

"Okay, how about yourself? What are you up to today?"

"Off to open the store. And if my nephew shows up on time, I'll go visit my dad." He downed the rest of his coffee, got to his feet and handed me Muffin. The cat promptly chomped on my forearm, leaped out of my grasp and disappeared in the back.

"How is your dad?" I felt bad for never asking.

"He's had Alzheimer's for a few years now. Doesn't know who I am most days and actually thinks I'm his brother. His memory from before I was born, however, is pristine."

"Ugh. That must truly suck. I'm so sorry." And I meant it.

"Circle of life and all that." He shrugged but those gray eyes flickered with pain before he recovered.

As he walked toward his pickup, I thanked him profusely for the battery and he gave me a backhanded wave.

The second he pulled away, I turned my key in the ignition and Bubbles roared to life without hesitation. I blinked back tears. It had been a really long time since I'd received any kind of a gift and this was a doozy.

"If he turns out to be a killer, I'm going to be really disappointed," I told Muffin as I corralled her and plopped her back inside her crate.

My phone dinged and when I saw the notification was a social media message I held my breath before opening it.

We're watching you killer! One wrong move and...

The last remark was followed by a skull emoji. I'd blocked the last person and this was a new anonymous account. I swallowed thickly as I took a screenshot and sent it to the marshal.

After taking a moment to compose myself, I put the van in gear and headed to town. The address Melody gave me turned out to be a carriage house in the back of a sprawling ranch home just off Main Street.

Melody flung the door open before I could even raise my hand to knock.

"Come in! Come in!" She blocked the escape plan of an overweight tabby with one of her legs and I hurried inside and shut the door before the cat could get past Melody's foot.

I removed my sunglasses as I walked inside and tucked them into my shirt pocket.

"Cool shades," Melody remarked with a big smile.

A staircase to the left brought you to a loft bedroom, and the main floor living area was one large room with a kitchen at the back. As I kicked off my flip-flops I counted at least four cats.

"Your place is—" *so-o-o covered in cat hair I'm going to gag* "—cute. It's just the right size for a single person."

"Thanks! My parents live in the main house and they built this for me when I turned twenty and brought home my first cat. My dad is allergic." She sighed sadly. "Can you even imagine how hideous that would be?" She waved me to follow her. "I just brewed some coffee and I have day-old doughnuts that I brought home from the store yesterday."

As we walked through the living room, tumbleweeds of hair scurried away from our feet and under furniture. She had a round oak kitchen table with seating for four. The centerpiece of the table was a long-haired white cat chomping on one of the doughnuts.

"Oh, Arthur." Melody giggled. She lifted the white cat off the table, but he took the doughnut with him in his mouth as he was lowered to the floor. "Arthur is new. I just got him a few days ago."

"How many cats do you have?"

"Nine."

"N-n-nine?" I blurted. *Holy crap!*

"It's like having a bunch of naughty toddlers."

Melody bent to pat Arthur, who was chomping the doughnut at her feet, so she didn't see my mouth fall open and me gag as a cat hair flew onto my tongue.

Abruptly a brawl broke out between Arthur and two other cats determined to relieve him of the doughnut. Melody didn't seem to care.

"Nine is a lot of cats."

"They're all rescues." Melody grinned proudly. "Help yourself." She nodded to the coffeepot and doughnuts on the table. I poured myself a cup of coffee and discreetly pulled out a long cat hair when it floated to the surface. There was no way I was going to attempt a doughnut after Arthur had already drooled all over them.

"I was going to bring Muffin inside but I knew you had other cats, so I didn't know if that was such a good idea," I told her as I sipped the strong brew.

"Very wise." Melody looked at me seriously. "Introducing cats is something that has to be done slowly over time."

Just then a couple of felines tumbled by in a howling ball of hisses, and fur flew everywhere. Melody didn't even seem to notice the two fighting because she was too busy giving me advice on taking care of Muffin. I listened politely, waiting for her to take a breath so I could change the subject, and when she reached up to smooth her golden curls, I saw something that stopped me cold.

"Your nails." Like mine she had the nails on one hand painted bright pink and the other hand sported blue polish. I looked at my own nails as if to confirm what I already knew.

"I hope you don't mind." She giggled. "When I saw your manicure I thought it looked so cool I couldn't wait to try it myself."

"I only did it because I'd run out of enough polish to

do them all one color, and keeping them painted stops me from biting them."

"The best fashion trends come from happy little mistakes, don't you think?"

I didn't know much about fashion and couldn't remember the last time I even bought new clothing or makeup. If I needed something besides underwear and toiletries, I went to a secondhand store. As I sipped my coffee I looked Melody over and realized to my surprise and horror she was wearing a green plaid button-down shirt and black jeans. The exact same thing I'd been wearing yesterday when I came in to buy cat stuff and coffee. She'd also switched out her usual large hoop earrings for small silver studs, which were what I always wore. I didn't know whether to feel flattered or completely freaked out.

"Ummm…" I started to ask her about it, but didn't know how to begin. Instead, I changed tack completely. "Sure is sad what happened to Murray. Have you heard anything about it? Any rumors or ideas who could've done it?"

"Well…" She put her palms down on the table between us, leaned in and lowered her voice. "Do you want all the gossip?"

"Sure."

She clapped her hands excitedly and began to regale me with the tale of how Penny and Murray met at Tess's wedding and fell in love but the romance didn't last long. This was all stuff I already knew but I didn't want to interrupt. Melody said that he had a successful handyman service in Seattle but when he moved to Hope Harbor he, of course, left all that behind. He figured that he'd have no problem starting his service up here.

"It did pretty well at first." She lifted the coffeepot and asked if I wanted more. I declined and she took a moment to refill her own mug and dig into a doughnut. A long dark cat hair dangled from the corner of her mouth as she chewed.

"You have a—" I began but then she licked her lips and the hair was gone with the doughnut. "Never mind." My stomach flip-flopped. A scrawny gray-and-white cat jumped into my lap and began kneading my thighs.

"Oh my God!" Melody slapped her palms to her cheeks in surprise. "She *never* likes new people." She smiled sweetly at me. "Now I know for sure you're a good person. Cats are an excellent judge of character."

"She's a sweetie." I gave the cat a stroke on her back and then I tried to get Melody back on track. "Since Murray was working at Pincher's when I moved here, I'm guessing the handyman business didn't work out?"

"It started out fine, he was mostly doing work for some of the older people in town and even in some of the outlying towns and farms. Repairing fences, painting, cleaning gutters…that kind of thing. Business had been slow at Pincher's and I remember Penny saying he was helping her out financially so we all felt bad when…" She made an exploding motion with her hands. "Kapow! It all blew up."

Melody's exploding sound caused the gray cat to leap from my lap and bolt out of the room.

"What do you mean?"

Again, she leaned forward and lowered her voice. "Word got around to watch out for Murray because, as you probably know, he was very handsy." She rolled her eyes. "You didn't dare turn your back on him because he'd just grab your ass or a boob and then turn away as if it wasn't even him. One time I was stocking shelves at the store and he reached in front of me for a can of beans and copped a feel." She grabbed her own breast and gave it a squeeze. "I yelled so loud the manager just about had a heart attack." The memory made Melody giggle.

"I guess that kind of behavior didn't exactly improve his business."

"Yeah, but people were still asking him to do stuff. Women just wouldn't be in the same room as him. My mom had him replace some fence boards one time and when he asked to come into the house to use the washroom, she locked herself in her bedroom until he was done."

"Were people that hard up for minor repairs they didn't mind hiring a pervert?"

She shrugged. "I think it was mostly out of loyalty to Penny. She's an institution here in town. Everybody loves her." She dusted doughnut crumbs off her shirt onto the floor and then added, "Besides, Murray would always laugh and make it seem like it was all in good fun. I think a lot of the older men in town found it harmless and thought he was just a practical joker. Even the store manager told me I was overreacting."

Misogyny was alive and well in Hope Harbor.

"Okay. What happened to make Murray's business blow up?"

"Tanya Smith happened." Melody just left it there without explanation as she reached for another doughnut. This one she blew the hair off of first and offered to share it with me.

"And who is Tanya Smith?" I asked, shaking my head no to the half doughnut.

"You know Liz and Joe?"

I squinted as I tried to think. "They run the diner?"

"Yup and they're Tanya's mom and dad. Tanya used to work there washing dishes on the weekends. Now she's a dental hygienist working in Bellingham. She's really good so if you ever need any dental work done, you should look her up."

"I'll do that." Dental care was literally so far down my list of things to do I knew it would never happen. "Did Murray grab Tanya's butt and her parents didn't handle it well?"

"Exactly! Except it was more than that. I heard that Tanya's dad strolled into the walk-in freezer and found the two doing the tongue tango and their clothes were disheveled."

Ewww. I thought about Murray and couldn't imagine him kissing Penny, never mind someone younger.

"And here's the kicker..." Melody licked doughnut icing from her fingers. "Tanya looked like a mature young woman, but she was only sixteen."

"Holy shit!"

"Exactly. It was one thing when he was slapping ladies' asses around town but once it involved a child, people lost their ever-loving minds."

"Did the cops get involved? Were there charges?"

"I remember asking Joel about it..."

"And what did Marshal Cobb think?"

"He looked into it, but Tanya claimed it was consensual and sixteen is age of consent in Washington so..." She shrugged. "But nobody would hire him to change a light bulb after that."

"Yet Penny stayed friends with him and hired him at the store even after the rest of the town shunned him."

"She has a very forgiving nature."

In my opinion, that was some serious messed-up loyalty. "You call Marshal Cobb by his first name? I take it you're friends?"

"We go way back." She nodded. "He's a nice guy."

"The way he was looking at you at the store, I thought he might have a thing for you."

"Nah." She wrinkled her nose. "We dated one time after high school and it was a disaster. No spark at all."

We made small talk about the cats, and Melody overwhelmed me by rattling off lists like all the household plants that were toxic to cats. I interrupted her to tell her I didn't own any plants so then she started telling me about some of the naughty stuff her own felines had done. I let her go on for a while but after I'd spent an hour with her, I was still at a loss about why something that looked like Melody's hair showed up in my visions. I tried to think of a way to ask her where she was when Murray was killed.

"I don't remember seeing you in the crowd that gathered outside of Pincher's when I found Murray's body."

"Oh I heard about it but we were receiving a dairy delivery at the store so I was in the back watching them unload. I couldn't get away, but I would've loved to be there! From the talk inside the grocery store, everyone was freaking out about it."

"That must be hard, getting up early, especially since you probably stayed late and closed up too…" If Melody stayed late and opened the store early she would've been across the street from Murray at the time of his death.

"I went home early." She leaned in and whispered, "Cramps."

It wasn't exactly a definitive alibi, but I really wasn't getting a murderer vibe off Melody. Even if she was across the street, that didn't mean she'd snuck in the back door of Pincher's, shot Murray in the head and returned to the store. Felt really unlikely. If it wasn't for her hair being similar to my visions, Melody would be pretty low on my suspect list.

"By the way, your hair is really nice." If you liked big platinum hair. "It's very unique. I bet there isn't anyone else in town with your style."

"Nope, I do it myself." She patted a big curl. "Do you really like it? Most of the other blondes in town are using a straightener but I just don't think that style suits me. As for the color, I was thinking of trying out red next time." She eyed my hair and I resisted the urge to cringe.

"Oh, I think you look better as a blonde." Well, this meeting had been a bust, but at least I'd found out the truth about Murray the perv. There was one more thing. "People have been saying some pretty nasty things about me online."

Melody frowned. "Yes, I saw a couple of the posts on the Hope Harbor page. I reported some of the worst comments and the moderator deleted them but, honestly, it's like swatting flies. You'd be best not to look at them at all."

I told her I left the group and then mentioned about the threatening messages I was getting and she sighed dramatically.

"Make sure you tell Joel about those! Sending threats is illegal."

"Do you think I should be worried for my safety?" I asked, nibbling a cuticle.

"Oh I think it's all just talk. You know how people get."

"I sure hope it's just talk," I told her worriedly. I got to my feet. "Thanks for everything. My sister is paying me a visit so I should get going."

"Oh! I heard she's a witch or a scam artist or something."

"Who said that?" My voice was sharper than I intended.

"Maxine at the gas station was talking to Jane who works at the sheriff's office and—"

"Don't believe everything you hear."

"Gotcha." Melody winked comically as if she was now in on the joke.

As I was slipping on my shoes, I told her, "You know what? I will take the name of the dentist office where Tanya works. I'm overdue for a cleaning."

Melody scrolled through her phone and then texted me the information. "Dental health is very important."

We left the house together because she wanted to stop at the van and meet Muffin. She scooped my kitten out of the carrier and cooed and cuddled her before putting her back in her crate.

"You're going to be an awesome cat mom," Melody said with a smile. "Already I can tell you're just looking out for her best interests."

"Thanks for everything." I meant it. Melody might be a bit odd with her copycat behavior, but she seemed like a pretty sweet woman. Lord knows I needed as many friends in town as I could get.

"No problem, let's do it again soon." She nodded her

chin toward an older man pruning a hedge a few feet away. "Ugh, he's doing it all wrong." She rolled her eyes. "Guess I'm going to need to chat with my dad."

I slid the door shut and climbed into the driver's seat. As I was backing Bubbles up, I heard Melody shouting. Her face was purple with rage and she had her elderly father by the shoulders and was shaking him hard.

"Holy crap!" I pressed the brake and stared.

Was she going to hit the old guy? Did I need to do something? Abruptly, Melody stomped off toward her carriage house and left her dad to his pruning.

"Muffin, I think our cat-loving friend isn't all sweetness and light."

Muffin meowed in reply.

I stopped at the service station and had them top up my propane tank. Customers either blatantly stared at Bubbles or gave me sidelong stink eyes. A group of teen boys were leaning against the building and puffing on e-cigarettes. When I caught their eye, one of them put his fingers into the shape of a gun firing at me and then blew on the tip of his finger like it was a smoking revolver. My throat grew dry with fear as I averted my gaze.

Brandy called as I was pulling away and I put her on speaker.

"Am I coming to the bubble-mobile or is it coming to me?" she asked.

There was a nearby park that was right on the ocean. I gave her the address and told her I'd meet her there. When she showed up, I had two lawn chairs on the grass behind the van and I was sitting on one with Muffin at the end of her leash stalking a leaf.

"I've brought sustenance," Brandy announced and then stopped short. "What on earth is that?"

"You remember my cat, Muffin. You met her last night when you were pointing a gun at Noah."

"I thought you were joking, or at least only cat-sitting."

"Nope. She's all mine."

She let out a dramatic sigh and sank into the chair next to me. "Here." She handed me a coffee in a to-go cup and I protested.

"Thanks but I've had way more than my usual amount of coffee today."

"It's a chai latte."

"Oh. Thanks." I placed it into the cup holder of my chair and then took the paper bag she held out and looked inside at the chicken wrap. "Thanks again." Eating out was a luxury I didn't allow very often but I figured if my sister could afford the sports car she was driving, I could allow her to spend a few dollars on me. Which brought me to the first item of business.

"I've heard you're a con man, shyster and also a witch." I took a sip of my chai latte.

"I've been called worse by worse." Brandy pulled out a sandwich and took a big bite. "Is that your way of asking what I do?"

"If it's anything illegal, I don't want to know. That way if they come to arrest you, I can be innocent and will even pass a polygraph."

She snorted, pulled out her phone and handed it to me. "What am I looking at?"

"That bright yellow app is me."

I pushed my sunglasses onto my head and then narrowed my eyes, clicked on the yellow circle and read what propped up: *Psychic Brandy is a spiritual healer, medium, reader and advisor. Contact Brandy today to help you uncover mysteries of your past, present and future.*

"Huh. Really? This is what you do?" I scrolled through the app.

"Yes, that's my own personal app and I advertise on all social media platforms to do palm readings. People send pictures of their palms and I tell them their future."

"You've gotta be kidding me." But I could see she was telling the truth. On the contact section of the app was an address in Seattle.

"That's where you live?" I pointed to the section on the phone and she shook her head.

"That's my office. There's no way I'd put my home address on there for all the weirdos to find me. But I'm actually in an apartment across the street. Short commute." She laughed.

"Wait a second, I know that street. Nan and I used to go to the butcher shop on that block."

"The butcher shop closed a couple weeks ago. It's been replaced by a bakery. It has an annoying dancing cupcake sign that glows twenty-four-seven into my apartment window on the second floor."

I handed back her phone and pushed my sunglasses back onto my nose. "So I get it. You're a professional bullshitter."

"First of all, it's not all bullshit. Unlike you, I've been able to harness my ability to do readings. Is it perfect? No. The palm readings are all done electronically. The palms are read within the app and it spews out results I don't even see but the rest…" She lowered her sunglasses and looked at me seriously. "I gaze into a scrying mirror and tell people enough truth to make the hairs on the back of their neck stand on end, and then they gladly hand over their credit card. Do I love it? You betcha."

"Through an app?" I shook my head. "How is that a thing?"

"Some people want to have in-person readings and I accommodate that for a hefty fee. Like the guy I saw in Bellingham last night. But I don't need to be sitting with someone to read them. I just need something. Sometimes they use the app or my website to send me a picture of an item, sometimes they just send me a message telling their story, but it works best if I have something tangible. Once they've sent my fee, I give it the old college try."

"And you've perfected your skill so that you can give every single person an accurate reading?" I reached down and took a twig out of Muffin's mouth and tossed it out of her reach. "I'm not buying that."

"Six months after getting clean I walked into a car dealership and paid cash for that Corvette." She turned her chair sideways and offered me a big smile. "Scarlet, I can teach you. You can have this too. You could even—" she sneered "—get a working refrigerator. Imagine the joy."

"First of all, I can't see myself turning into a pay-per-view psychic even if it means a fridge, or a sports car. Second, if you're so good, how about you help me solve this town's murder so I can get the hell out of here."

"Do you think I haven't tried figuring this out for you? It doesn't work like that. I wish it did."

"So complete strangers can send you a picture and

you can give them an accurate reading but for me you get nothing?"

"Honestly, I've tried. Maybe it's a family connection. I get snippets but…" She shrugged and then changed the subject. "By the way, you looked pretty cozy with bonfire guy last night." She playfully punched my shoulder. "Are you sure you want to leave this town?"

"He's a nice guy who gave me a new battery for Bubbles, but that doesn't change the fact that the first vision I had about Murray's murder was all about Noah's hate for the victim." I sipped my chai. "But after a bit of research it turns out that the entire town hated the victim so, basically, all five hundred thirty-three remaining people in this town have a motive to want him dead."

"Sounds like someone did the town a favor."

"Remember how I told you they did a gunshot residue test on my hands on the day I found Murray? It came back positive."

Brandy tucked a strand of long dark hair behind her ear and turned to face me. "And remember what I told you, that doesn't prove anything. You were in the room where he was killed. You touched something that the killer touched." She shrugged. "It means nothing."

It didn't feel like nothing.

"It might be nothing to you, but to small-town Marshal Joel Cobb, I might've just as well have confessed."

"Say the word and I'll put you in touch with my lawyer."

"No." Then I reconsidered. "Not yet, anyway."

We ate in silence, watching the tide roll in and listening to the seagulls squawk as they dove in the surf. Muffin fell asleep on top of my feet. It was warm for September and the breeze off the water felt good. Sitting with my sister at the ocean gave me a kind of peace that made me ache for a home I'd almost forgotten existed.

Then Brandy ruined it when she opened her mouth. "Tell me about the shitstorm you were up to in Seattle and Aberdeen. What happened there?"

My instinct was to deny everything, but this was Brandy, not some cop, and she was far more likely to believe me. "Shortly after Nan's funeral I was boondocking around Seattle and working at a shoe store in the mall."

"Boondocking?"

"Just means I'd pull over somewhere like a street or a parking lot to park the van for the night instead of paying for a campground." I nervously gnawed at the cuticle of my pointer finger until I caught myself and tucked my hand beneath my thigh. "Sometimes I'd park behind a local 7-Eleven. The guy who worked the night shift didn't mind. He was nice to me." The memory hurt down deep in my gut. "Anyway, one night I decided to stay overnight at the mall parking lot instead because I had an early shift at the shoe store. That night there was a robbery at the 7-Eleven and my friend the clerk was shot. When cops reviewed the security footage for the last few days they saw Bubbles parked out back and tracked me down to talk to me."

"You were a suspect?" She pulled her favorite lipstick from her bag and applied it to her mouth. As she did, Nan's ruby ring caught the light.

"Briefly, but I told them about parking at the mall that night. After they checked the security footage there they saw that I stayed inside Bubbles all night."

"And then what?"

"There was a house fire a few days later. It had nothing to do with me or the murder, but I happened to be parked not far away that night so I walked over out of curiosity." I sighed. "Correction—I walked over because I felt called by the fire. It was like a magnet." I slid a sideways glance at my sister and she just nodded. "Anyway, the old house was fully engulfed when I arrived. Luckily, nobody was inside."

"What did you see?"

"The murderer who killed that clerk at the 7-Eleven. I saw the entire thing like it happened in front of my face. When the police reviewed store video they saw the guy wore a black ski mask so they had no idea what he looked like. In my vision, I saw him run down the road, climb into a red Nissan and pull off the mask. I even saw the license plate." I turned to Brandy. "That's the thing about my fire visions. They are completely random. Why would it be so clear that time and not now when I really need it?"

"You'll get a knack for this thing over time," Brandy promised. "So you told the cops about your vision."

"Yes, I called the police. I made up a story about how I'd gone for a walk that night and told them what I'd seen."

"They didn't believe you."

"The mall was five miles from the 7-Eleven and the mall security cameras never showed me leaving Bubbles so they couldn't figure out how I saw what I did. Then they found the red Nissan, found the ski mask still inside and the guy still had the gun and cash on him."

"The cops didn't push because they were just happy to get their man."

"Right but the media caught wind and my name was in the paper along with a picture of me and Bubbles:

Eyewitness Comes Forward." I blew out a breath. "Now my name is forever linked with the killing."

"And then in Aberdeen?"

"It was a drowning. Young woman jumped off a bridge." I cleared my throat. "I was staying in a campground that time and felt like barbecuing some burgers. Got a newspaper from the campground office to use as fire starter and read about the woman in the paper as I lit my fire."

"And you saw her jump off the bridge in your fire?"

"I saw it. But she didn't jump. She was pushed by her ex-boyfriend."

"Again, you told the cops you just happened to be walking by?"

"Yeah." I nodded. "And once they had my information they checked around. A gas station close by had security cameras that caught the ex grabbing her and putting her in his car. She had a restraining order against him. When the cops told him they had a witness who saw him push her off the bridge, he confessed. And again the papers got hold of the story and I was the witness that saved the day. Obviously, that made the cops look harder at me and I began to realize that I couldn't keep coming forward because, eventually, it would look like I was a serial killer or something."

"You could've just admitted to being psychic."

"I'm not ready to become that level of a freak. Not that you don't rock it like a superstar," I added quickly. "But I'm not like you. I'm an introvert. The idea of that kind of spotlight makes me want to crawl under a rock and hide."

"There were other cases though." She said it like a fact, not like a question.

"Yes."

"And those you just sent in anonymous tips?"

"Yes." I dragged my fingers through my hair. "Something happened when they removed that tumor from my head. It turned me into this person who can see things in fire, and I don't want that. I don't want it at all. I'd love if it would just stop."

"Are you kidding me right now?"

"What do you mean?" I got irritated. "We can't all be like you, embracing this weirdness."

"Remember when Mom rented that cabin for a month at Ross Lake?"

"I sure do. You were sixteen and a pain in the ass."

"You were ten and a bigger pain. Neither one of us wanted to go. We fought in the car the entire way. It was so hot and the cabin smelled like mothballs and dead rodents. We were covered in mosquito bites from head to toe and ate peanut butter sandwiches for every meal."

"But it was such a good time," I said wistfully.

"Yeah." Brandy smiled and exhaled. "But you know she rented that cabin because we got evicted from the apartment after Mom lost her job."

"I didn't know that." I turned to face my sister. "I remember her saying she'd be starting a new job soon and so we deserved a vacation."

"She didn't want us to worry. I heard her on the phone to Nan. She was freaking out. Two pain-in-the-ass kids, no job and no place to live. Nan wanted us to live with her, but Mom refused." Brandy got up from her chair and picked an armful of long dandelions and began tying their stems in knots. She turned to me. "Do you remember all the local cabin ladies coming over for tea?"

I nodded slowly as the memory came back. Seemed like all of a sudden our mom had a lot of friends in the area. I spent every waking moment swimming in the lake and had hardly noticed then but now it all came together. "She was reading tea leaves for money."

"Yes. After a month she had enough money to rent a new apartment and some spare to keep us in groceries until she found a new job." Brandy walked over and placed a dandelion crown on my head. "So you see, Princess Scarlet, Mom would've wanted you to use your talents to help yourself. Not just with this murder, but to make a living using what you've got."

"I don't believe that." I shook my head. "She rarely took out her tea leaves after that time at the cottage. I don't ever remember even having tea in the house after we left the cabin. She sure didn't make a living at it."

"It gave her headaches. Just like you." Brandy shrugged as she lowered herself back into her lawn chair next to mine.

"Then why didn't she or Nan tell me about it? Why didn't they give me a heads-up and give me instructions and—"

"Yours is a more…" Brandy fumbled for the word. "You're just more complicated than the rest of us. There was discussion about when to tell you and I guess they thought they had time."

I thought back to Nan's last days and a time toward the end when she held my hand in hers and told me she had so many regrets. When I assured her she shouldn't have any misgivings about her life, she became agitated and the nurse gave her more painkillers. In her doped-up state Nan had made me promise not to get rid of Bubbles and I'd agreed. It was the last conversation we had because even though the doctors had told both of us that she had a few more months, she'd passed in her sleep that night.

Abruptly Brandy clapped her hands and startled me from the memory. "Tell me everything you've been able to find out about this dead guy, Murray, and what your visions have shown you so far."

There wasn't much to tell but I told her about seeing how much Noah loathed Murray in the flame of his lighter, and then seeing blond curly hair in my candle, at the bonfire and in my dream. I mentioned my coffee date with Melody as the only curly blonde I knew and even brought up her copying my look and then I just shrugged. "That's all I've got."

I was expecting Brandy to mock me for my lack of skill, but she listened and then patiently explained her own technique.

"When I look in a mirror seeking a vision, there are times when it's crystal clear but other times it comes in bits and pieces and it's up to me to put the story together. I tried to get a read on what happened to this Murray guy," she admitted, "but I couldn't get a thing. Sometimes, when the message belongs to another psychic, she's the only one who can piece it together. This is your puzzle."

"So it's all on me." I blew out air between my lips. "That sucks."

"Yeah, but I'm going to show you everything I can before I leave today and, hopefully, that'll help."

"You're leaving?" I tried to keep the disappointment from my voice, but it slid in anyway. Tomorrow was my birthday. I'd spent the last ones alone after Nan died and was hoping Brandy would at least remember. "No worries. I know you've got a life. Plus, I'm back at work at the dollar store tomorrow anyway."

"Something's come up. It's a big work thing. I can't miss it because it means a huge amount of cashola. But Seattle is only a couple hours away. I'll be gone a few days but then I'll be back. Who knows? By then you could have this entire thing wrapped up and, if you do, roll Bubble down I-5 and stay at my place awhile."

Brandy got up and dusted her hands on her knees. "Let's get this lesson rolling."

I picked up the sleeping Muffin and placed her gently in her carrier before putting the lawn chairs in the trunk area under my bed at the back of the van. We climbed inside Bubbles and got comfortable at the table.

"With mirror scrying being my forte, I can call on my skill pretty much anywhere." Brandy dug into a tote bag, pulled out a silver-edged mirror about twenty inches in diameter, and placed it on the table inside a stand. "Having fire as your skill set makes things more difficult."

"Just a little," I said sarcastically.

"But I'm going to show you how I take on a case and maybe you can apply some of this to your talent." She scrolled through her phone and then showed me a picture of a middle-aged woman. "This is Vera. See the black pearls she's wearing in the photo?"

"Yes."

"They were left to her by her mother and have a lot of sentimental value. They went missing about a month ago and she's torn her house apart looking for them. She suspects her housekeeper but doesn't want to accuse her without confirmation."

"And you're going to be able to look into your mirror and tell her where the necklace is?"

"Hopefully." Brandy brought out a hair elastic and tucked her long black hair into a high ponytail. "And if I can't figure it out, I'll fake it."

"Excuse me?" I blurted. "How is that even remotely ethical?"

"Ethics shmethics," she laughed. "Vera has paid me a five-hundred-dollar advance for my services and I'm going to do my best. She's well aware there are no guarantees." She took out a business card. "This card is the housekeeper's. Sometimes having an item from the person I'm trying to see is helpful." She wiggled in her seat, adjusted the mirror position so she was looking directly into it and then said, "Watch and learn, sis."

First, Brandy closed her eyes and took in a few deep breaths, releasing them very slowly. Then, she half opened her eyes and gazed sleepily into the mirror while holding the business card in one hand. With her other hand she used her thumb to slowly turn our grandmother's ruby ring. Her eyes grew huge as she stared into the mirror. At one point she didn't appear to be breathing at all and her pale face went chalk white.

I clenched my hands tightly in my lap. She wasn't moving. I couldn't even see her chest rise or fall with breathing. Should I give her a shake? Was she going to be all right?

Abruptly, Brandy drew in a gasping breath followed by a full-body shudder.

"Could I get some water?" Her voice was hoarse, but the color was returning to her face.

I jumped up and got her water from the tap.

"Fridge doesn't work so I've got no ice. Sorry." I

handed her the glass and she took a couple of gulps, then wiped beads of sweat from her forehead with the palm of her hand. "You scared me. You looked so-o-o…out of it. Like you were dead with your eyes open." I dragged my hands through my hair. "Did it work? Do you know what happened to the necklace?"

Brandy held up her hand to ward off questions and then punched a number into her phone.

"Hi, Vera, this is Brandy… Yes, and no, your maid did not take them… Last weekend your granddaughter used the pearls to play dress-up. You'll find them in the bottom of the toy box… Yes, I'll wait." Brandy rolled her eyes at me and soon the woman was back on the phone. "Oh good… Although your housekeeper didn't take them, there's one more thing you should know about her." She paused before adding, "She is sleeping with your husband. If you hurry, you may catch them at the Holiday Inn just up the road." Brandy tilted her head and tapped her chin. "In room 310."

The slew of curses that followed came crystal clear from the other end of the call.

"I'll be sending you an invoice for the balance."

After she ended the call, Brandy tucked the mirror and her phone back in her tote then dusted her hands together with a big grin on her face. "See? Easy peasy."

"Easy for you." I let out a low whistle. "Wow. I have to admit I'm impressed."

"It's not always that simple, or dramatic, or quick. Take the case I'm dealing with in Seattle tomorrow. Parents messaged me a month ago about their missing kid. I don't like to take those kinds of clients."

"Too emotional?"

"Yes, and usually my skills won't let me get that

dark. You've solved murders? I catch cheaters and find jewelry." She released her hair from the elastic and it fell freely down her back. "Also, it means dealing with cops, who aren't my favorite people."

"But you're going back to talk to them about their missing child?"

"I had a dream. What I saw might be helpful to the investigation. I couldn't live with myself if I charged them a fee and any inklings I got turned out to be bogus."

For once, I felt a little proud of my big sister.

"Mom and Nan had the same issue dealing with darker situations," Brandy mentioned.

"How do you know that?" I frowned.

"I heard them talk about it. Mom said that if a woman came to her wanting to hear about someone who passed on, she got an immediate block. Nan said it was the same for her and, I guess, it's been the same for me too." She pointed a finger at me. "You, on the other hand, have a knack for finding the dead inside flames."

"You don't know that."

She exhaled loudly. "Scarlet, your fire-seeing didn't start with the tumor. That summer we were at Ross Lake, Mom forbade us from having campfires on the property or going to anyone else's fires. Do you remember that?"

"Sure." I thought back. "It was a dry summer. It was because of the risk of forest fires."

"No, that's just what she told us. It was because that very first night we were all sitting around the campfire roasting hot dogs and you got this faraway look in your eyes and in this weird, freaky voice you told

Mom that Grandpa had been married before and killed his first wife."

"That's ridiculous!" I got to my feet and wrapped my arms around my body to stop from shaking. "I never said that! Why would I say it, if it wasn't even true? Now you're just making stuff up!"

"Scarlet, it was true and, until that moment, Nan was the only person who knew it."

SIX

"You're telling me our grandfather was married before and killed his first wife?" I felt physically sick. Although I'd never met the man, it wasn't the kind of family history to be proud of. "Nan said that he was killed in a hunting accident when Mom was just a baby."

"Apparently, the person he hunted was his first wife and, years later when the cops came asking questions, he was already married to Nan, and Mom was a baby. He turned the same gun on himself."

I sat back in my seat and held my head in my hands. "Poor Mom." I moaned. "To learn that must've been devastating, but to hear about it from me..."

"To be fair, Nan should've been upfront about it. She should've shared the skeletons in our closet and she should've told you about your talents."

"Why can't I remember that?"

"The next day when you tried to bring it up, Nan told you that you'd had a bad dream. I guess your subconscious decided that was reason enough to put it aside." Brandy put her palms on the table. "Anyway, back to your situation. You need to practice. A lot. Big fires. Little fires. Clearing your thoughts through meditation and focusing on what you want to know." She tapped a fingernail on the table. "The more you practice, the clearer things will come to you, and the sooner the better. Next time we get together I'll observe you around a fire and see if I can offer any tips."

"Okay." My mind was still on my grandfather.

She got to her feet then and picked up her tote. "If you're still not getting clear visions, we'll figure out a way to get a personal item that belonged to the dead guy. That should do the trick for sure."

When she stepped outside, she turned and looked at me. "I get bad vibes from this town, Scarlet. You need to get out of here."

After she left, I approached Nan's picture on the wall and touched it with longing.

"I wish you would've told me this stuff." I felt a ball of anger in my chest but it sizzled out and left a hollow longing. I closed my eyes, and a tear slid down my cheek. "I wish you trusted me enough to tell me the truth. Why didn't you show me what I needed to know?"

We had been so close and yet Nan hadn't felt safe enough to open up to me. That stung. My mind and heart were racing with all that I learned and I felt like I was on the verge of a panic attack.

I opened the rear doors of my van and zipped up the back screen so that I had a clear view of the ocean behind my bed. I sat cross-legged in the center of my mattress and gazed out at the sparkling water, watching the returning tide slowly eat up the sand. The sound of the waves and movement of the water was hypnotic and I allowed my mind to clear and my breathing to slow.

It was soothing, but try as I might, I couldn't get Brandy's warning out of my head. She was right about this town. Since Murray's death I'd had the same uneasy feeling about Hope Harbor. Something was rotten here, and I needed to help get this thing solved so I could leave. Permanently.

At one point I fell asleep with Muffin tucked up against me curled into a ball. I woke up to the startling sound of a child shrieking. I got to my knees and frantically scanned the beach behind me only to realize it was a family playing in the surf.

But then there was a loud rap on my windshield and I whirled around to see Marshal Cobb's face.

"Oh great," I grumped as I scrambled out of bed and made my way to my driver's seat. I rolled down my window and smiled. "Hello, Marshal. Something I can help you with?"

"This is a day-use park. There's no camping."

"I'm confused…" I pointed up at the sky. "That's the sun, right? Are you telling me I'm not allowed to use the park in broad daylight?"

"I'm just reminding you of the law."

Muffin clawed her way up my pant leg then my shirt to perch on my shoulder and hiss at the marshal.

"Don't you have a murderer to catch? Is this really the best use of your time?" I was smiling sweetly but I wanted Muffin to leap onto his face and claw his eyes out. "I've gotta say, this is starting to feel a lot like harassment."

"I heard you and your sister were here and…" His voice trailed out.

"We had the audacity to sit in lawn chairs, eat sandwiches and have a picnic. Wow. You'd better arrest me right now." I thrust my wrists out the window. "I just bet there's some obscure Hope Harbor law against eating a sandwich on the beach without a license?"

"Don't get smart with me, Red. I just want you to know I'm keeping my eye on you."

"Same." I narrowed my gaze at him.

"Excuse me?" He tilted his head and then laughed.

"Well, don't you think you should be working this murder case night and day? Don't the people of Hope Harbor expect that their marshal will be all over this so they can feel safe in their beds?"

"I encourage you to worry about yourself and not about me," the marshal drawled. Then he spoke up loudly to ensure people nearby heard him, "From where I stand, I am closing in on my suspect." He shook a finger in my face, then strode back to his car and drove away.

Even after he'd left I received blatant gawks from people close by.

"Oh, brother." My hands were balled into fists and I had to force myself to relax. I pulled Muffin toward my face and kissed her nose. "Can you believe that guy?"

Hope Harbor was only twenty minutes from the Canadian border and I'd never felt such a strong urge to escape my country as I did in that moment, but I knew there was only one way to get out of this situation and this town: find Murray's killer.

Brandy's reminder to practice rang in my ears and I got down my three-wick candle and took out my lighter. As I was placing both on the table I noticed the parking lot filling up with beachgoers. There weren't going to be many more warm autumn days so everyone in town seemed to be taking advantage of the nice weather.

I even spotted Tess and Penny climb out of a red sedan and make their way to a picnic table. I debated approaching them to say hello. It seemed impolite not to, but they appeared to be having a pretty deep conversation. Tess sat on one side of the table leaning forward and talking animatedly, waving her hands in the air while Penny just looked sad.

Suddenly Tess turned her head and stared right at me. She said something to Penny, then got to her feet and strode toward Bubbles. I placed Muffin down and hopped out of the vehicle.

"Hi!" I smiled. "How are you doing? How is Penny holding up?"

"Are you following us?" Tess asked.

"Excuse me?" What kind of an accusation was that? "No. I've been here for hours. Had lunch with my sister and I was just getting ready to leave." I'd actually planned on staying but this was the last straw.

"I'm just joking!" She giggled. "Sorry, my humor isn't for everyone." She ran her hands through her hair. "It's a beautiful day so I told Mom we needed to get out and enjoy it before the rains come. Besides, all the phone calls from everyone in town is getting to be a bit much. Everyone is digging for information for the gossip mill. And some are so persistent!"

"Anyone in particular bugging you guys?"

"Yoo-hoo! Red!" Penny called out from the picnic table with a friendly wave. I raised my hand in acknowledgment, then looked at Tess, waiting for her to answer.

"I'll just tell you tomorrow at Pincher's."

"Oh. Are you, um, so you're going to…"

"Work at the store? Yes. I told Mom you could probably use a little help getting the boxes unpacked from the storeroom. I'm hoping to head back home in a few days so trying to help out where I can in the meantime."

"Okay." That made sense. "I'll see you at the store

tomorrow then." I started to walk away and then turned back. "You know, if you need to talk or if you two need anything at all, please don't hesitate to ask me."

"Thanks. That's sweet."

As she walked away I got the feeling that she not only would never ask me for a damn thing, but I was betting she didn't trust me like half the town. Was she coming into Pincher's tomorrow to help out, or to keep an eye on the town suspect?

I returned to Farmer Miller's field because being in the park was just attracting the wrong kind of attention. Before I settled in for the afternoon, I dialed the number for the dentist office that Melody gave me and I asked to speak to Tanya. I was told she was away on vacation and would be back in a few days.

Damn. I was hoping to talk to her. As a young victim of Murray's she could be a suspect. Her so-called vacation could've involved murder and I wondered if the marshal had even thought to look into her yet. I tried to research her name to see if I could get a home address but nothing came up. I did find her social media pages but her privacy settings were too good for me to get a true glimpse into her schedule. I set a reminder on my phone to try calling her again in a few days.

The rest of my day was spent tossing a toy mouse to Muffin, staring at my three-wick candle for messages from beyond that didn't come, and arguing with Nan's picture about why she never mentioned the revelation that my grandfather was a murderer.

"I thought we were close," I told Nan's picture as I brushed my teeth for bed. "You taught me useless stuff like how to fold a fitted sheet but failed to teach me the basics of my psychic abilities." I spat toothpaste into the sink. "And left out all about our family's history of psychic talents." Slipping out of my clothes and tucking them away into the cabinet above my bed, I continued to fume. "We spent months on the road in this tiny camper together. There were plenty of quiet times before you got too sick when you could've said, 'Hey, there's a couple of important things I need to tell you.'"

MY PHONE ALARM went off promptly at seven. Even though the store didn't open until ten, I wanted to have a non-rushed morning. I wanted to be there early and get things tidied up before I had to spend the day with Tess. I was hyperaware that there would be blood on the floor of the storeroom waiting to be cleaned. It would be a kindness to do it for Penny and Tess, but it wasn't something I was looking forward to.

I had my morning coffee, dangling my legs out the sliding door of the van with Muffin on the leash pestering a butterfly. My supplies were low so breakfast was peanut butter on half a stale burger bun. A reminder of that time spent at the lake with Mom and Brandy. An innocent childhood memory that now had a darker feel since Brandy had filled me in on the struggles my mother faced and the way my family conspired to keep me from fire.

Muffin attacked my shoelaces and I laughed, grateful for the comic relief the kitten gave. She seemed to be getting used to the leash and was using the litterbox regularly but I was concerned about leaving her in the van all day while I worked. Thankfully, the temperatures were cool enough outside that the van wouldn't get too warm.

Living in a camper van meant things always had to

be tucked away into cabinets before I drove or they'd become projectiles at a speed bump or sharp corner, but today I also took extra care to be sure Bubbles was Muffin-proof. I didn't want to keep her in a crate all day. When I turned off the van ignition in front of Pincher's Dollarama, I opened the roof vent and all the side windows so that there'd be good air flow. She'd already been fed but I left some fresh water in her bowl and a bit of kibble as well and I cleaned her litterbox. There was no great farewell from the cat. She was curled up on top of my pillow and snoring softly.

Main Street was virtually empty at eight in the morning but there was one vehicle down the road by the bakery and it looked a lot like Tess's sedan. Maybe she was grabbing breakfast before work. Thankfully, the crime scene tape had come down from the front door and I took a deep breath as I slid my key in and turned the lock. I thought about the last time I was here and Murray was sprawled in the back room with a hole in the back of his head. A shudder went through my body as I opened the door.

When I stepped inside and flicked on the fluorescent store lights, the familiar scent of cheap plastic and pine floor cleaner greeted me. I locked the door behind me and procrastinated a bit before heading to the stockroom. I took my time checking the shelves to see what needed to be restocked and then put my purse and jacket on a chair behind the register. After a few minutes of dusting, I realized there was no more putting it off. I needed to clean that back room now so that it was done before Tess showed up.

"You can do this," I murmured, giving myself a little pep talk to help with mopping the blood.

As I walked toward the back of the store, I heard a noise coming from the storeroom and I froze. I covered my mouth with my hand to make sure I didn't scream and took a quick step backward.

The murderer has returned to the scene of the crime. Get out!

As I was making a hasty retreat, I heard a crash from that back room followed by a slew of colorful curse words.

"Oh God, it's Tess." I let out a sigh of relief as I rushed forward to the storeroom. When I flung open the door, she let out a squeak of surprise and grabbed her chest.

"You just scared the hell out of me."

"Same," I told her. "I heard a sound back here and wasn't expecting you to be here so early."

A large box of notebooks had fallen over and emptied its contents all over the floor. As I began scooping them up and putting them back in the box, I took in the strong scent of pine cleaner. "I was hoping to get here early enough to clean up the mess from, you know… so you wouldn't have to."

But Tess had already tidied up. I looked down at a pale pink stain on the concrete floor that hadn't been there last time I worked. It was obviously a faint mark of blood. My throat went dry.

Tess saw me staring at the floor, walked to a corner of the room, and dragged over a ratty old rubber-backed area rug and laid it out on the floor.

"There. It's done." She dusted her hands on her pants. "When Marshal Cobb told me the tape was down last night, I came right over and took care of it. The place was a mess. Fingerprint dust everywhere, and half the boxes were turned upside down. Even Mom's paper-work was all over the place."

"Guess they would've been looking for the murder weapon."

Tess had tidied Penny's corner desk as well and moved it tight against one wall.

"I'm sure the killer would've taken that with them, don't you think?" Tess grunted as she hoisted a box, and I rushed to help her place it on a shelf. "Let's just put as much of this stuff out on the floor as possible, okay? What good does stock do in here? Last I checked customers didn't come back here to shop."

"Penny thought if the shelves were overcrowded it made the store looked unkempt."

"My mother doesn't always have the best judgment."

Just like that I realized I had a new boss. If Tess wanted to be in charge, I had no problem with that. I was just here to make a paycheck and get out of Dodge as soon as I was allowed.

"Great idea moving the desk over," I commented, reaching for a compliment to put Tess at ease. "It looks much neater in here having the desk against the wall."

"It just makes sense." Tess smiled. "Also, she had so much stuff on it, I don't know how she had any room to do paperwork."

Penny did keep a ton of paperwork and also some photos on the desk and they did take up a lot of space but now they were gone. My cell phone rang but I didn't recognize the number so I just sent it to voicemail. It rang again almost immediately and Tess looked at me with annoyance.

"I hope you're not one of those workers who spends all day on her phone."

"Nope. I'll turn it off," I said through gritted teeth.

"Sorry." Tess sighed. "Mom told me you're a good worker so I don't know why I'm being such a bitch." She offered me a forced smile. "Things are just really tense right now."

"No worries. It's a stressful time for everyone."

"It sure is." She drew her hand through her short blond hair and then patted it down when it stuck up. "Can't wait to be out of this town."

You and me both.

Before the store opened, I hauled out as many items as the overfilled shelves could hold and dusted as I went. Just before ten I walked to the storeroom and asked if there was anything else she needed me to do before we opened. Tess was currently balanced on the top rung of a six-foot ladder and was opening boxes and moving things around, grumbling to herself.

"Oh I'm sure you don't need me to tell you what to do, just go ahead and go about your day as if I'm not even here." She waved her hand as if to shoo me out of the room.

There was an actual lineup of half a dozen people waiting outside Pincher's for me to unlock the door. I wanted to believe that people were just anxious to get shopping but the whispers, sidelong glances in my direction, and the number of times people looked toward the storeroom door told me the gossip mill was alive and well in Hope Harbor and the locals were getting a thrill out of shopping at a crime scene. I should've charged a buck a head to take selfies with me. I could've put up a sign saying: Get your picture with a murder suspect now before she's behind bars!

I tried to make light of it in my head but it was growing old quickly.

Tess never left the back stockroom until noon, when she announced she was going for lunch. "I'll take over for you when I get back."

Once she was gone, a freckle-faced girl of about ten with short dark hair approached the counter. "I'm looking for a wig. It's for Halloween."

"We don't have any of the Halloween things out yet. It's still six weeks away." I waved my hand in the air. "We still have all the back-to-school stuff on the shelves so there's no room."

"Yeah, but every year you run out of costumes almost right away and last week Ms. Penny said a box of wigs just came in but she hadn't unpacked it yet." She put her hands together and begged, "Puleeeze."

There was no one else in the store so I locked the register and told her I'd take a quick check in the back.

There were two cardboard boxes labeled Halloween pushed off into the corner. The packing tape had already been removed so I popped the first one open. It was full of costume makeup, vampire teeth and tubes of fake blood. I closed that one up and moved on to the next. Bingo! It was filled with boxes of cheap nylon wigs in various colors and lengths. The girl hadn't said the color she wanted so I snagged one labeled Princess Blonde, one that said Vampira in black and white, and a multicolored clown wig. I returned out front with the three in my arms.

"Ta-da!" I dropped the three boxed wigs onto the counter and the girl immediately snatched up the clown one and clutched it to her chest.

"Yesss! This is perfect!"

It brought a smile to my face thinking of trick-or-treating when I was a kid. After I rang it up, I placed the other boxes under the counter to be put back in the storage room after I closed up for the day.

I took out a bottle of Windex and sprayed down the counter, then moved on to the glass front door and sprayed it down as well. There was no one in the store so when someone spoke behind me, I whirled around, pointing the glass cleaner like a gun.

"Didn't mean to scare you." It was Noah with an amused look on his face and not appearing the least bit sorry.

"Did Tess leave the back door unlocked?"

"No, I used my key. I came to deliver Penny's heavy-duty paper cutter. I left it on her desk."

"I'll let her know."

"The paper cutter isn't the only reason why I stopped by. If you promise not to mace me with glass cleaner, I'll tell you."

I hadn't realized I was still holding out the bottle. "It isn't?" I moved from the front door back behind the counter.

"I wanted to see if I could take you to lunch at the diner."

My heart did a little flip-flop. Just then Tess returned looking like she'd had a chill pill with her lunch because she smiled warmly at Noah as they said their hellos.

"I was just asking Red if I could take her to lunch. Is that okay with you?"

"Of course, Noah. You two take your time. Looks like it's been absolutely dead in here anyway."

I wanted to argue that there'd actually been a lot of

sales already. More than usual even. But what was the point? "Let's go."

I told him I needed to stop and check on Muffin. When I slid the door open Muffin leaped onto my chest with her murder mittens digging into my breasts. I untangled her from my shirt and gave her lots of pets, pats and scratches. She'd obviously missed me and didn't appreciate being cooped up.

"Do you mind if we don't go to the diner?" I cuddled the squirmy cat before releasing her in the van. "This is the first day I've had to leave her alone and—"

"Say no more." He held up a hand. "I'll get us a couple sandwiches to go and we can eat in Bubbles. How's that?"

"Perfect. Thanks."

While Noah went off to fetch lunch, I grabbed my sunglasses from the dash and slipped them on. Then I put Muffin in her harness, snapped on the leash and let her wander the pavement around Bubbles and onto the grassy boulevard. Locals took one look at me walking a cat and glanced hastily away. I was living up to my reputation as the weird new girl.

A loud squeal preceded the arrival of Melody. "Oh my God she's getting so-o-o big!"

"Yeah," I replied even though it was not like Muffin could've grown much since the day before.

Melody scooped up Muffin and snuggled her against her face and was met by the kitten chomping her on the cheek. Melody wasn't fazed at all but she put the cat down and smiled at me. Her eyes were hidden behind dark sunglasses with white rims, which were identical to ones I'd purchased at the gas station.

"Look at you being the very best fur mom." She

grinned from ear to ear and all I could think of was her face contorted with rage as she yelled at her dad.

"You on your lunch break?" I asked.

"No, I'm just about to start my shift." Melody held up a takeout coffee that she must've gotten from the coffee shop up the road. "I should've grabbed you a coffee too. Sorry about that!"

"Oh. No. Really, you don't have to worry about me."

Just then my lunch date returned from the diner with a sack of food. "Hey, Mel," Noah said, handing me the bag and adding to me, "I hope you like chicken salad."

Melody looked from Noah to me and back at him, her eyes ping-ponging comically and a smile frozen on her face.

"Hey, did you know you guys have identical sunglasses?"

"Well, I've gotta get to work," Melody announced loudly and with a nervous smile. "You two have fun now…" She got all flustered. "I mean enjoy your food." She twirled around and started fast walking in the opposite direction of the grocery store, corrected herself and then turned around.

"She's a bit of an oddball, isn't she?" I murmured.

"Yeah, that's putting it mildly." Noah laughed.

I grabbed a couple of room temperature glasses of water for us and we sat at my table eating the sandwiches.

"That was delish. How much do I owe you?" I asked, dabbing my mouth with a napkin.

"Nothing. My treat."

"You can't keep buying me stuff. People will talk."

"Oh, darlin'…" He slapped his knee and gave me a dramatic wink. "Folks are already talking."

"Yeah, well, I don't like that." I frowned. "Citizens in this town should just learn to mind their own business."

"That ain't gonna happen but you keep on dreaming."

We were quiet for a bit and then I blurted out about the online threats.

Noah grew very still and his eyes darkened. "What did Joel say?"

"Not a thing," I said, exasperated. "I've sent him screenshots but not a peep from him."

"I'll have a word and tell him—"

"You'll do no such thing. The marshal already has a big-time hate on for me. I don't need you saying anything to him to make him more angry."

Noah gave me a sharp nod in agreement and then a few minutes later I asked him, "Who do *you* think killed Murray?"

"Me?" He rubbed the scruff of stubble on his chin. "I'm not sure."

"So you're sure it's not me? Because everyone else around here seems to have me convicted and locked up."

"Nah. You're much too pretty to shoot someone in the head."

I hated that my heart squeezed because he called me pretty. "You're saying pretty girls can't kill someone?"

"Whoa. I'm not saying you aren't physically capable of murder." He held up his hands. "I think, given the right circumstances we are all able to take a life." He crumpled his napkin and then took a drink from his water glass.

"If not me, then you're basically admitting a longtime resident of your quaint little town killed him."

He nodded. "Well, not necessarily. Could be a transient who happened to come into town."

"You don't believe that."

"It's unlikely but possible." He shrugged. "What about me? Do you still think I could've killed Murray?"

"Like you said, we're all capable given the right circumstances." But I had to admit he'd fallen down my list of suspects. "But, no, I don't think it was you."

"Well we've just taken two people off the suspect list then. Only five hundred thirty-one to go." Noah looked at his watch. "I gotta get back and relieve my nephew for his break before he forces people to make purchases they instantly regret."

"Thanks for the food and, I really have to say, thank you again for the battery. It's a great feeling not having to worry if Bubbles will start every morning."

"You're very welcome." He flashed his dimples.

I watched the sway of his hips as he headed down the street and fanned myself.

When I went to enter the dollar store, the door was locked and the closed sign was up. A sticky note on the closed sign said Back at 2:00.

That was still fifteen minutes away. Something must've come up that Tess couldn't wait for me but why wouldn't she call? She could've gotten my number from Penny. Also, I was literally parked out front, so she could've come to the van.

Using my key, I opened the store and flipped over the closed sign. There were some boxes of school supplies stacked in front of the counter and I went to work unpacking and shelving the notebooks and pens.

It was getting close to five o'clock closing time when Tess burst into the store from the back room. I was carefully placing crayons on the shelves near that door and she almost bowled me over. She looked a hot, sweaty mess.

"Are you okay?"

"Yes, of course I'm okay." She ran a shaky hand through her hair that was damp with sweat and sticking up in all directions. "I've just been working my ass off in the back room and realized I had the closed sign up."

"I've been back for hours," I told her. "If I knew you were in the back room I would've come back there to help you with whatever you're doing. As a matter of fact, how about we close up a few minutes early and I can help you in the storeroom."

"Nope." She made shooing motions with her hands. "I'm almost done and I'd rather just get it all finished myself tomorrow. Mom said she's got some steaks out to barbecue and I'm starved so I'm leaving now."

"Okaaay." I nodded. "I'll just lock up and leave in a few minutes."

"We might as well leave at the same time." Tess shrugged and tried to appear casual, but she was acting strange.

"Okay." I grabbed my purse from behind the counter and we turned off all the lights before leaving.

"See you tomorrow." Tess gave me a little wave as she quickly walked over to her little car.

I climbed inside Bubbles, turned the ignition and waited until Tess was out of sight. Then I grabbed my keys and walked back to the store. Once inside, I made my way to the back storeroom, convinced there was something inside Tess didn't want me to see.

However, it was spotless. Many of the larger boxes had been emptied and the stock shelved in an orderly fashion. She'd even flattened and stacked all those boxes by the rear door. Penny's desk in the corner was still devoid of the usual clutter of paperwork but Tess had placed a cup full of pens and some notepads at the ready.

Even all the heavy boxes on the shelves were arranged neatly. Tess had arranged the containers so that labels on the boxes were facing out and clearly marked, which would make restocking and finding things so much easier than the haphazard way Murray had done it before. Honestly, I was impressed.

"I guess she was working up a sweat really just working," I murmured to myself with a little disappointment. "No drama here after all."

I was making my way back through the store to leave through the front door when I remembered the boxed wigs behind the counter. I didn't want Tess to get in earlier than me tomorrow and see I hadn't bothered putting them away. I picked up one box in each hand, immediately noticing that one box was significantly heavier than the other. I looked in the small plastic window of the heavier box containing the blond wig and gave it a shake. Something of weight moved from side to side and it sure wasn't the golden hair made with plastic fibers that was meant to turn everyone into a princess.

"What the hell?"

Curious, I opened the top of the box and shook the contents onto the counter.

A wavy blond wig toppled out, and nestled within the bright synthetic strands lay a shiny black revolver.

SEVEN

My HANDS FLEW to my mouth to stifle a scream as I stared at the gun nestled cozily within bright yellow curls.

Okay, think! I covered my face with my trembling hands.

On shaky legs, I ran out the door and jumped into Bubbles. I dumped out my purse, searching for my phone. I'd powered it off earlier in the day and had to wait for it to start up. I ignored a half dozen missed calls while dialing Cobb's digits. It went to voicemail. I left a frantic message and then called Sheriff Duthroyd. He picked up on the third ring.

"I found the gun in fake hair and I don't know what to do," I blurted then added, "This is Scarlet."

"Don't leave," he instructed.

I locked the store and sat in my van out front trying not to throw up. Marshal Cobb showed up first and then the sheriff's car arrived before Cobb had even unbuckled his seat belt. I was locked inside the van, arms wrapped around myself and rocking back and forth. Cobb rapped on the window, and my heart nearly came out of my chest as I rolled down the window.

"It's on the counter. Inside." I nodded to Pincher's.

"Wait here," he told me as if my shaking hands could possibly drive right now.

He disappeared inside the store, and Sheriff Duthroyd approached me next.

"Tell me again where you found a gun." He gave me a friendly smile. "Your comment was a little confusing."

I took a breath and explained all about the little girl wanting a wig and about gathering three choices from the box in the storeroom so she could choose a style for Halloween.

"I thought she'd go with the blond princess wig but I'm so glad she decided to be a clown." My words tumbled out furiously and my voice shook with emotion. "Could you imagine what would've happened if I'd sold her a wig with a gun inside? What if she thought the gun was a toy and then what if—"

"Take a deep breath and let it out slowly," the sheriff suggested. Once I'd done what he asked, he said, "Okay so the little girl left with the clown wig and then…"

"And then I put the other two wigs behind the counter so I could bring them back to the storeroom at the end of the day. I was closing up and I remembered the wigs behind the counter so I figured I'd better put them back where they belonged in the back because we don't have Halloween stock out on shelves yet. When I picked up the two boxes, I noticed one was a lot heavier."

I explained how I dumped the contents of the box onto the counter and the gun had come out on top of the wig.

"Did you touch the gun at all?"

I shook my head.

"Are you sure?"

"Positive. I touched the box and shook the contents onto the counter, but I absolutely did *not* touch the gun."

"Good job," he told me. "I'm going inside. Please just stick around a bit longer, okay?"

I nodded. Once he disappeared inside I grabbed Muffin from off my bed and brought her to the driver's seat where I snuggled her against her will. The kitten squirmed and resisted but then settled in to painfully knead my chest. In a horrible repeat performance, townspeople began to gather, curious about why the law was back at Pincher's.

From where I sat I couldn't see more than a couple feet inside Pincher's glass door. It wasn't long before Cobb emerged from Pincher's, phone pressed to his ear. His eyes were granite as they cut to me. After he got off the phone he walked over but just before he reached the van, Sheriff Duthroyd stopped him and sent him back inside, then the sheriff approached me.

"It's the murder weapon, isn't it?" I nibbled the corner of a nail.

"It looks that way but we'll need to do tests to be sure. Can I come in?"

I opened the sliding door and he climbed inside and took a seat while I placed Muffin on the floor.

"Marshal Cobb will retrieve the evidence and it'll be tested. In the meantime, I need you to start from the beginning. From when you first showed up to work today, right up until you called me."

"Okay." I wove my shaking fingers together on the table between us, drew in a deep breath and recited my day right from when I pulled up to Pincher's until the moment I found the gun. As I talked, Muffin climbed up the sheriff's pant leg, perched momentarily on his shoulder, then jumped onto the table between us. I gathered her up and buried my face in her fur.

"The girl who bought the clown wig, do you know her name?"

I shook my head.

"Describe her to me."

"Maybe ten years old, short dark hair, and lots of freckles."

"Ah. Sounds like little Meg." He smiled. "Her mother used to do administration work at my office and sometimes Meg would come to work with her."

The sheriff got to his feet and told me he'd be right back. He made a phone call and I could make out snippets that told me he was talking to Meg's mother or father to verify what I'd told him. Then he returned and asked me to show him where the box of wigs was kept in the storeroom. Careful not to let Muffin escape, I walked back in the store with Sheriff Duthroyd following. We passed Marshal Cobb, who was on his way out the door with an evidence bag.

In the storeroom I pointed to the cardboard box in the corner. I explained to him that Tess had spent a lot of the day reorganizing the room and we'd put a lot of stock out front on the shelves today but not the Halloween boxes. "We're waiting until a lot of the back-to-school items sell out before we start shelving Halloween and fall stuff."

"So lots of stuff got moved today." He frowned. "Now I want you to think hard. Where do you think this box of wigs was on the morning of the murder?"

I walked around the room, staring up at the shelving. Finally, I pointed to a shelf about chest height in the back corner. "I can't be positive, but I remember Murray mentioning the day before that he had cleared that space specifically for Halloween stock." I tapped my chin thoughtfully. "That day the Halloween boxes were stacked by the back door waiting to be shelved by Murray. There had been a couple boxes of bath products here before that I'd brought out front. It would've been the most logical place for him to slide in the Halloween stuff."

"You don't think he would've rearranged stock to put them somewhere else?"

"It's possible but..." I stopped myself, not wanting to speak ill of the dead but then went ahead anyway. "Honestly, Sheriff, Murray was kind of lazy. If he could slide those boxes onto an empty spot on the shelf, that's what he'd do and not a tiny bit more." I wondered aloud, "Of all the places to put a gun, why would it be in a box of wigs?"

"If I had to guess—" Duthroyd scratched his head "—the murderer was surprised by someone and stuck that gun in the first place they could find."

"Surprised by someone?" I frowned. "You mean me. They heard me walk in that morning, stashed the gun and ran out the back?"

"That's very likely."

"Why wouldn't the killer take the weapon with them?"

"Panic?" The sheriff shrugged. "Probably planned on coming back for it eventually."

"I know this is a small town but many people have keys to Pincher's."

"Yeah, it's a small-town thing all right, but I'll have Marshal Cobb reach out to Penny. She should change her locks at the very least."

"That would be a good idea."

We made our way back outside. Sheriff and the marshal talked for a couple minutes and then Duthroyd got in his vehicle and Marshal Cobb walked over to me.

"I should call Penny." I wrung my hands. "And let her know what happened."

"Already done," Cobb said quickly. "Don't be telling everyone and anyone what was found and where it was discovered, okay?"

I nodded but there were already townspeople around and I was guessing they'd figure it out.

"The sheriff is heading over to interview Tess to confirm your story." He rubbed the back of his neck in irritation and I got the feeling he would rather be doing the interviewing himself.

"So I'm free to go?" I pointed to the van behind me. "I already gave a statement to the sheriff so…"

Cobb seemed distracted and was frowning at the crowd milling about. To me he said, "Just hang here a few more minutes."

The marshal headed back in the store. As I climbed back inside the van, my phone rang in my hand. It was the same unknown number that had called me throughout the day, so now I was curious and answered.

"Hello?"

"Is this Scarlet Hooper?"

"Yes. Who's this?"

"My name is Fred and I'm calling from an RV store in Bellingham. First of all, happy birthday."

"Um. Thanks?" I gave my head a shake and slid the van door closed behind me. "How do you know it's my birthday?"

"Your sister, a Ms. Brandy Hooper, has arranged for your camper van to be outfitted with a new refrigerator as a birthday gift."

"What? Really?" I lowered myself onto a seat and blinked back tears. "I—I don't know what to say…"

"Just give me the year and model of your van and then I'll see if it's something we have in stock or if I have to order it in."

Choking back tears, I rattled off the information.

"We don't have one here at the moment, but it'll only take me a day to get it from our other location. I'll order it today and you just give me a shout when you can make it in to have it installed."

I thanked him profusely and then grabbed a pen so I could take down his contact information. When I hung up the phone, I lowered my face in my hands and sobbed. Once I was able to stop crying, I tried calling Brandy but it went straight to voicemail.

"Thank you so-o-o-o much! You didn't have to give me a fridge but I'm really, really, truly grateful." I blew out a breath. "Also, I was right about the blond hair. Kind of. It's complicated. Call when you can."

Muffin was pouncing and stalking her shadow. I was a bundle of nerves because of what was happening outside the van but, even so, for a split second I did feel a glimmer of happiness. My sister had not only remembered my birthday but bought me a new fridge, which would improve my life immensely.

Provided I didn't end up in a prison cell for a murder I didn't commit or stalked and killed by some fanatical vigilante.

Everything to do with Murray's murder wrapped around me like a heavy dark blanket. The only comfort was that my vision had been correct about the importance of the wavy blond hair. As I thought about that, my phone rang and it was Noah.

"What's up? Why are the police back at Pincher's? Don't tell me there's another body?"

"I'm not supposed to say…" I blew out a puff of breath and my fingers shook. "I guess it's okay to tell you there's definitely *not* another dead person."

"Are you okay? You sound stressed?"

"That's probably because I *am* stressed. Was just planning on spending my birthday evening drinking wine and eating some of the stale crackers in the back of my cupboard but even that sounds like too much work now." I laughed mirthlessly. The weight of the day sat heavy on my chest. "I'm just so sick and tired…" A sob escaped my throat and I stopped my rambling. "I'm sorry. This week has been a year. I gotta go."

I disconnected the call and flopped down on my mattress in the back and stared at a spot on the ceiling until there was a heavy knock at my door. It was Marshal Cobb.

When I opened the door he said, "You're free to go."

As expected, even more locals had gathered in a clutch on Main Street and were eying us curiously. I was annoyed when the marshal simply turned away, leaving me to call after him, "Hey, so is it okay for me to come to work tomorrow?"

He walked back to the van. "Sure. It's not like you should expect to find any more murder weapons or another body."

"I could do without the sarcasm." I crossed my arms.

Marshal Cobb looked at me. "Nothing's changed. Keep your mouth shut about what you've found and, just like before, you need to stick around town until all this is figured out."

"Yeah, yeah, I know…" I scanned the curious crowd

of onlookers. "What about the threats I've received? What are you doing about those?"

He took off his hat and scratched his scalp, then looked at me wearily. "Red, I'm doing the best I can, okay?"

Suddenly I felt sorry for the small-town marshal thrust into a big-time investigation.

I watched him walk away pausing only to tell people to disperse immediately.

"Please just hurry up and solve this thing," I whispered to his back.

This town was fraying my last nerve.

My plan was to drop by and talk to Penny, but when I pulled up to her house, I didn't see any cars in the driveway. I parked Bubbles at the curb in front of her driveway and called her cell phone.

"Oh, Red, you must be just sick after finding the murder weapon," Penny exclaimed.

"I'm doing okay, I just want to know how you're doing?"

"I think I'm in a bit of shock, actually. Marshal Cobb said I should have the locks rekeyed. Do you really think that's necessary?"

"I do. Do you want me to see about getting a locksmith out to take care of that for you?"

"Oh, I'll just ask Noah. He won't mind."

I frowned because despite his kindness and sexy dimples I still thought it would be better to get someone outside of this town to handle the lock change. But it wasn't my store. "Or you could call in a locksmith from Bellingham even. Is there anything I can do?"

"No, I'm fine. Tess is here and she just finished her interview with the sheriff. We're just going to spend a quiet evening together. She said to tell you she'll see you at the store tomorrow."

"Okaaay." I stared at the dark house that had no cars in the driveway and said goodbye to Penny, all the while wondering where she was. She hadn't come out and said she was home, but it was implied.

"Lord, get me out of this freaky town." I returned to Main Street and popped into the grocery store to get some dinner because the stale crackers in my cupboard weren't going to cut it today. The store was empty, and I was guessing that was because everyone was gossiping outside of Pincher's. The deli section sold hot roasted chickens and I decided to get one as well as a bag of ice to stuff in my fridge to keep the leftovers. At the last second, I decided to splurge on a cheap bottle of wine.

Melody startled and then looked physically pained when she saw me approach her register.

"Hi." I offered her a tired smile. "I guess you heard there was more drama at Pincher's."

"Yes, I heard." She bit out her words curtly along with the total.

I got out my debit card, paid for the order and declined a bag. She methodically put my items aside without her usual chatter.

"Is everything okay?" I was puzzled by her sudden coolness.

"You know, missy, not everyone likes a show-off," she hissed.

"A what?" I blinked at her in confusion.

"Oh, you know what I mean…" She huffed. "Throwing yourself at the coolest bachelor in town." Then she frowned. "Well, the *only* good-looking bachelor in town, if you must know."

"Throwing myself?" My mouth fell open and I had to gather the urge not to leap across the counter and slap her right across the face. "Look, if you're talking about Noah, he's been very kind to me, but we are not an item *at all*, and I assure you that I am not looking to change that anytime soon." I furiously added, "As soon as this murder is solved, I am leaving this town and I'm never coming back."

"Really?" She closed her eyes and covered her heart with her hands as she exhaled with relief. "That's great."

Ouch. "Well, thanks for making it easier to leave this crappy town."

I turned to leave and she called out hurriedly, "No, I mean about you not being interested in Noah. Not great about you leaving. I like you. It's just that I think I have a real chance with him, you know? His wife—God rest her soul—never really took care of him properly. She was always take, take, take."

"I thought they were divorced, and she had cancer and he was just, you know, being the good guy taking care of her?"

"Well, yes, but he needs a woman now who will be there shoulder to shoulder in the store working and cooking and cleaning and taking care of allll his needs. If you know what I mean."

Oh I knew exactly what she meant and I didn't want to be the one to break it to her that Noah did not give the impression that she was next in line to be his missus.

"After the funeral I baked him a pie and he said it was the best one he ever had and then there were the roses."

"Roses?"

"Yes, for weeks there was a rose left on the hood of

my car and I couldn't think of who they could be from but one time Liz from the diner said she saw Noah walking by just before I found the rose." She smiled broadly and then held up a hand. "I know what you're thinking and he's being discreet because he doesn't want the whole town to know." She sighed. "I love a man who takes his time."

I tried to imagine Noah leaving roses for Melody and it didn't compute.

"We've also shared a few, um, moments." She winked. "If you know what I mean."

I didn't know what she meant but had zero desire to try and climb inside her head and sort out Melody's fantasies from reality. "Well, good luck with that and have a good evening," I said, running out with my still-warm chicken in one hand, a bag of ice in the other, and the wine tucked under one arm.

By the time I pulled onto my spot on Farmer Miller's back field I was desperately wanting that chicken, cuddle time with Muffin and a large glass of wine and not necessarily in that order. What Melody said about Noah caused me a pang of something in my chest.

"Look at me," I said to Nan's picture. "Getting jealous over a guy I want absolutely nothing to do with." I shook my head. "I know what you'd say. You'd tell me it's okay to settle down and have a family but, yeah, I don't see that happening anytime soon and I sure don't see it happening in Hope Harbor."

I fed Muffin and while she was munching, I slid the sliding door open but zipped up the screen so I could have the fresh breeze without worry of mosquitos or having the cat escape. Then I unscrewed the bottle of red wine and poured a hefty portion into a plastic tumbler. I was just about to dig into the chicken when I heard footsteps crunching on the gravel near Bubbles. I leaped toward the sliding door to slam it shut and there stood Noah.

"Knock, knock." He offered me a sheepish smile. In his hands he held a white birthday cake with yellow icing flowers. In pink cursive icing it said Happy Birthday, Red.

"Awww. Are you kidding me?" I put a hand on my heart and felt my insides melt. "Come in!" I hurriedly unzipped the screen and closed it quickly behind him. It was a good thing I was no longer convinced he was a murderer because, apparently, I could be won over with frosting.

"A little birdie told me it was your birthday." He put the cake down on the table.

"That little birdie was me." I chuckled. "Have you eaten? I have roast chicken and wine."

"Is that the chicken?" He pointed to the counter where Muffin had straddled the chicken and had her tiny teeth sunk into the back.

"Eek!"

While Noah laughed until he was doubled over, I wrestled the bird from the cat and stuffed Muffin into her carrier but not before receiving a number of gashes for my trouble. I went to work picking off any cat hairs and then brought it over to the table.

"Sorry. I'll understand perfectly if you can't bring yourself to eat it after witnessing that furball's attack."

"I'm sure the alcohol from that wine will destroy whatever germs the cat put on your dinner."

"Let's hope so!"

We laughed and then he said he would've called first

but still didn't have my cell number. It was a hint and I smiled.

After I poured him a glass of wine and put out a couple of plates I rattled off my cell phone number. He texted me back with a heart emoji that stupidly made my heart pound in my chest. We ate and chatted about the balmy September weather and eventually got around to the big news of the day.

"So...a gun in a wig box, huh?" he said.

"You didn't hear that from me." I shook my head and frowned. "I was instructed not to talk about it."

"That same rule doesn't apply to everyone else in this town." He laughed and then got serious. "But, really, a gun in a wig box..." He whistled in disbelief. "That's so messed up."

I nodded in agreement and told him the sheriff believed the killer was surprised by someone, possibly me, and hid the weapon in the box just because it was readily available.

"I guess that makes sense."

"As unsettling as it was to find it, I'm so glad they've got the murder weapon. Who knows? Maybe it's covered in the killer's fingerprints. I'm just hoping they can find Murray's killer."

"I agree. Can't wait until Hope Harbor returns to the days when the biggest excitement is when the diner has a two-for-one prime rib night, or when the Fourth of July fireworks accidentally start someone's field on fire."

"Hope Harbor really knows how to party."

Muffin was loudly howling and protesting from the crate, but I ignored her and eventually she quieted.

When we'd eaten a bunch of the chicken, I put it on

the counter, and got out a knife and a couple of smaller plates for the cake. I handed Noah a slice and dug in.

"This is so good," I said around a mouthful of gooey sweetness.

"Well, when you said you were going to have stale crackers for your birthday dinner, I figured I needed to stop that crime in its tracks."

"Greatly appreciated."

I was stuffed by the time I took our plates and put them in the sink, and loaded what was left of the chicken carcass and cake into the fridge, which had cooled thanks to the bag of ice.

"Guess it's safe to let the chicken thief out of her crate." I laughed and opened the door but Muffin was curled up fast asleep in the back so I just left the container open so she could leave when she wanted.

Noah refilled our plastic wineglasses. "I propose a toast."

I sat back down across from him and picked up my glass. "What are we toasting to?"

"To you, of course. Happy birthday, Red."

I tapped my glass to his and took a drink. It had certainly been a day with all the ups and downs of a roller coaster.

We made easy small talk. I told him about Brandy buying me a fridge for my birthday and he filled me in on some of the sillier local gossip around town and that brought something to mind.

"Melody told me someone was leaving roses on her car. I guess she has an admirer."

"Huh." He smiled. "Well, good for her. It would do that girl some good to get some attention from a guy.

Maybe it'll stop her from adopting ten more cats." He chuckled.

Since he looked genuinely surprised by the flowers, I think Melody had better look elsewhere for her secret admirer.

"Okay, Mr. Adams, we've talked about everyone else, now it's your turn. Tell me something about yourself," I said, sipping my wine.

"Like what?" He gave me a lopsided grin.

"Something most people don't know."

He took a drink and leaned back to give it serious thought. "Now, no making fun of me for this, okay?" He pointed a finger at me.

"Sorry. No guarantees."

He sighed dramatically. "Sometimes I listen to country music." He said it in a whisper.

"Oh come on." I rolled my eyes. "That's as common out here as dirt roads and seagulls."

"Maybe, but the kind I listen to is the old whiny your-dog-ran-away-and-then-your-wife-left-you twangy stuff." He looked genuinely embarrassed.

"Well, that is pretty unforgivable," I joked. "If the town knew this, you might have to turn in your most eligible bachelor card."

I scrolled through my phone, brought up an old Merle Haggard song about misery and gin, and turned up the volume. He tossed back his head and laughed while I got up, put my phone down, and found a spoon to use as a microphone to mockingly sing along. Noah jumped up and put out his arms, and then we danced along in a goofy manner, singing badly until we had tears in our eyes and couldn't catch our breath. My phone moved on to a slow country ballad. I reached for it to turn the song off, but Noah put his hand in mine, spun me around and then drew me close.

We slow danced in the very confined space of my van. As he pulled my body against his, I laid my head on his shoulder and wondered if he could feel my heart pounding through my shirt.

When the song wrapped up, he lifted my chin with the tip of his finger. There was a split second when my mind considered protesting the kiss that was coming, but the rest of my body had other plans. His lips were tentative at first but then, as I wrapped my arms around his neck and replied with my own need, things began to heat up.

It was only a few steps from my cramped hallway onto my bed, and we collapsed on top of the mattress without even separating our mouths.

"Are you sure?" he murmured against my mouth.

"Yes," I panted, lowering my mouth to nibble his neck.

Even though my mind was trying frantically to remind me this could be a horrible idea, my entire body was on fire and yearning for his touch.

"Are you really, really sure?" he said hotly against my collar bone.

"Oh God, yes," I breathed.

We began making love like we were frantic to devour each other, but as the evening wore on, frenzied sex melded into passionate lovemaking. Every place on my body that his hand touched ached and ached for more. The sun went down and the only sounds beyond the screened doorway were crickets as we lay content in each other's arms. The initial fervor was gone, and a languid peace hung over us.

"That was just…wow," I murmured into the crook of his arm.

"Double wow," he whispered back, kissing the top of my head.

Muffin hopped across the van and began kneading the sheet that covered us.

"Her little paws are like razors." Noah laughed, but he didn't push her away.

We lay in silence a long while but eventually I felt myself nodding off.

"I should go. You have to work in the morning and so do I." He sighed and reluctantly got to his feet.

I watched him dress and then I grabbed my own T-shirt from the floor and pulled it on to walk him to the door.

"I'll call you tomorrow," he promised, bending down to kiss me tenderly. "Try not to find another thirty-eight special while you're at work."

"Ha! I sure hope there's not another one."

I waved goodbye to him and watched the taillights of his pickup until they disappeared down the road.

Later, as I lay in bed enjoying the scent of Noah still on the sheets, an alarming thought sprang to my mind.

I'd never told Noah that the gun I found was a thirty-eight.

EIGHT

DARK CLOUDS WERE moving across Farmer Miller's field when I climbed out of bed. My body had that good ache in my limbs from enthusiastic lovemaking, but my head was fuzzy from tossing and turning through the night. It wasn't just the rolling thunder that had kept me up. Noah knew the type of gun that I found and that was hard to ignore. Sure, someone else could've told him, but who else knew besides the marshal and the sheriff?

And, of course, the killer.

With the kettle on for coffee, I fed Muffin and then put her in a harness and took her outside. I carried her away from the sticky mud surrounding the van and onto the damp grass. She jumped around in the weeds like usual but then sprang up and pounced on a brown leaf blowing past.

Muffin appeared to have adapted just fine to wearing a harness and I appeared to have adjusted to being owned by a cat.

While I contemplated what to do, I ate birthday cake for breakfast and washed it down with coffee. Once highly caffeinated and overly sugared, I opted to call Marshal Cobb. It wasn't even seven, so I expected it to go directly to voicemail but he picked up on the first ring.

"Cobb here."

"Did you tell Noah Adams that the gun found was a thirty-eight special?"

"Is this Red?"

"Yes." I rolled my eyes. "Well?"

"No." He paused a beat. "But he was at the bakery when I was there after you left. He could've overheard me on the phone with the sheriff, along with half the town."

This from the man who told me not to be talking about the case all over town.

"Okay, that's probably it. I was just surprised he knew the type of gun."

"Is there a problem? You're not still thinking Noah killed Murray, are you? Because I've looked into it but I'm just not seeing a motive."

"No, of course I don't think it's him." At least I hoped not. "It's just that he had a key, hated Murray and knew about the gun so I just found it…curious."

"Half the town had a key and the entire town hated Murray." He blew out a puff of breath. "Look, I get it. You're anxious to clear your name."

"This isn't just about clearing my name. It's about finding out the truth."

"Yeah, well throwing accusations around willy-nilly does not make you look good. Know what I mean? Let the law handle the case. You just keep your ass out of the way. If you're innocent, we'll know soon enough."

He disconnected the call, leaving me fuming. I grumbled to Nan's picture while I did my dishes.

"If I'm innocent, he said. *If!*" I shoved my cleaned coffeepot and kettle into the cupboard with far more force than necessary. "My name is not in question here.

If he thinks that, he's gotta have his head shoved so far up his—"

My phone rang and I saw it was Brandy. I took a second to calm myself and then answered. "Thanks so-o-o much for the fridge."

"Originally I was going to send you to the spa for a manicure, pedicure and massage but I realized you'd appreciate the fridge more." Her voice was tinged with fatigue.

"Absolutely!" Although I'd never had a spa day before and the idea was really appealing. Looking down at my chewed cuticles I asked, "So how did it go? Were you able to help find that missing child?"

"Sort of." She seemed to stifle a yawn before she changed the subject. "Your message said you were kind of right about the blond hair in your visions. What happened?"

I filled her in about how I found the murder weapon.

"There's something you're not telling me."

"Did I mention the part about everyone and their dog having keys to the store?"

"No, but that's not it." She waited but I was not about to tell her about sleeping with Noah. "Have you been practicing your divination talent?"

"Yes, but yesterday I ran out of time. Worked all day and then there was, um, birthday cake and stuff."

"You need to make this a priority. You'll never improve unless you work on it."

I didn't ask for this ability and my life would be a lot better without it, so I wasn't sold on how perfecting this skill would improve my life.

"We keep going round in circles having the same conversation, Scarlet. We both agree that Hope Harbor would sooner hang the title of killer on your head than one of its own." She yawned again. "You have a psychic advantage. You need to use it before you're hung out to dry for this murder."

On that, she had a point. If I could use my fire visions to find more clues, I could save my own ass. "You're right. When I'm off work tonight, I'll spend the evening working on it."

"Good. A little practice, and before long you might be able to actually see events instead of random clues like blond hair. Are you working tomorrow?"

"Yes, both today and tomorrow until five."

"Okay, I'll see you tomorrow evening. Together maybe we can get some real answers."

When I got to the store my keys didn't work in the lock but there was a sticky note on the inside of the store window saying: *Red, see me for a key. Noah.*

Guess she got Noah to change the locks like she said. I puffed up my cheeks and blew out a breath. I wasn't expecting to see Noah so soon after our evening together. This might be extremely awkward.

The store was still closed but Noah's nephew saw me approach and opened up.

"Uncle Noah said you'd be coming to get a key." He slid a key across the counter to me and smiled. "I tested it myself so it should be fine, but let me know if it doesn't work."

"So you were the one who retumbled the locks at Pincher's?"

"Yes, ma'am." He hurriedly added, "But don't worry. Uncle Noah showed me how to do it a while ago and I've done it lots of times on my own."

"I'm sure you did a great job. How many keys for the store did you make?"

He scratched his head as he thought and then began ticking them off on his fingers.

"Well, two for Ms. Penny and one for her daughter and I dropped those off at their place first thing this morning. Then there's one for Uncle Noah and one for Ms. Liz who runs the diner and Becky at the bakery and, of course, you."

"Jesus. The whole purpose of getting new keys cut is so that not everyone would have a key."

"But then how are people going to get in and get stuff when you, Tess or Ms. Penny aren't around?"

"They aren't." I pressed a finger to my temple because I was getting a headache.

"That doesn't make sense. Like last week when we needed new ribbon for the cash register before Pincher's was open, I used Uncle Noah's key and just helped myself. I left the five dollars on the counter, of course," he said. "And Ms. Penny needed some dinner rolls for her supper one time and so she used her key for the bakery because it was after hours."

"Oh my God, why even have separate keys for every store? Why not have every place keyed to use the same key then?" I demanded.

"That's a really good idea actually."

"I think Red is being sarcastic." Noah approached the counter and winked at me, causing my heart to skip a beat.

"Don't you think it's weird?" I demanded. "Someone was killed at that store and the marshal is trying to figure out who had access to the store, and changing the locks was to help with that but now seven people have keys and—"

"Eight," the nephew spoke up. "I forgot Melody."

"Good lord." I just shook my head.

"It's okay." Noah came around the counter and draped an arm around my shoulder. "It's just a—"

"If you say this is a small-town thing, I might just lose my mind," I grumped.

"Okay, I won't say it." He leaned and whispered in my ear, "But it is."

I punched him playfully in the shoulder and he proceeded to walk me up the road to Pincher's.

"I had a really nice time last night." He grabbed my hand and swung it in his as we walked.

"Um. Me too." I looked up the street and spotted a few locals gawking our way. "This might not be such a good idea." I reluctantly untangled my fingers from his. "People are going to talk."

"Oh, darling, you know they are already wagging their tongues. Consider it a public service that we're giving the town a little something to think about instead of poor, dead Murray." He reached for my hand again, but I took a step away.

When we arrived at the store, I stuck my new key in the lock and turned the dead bolt.

"It works," I said, announcing the obvious. "So thanks."

"Oh I didn't walk you over to check on the key."

"You didn't?" I frowned as I opened the door and then turned to him. "Then why—"

He leaned in and kissed me hard on the mouth and I stepped back.

"Noah!" My gaze skipped up and down the street. "You obviously don't care what people think, but—"

"You're right. I don't give a rat's ass what people think and neither should you."

If only life was that easy. "I am already the most hated person in town. People are going to get it in their heads that I'm coercing you somehow and—"

"Can I buy you dinner tonight?"

"Ummm..." I'd promised both Brandy and myself I'd work on my fire scrying but, still, I did need to eat. "Okay, but I have things to do afterward and—"

"I'll see you when you close up." He sauntered off then and when he was a few steps away he stopped and turned around. "I knew it."

"Knew what?"

"I knew you'd be watching my butt as I walked away." He winked.

"You're incorrigible."

I laughed as he began swinging his hips in a very exaggerated fashion while he strolled down the sidewalk.

"Man oh man, I'm in trouble." I exhaled long and hard and tried to shake that man out of my head.

Once again, I was early to the store, but this time Tess didn't beat me. I was determined not to give her any reason to ride my ass all day, so I spent the hour before opening dusting the countertops and shelving goods, then swept and mopped the floors. I went through the stockroom and took a glance around. No bodies, no more guns happened to be lying about, but I still felt uneasy in this small space where so much had happened.

We sold some cheap votive candles in the store and I thought I'd give one a go since I had a few minutes before opening time. I borrowed a lighter from the shelf, put the tiny candle on the counter and lit the flame as I hopped up on the stool. The vision that hit me was excruciating pain. I felt like my entire leg was broken glass. It was cold and dark but I was trying to run through a forest despite the pain in my leg.

A knock on the store's front door shook me from my stupor and I blew out the candle. The vision and pain had been so realistic that as I walked toward the door, I double-checked that my leg was functioning. Of course it was, but there was a surreal sinking feeling in my gut and I found myself wiping tears from my eyes with the back of my hand.

When I flipped the closed sign over to the open side there was already a gaggle of preteens waiting with money or debit cards in their hot little hands. The teachers must've given out school supply lists. Although I was shaken by my vision, Penny had warned me weeks ago about this event. Many locals would head into Bellingham and the mall to do the majority of their shopping, but most would try Pincher's first because we had better prices. I was eternally grateful for the bustle and the countless questions from the kids to locate this item or that. Time flew by, leaving me no time to think about what I'd seen in the candle.

It was early afternoon when both Penny and Tess rolled up. They stood chatting agreeably with Marshal Cobb for around ten minutes before coming inside. When they sauntered in it was with full smiles and a lackadaisical attitude that said nothing was wrong here and nobody had died in this establishment.

"Hi, there," I said to them as I finished serving a young mom with a howling toddler on her hip.

Penny walked over and scooped the toddler from

the mom and began making cooing noises and talking baby talk. Then she and the mom talked in hushed whispers about poor Murray as they made their way toward the door.

Once she was gone, Penny turned to me. "I bet you're itching to have your lunch break." She smiled but the bags under her eyes said she was more exhausted than I was. "Tess meant to come in and help this morning but we got caught up with other things."

"I don't mind working through lunch, if you need help." Although I'd really like to go check on Muffin.

"Nonsense, Tess and I can manage just fine." She glanced over at Tess, who nodded.

"Of course we can." Tess ran a finger along the glass case at the register then frowned as if disappointed there was zero dust to complain about. "As a matter of fact, how about you take the rest of the day off."

Penny clapped her hands. "Excellent idea." When I didn't reply right away, she added, "With pay, of course."

Who could argue with that? "Are you sure? The kids have their school supply lists so it's been super busy."

"Positive," Tess announced.

"Okay, but if you change your mind…" I grabbed my purse from under the counter and hooked it on my shoulder. "I won't be far so just give me a call if it gets busy again."

Outside, Marshal Cobb was playing peekaboo with the toddler who was in the store moments ago. The child was having none of it and the mom seemed intent on a serious conversation. At the sight of me she stopped talking and nodded her chin in my direction. Cobb glanced over and regarded me coolly. This business about being the target of local gossip was really getting old.

When I was climbing into Bubbles, the marshal walked over.

"That gun has gone in for testing."

"Good," I replied as I opened my door.

"They'll be checking fingerprints."

"Great." I climbed inside.

"Red, if there's something you want to tell me, now is the time."

"I never touched the gun. My fingerprints won't be on it."

"When you found it, you picked it up and—"

"I never touched it." I stared at him from the seat of the van and put my key in the ignition. "Did you check the registration? Find out who the owner is?"

"Don't tell me how to do my job, Red." He turned then and walked away.

My first thought was that I'd drive Bubbles over to the grocery store and get sandwich fixings for my lunch, but I couldn't stand to be in this town a second longer. As I drove down Main Street I slowed next to the marshal and rolled down my window.

"I have to go into Bellingham for a bit. Don't want you thinking I've left town for good."

"You'd better not be going any farther than that because—"

I didn't let him finish his warning. Instead I pointed the nose of the van toward I-5 and accelerated south. After I went through a drive-thru for a burger, I drove to a local park and ate at a picnic table. Muffin chased a fly from the end of her leash and pounced at her shadow.

"Look at the bubbles!" a young boy exclaimed, pointing at my camper. His mom smiled at me and then agreed with her son that the van was very cool. It felt good to be away from the judgmental faces of Hope Harbor.

Muffin tangled herself in her leash and then did it again after I freed the leash of her legs. A curious seagull tilted its head in our direction and I gave him the stink eye.

"Come near my cat and I'll be making seagull stew," I warned.

The breeze kicked up a notch, and knots of dark clouds gathered over my head. I managed to return to the van just as plump raindrops pummeled the pavement. Muffin hopped along the counter and eventually wound up in the center of my bed, where she purred and kneaded the blankets until she fell asleep.

A notification chimed on my phone. Another anonymous message: If you don't get locked up soon I'll take you out myself.

At the end of the message were emojis for a gun and knife.

"Nan, if you've got any pull from the other side, please help me figure out who killed this guy." I retrieved my three-wick candle from the cupboard and placed it on the table. I did not want to return to my earlier vision, which was nothing but pain, but I also needed to put these puzzle pieces together.

Brandy performed her scrying so effortlessly. Even though she told me practice was all I needed, I felt there was more to it than that. After cracking my knuckles, I lit the wicks, rolled my shoulders and drew in long, slow breaths.

This time there was no leg pain; only blurry snippets

appeared to me inside the flames. A long dirt road. A golden sunset. A hazy vision of me stretched out on my bed in the camper followed by the strong smell of vanilla, ending with a thunderous clang that reminded me of the time Bubbles and I'd been caught in a hailstorm.

My gaze became unfocused as I woke from the vision to the sound of wind chimes and the smell of burning. I felt off-kilter and even more confused than ever. I stepped outside briefly to let the cold rain help me come around and then I took a seat in front of my candle and tried again.

And again.

Every time was the same: dirt road, sunset, vanilla smell, and the finale was the van being pelted with hail.

"Argh!" I slapped the table with my palms. This was infuriating. It reminded me of the time Nan and I bought a thousand-piece puzzle of a field of sunflowers. So many yellows, greens and blacks that it took forever. My mind was now giving me a large puzzle to assemble but only offered me a tenth of the pieces.

"This is bullshit."

My head ached as I sprawled out on the bed with Muffin and figured I'd close my eyes for a few minutes. Next thing I knew my phone was ringing. I fumbled around until I found it in the bedding then answered sleepily.

"Hullo?"

"You stood me up for dinner," Noah said.

"Ugh." I sat up and squinted at the time. It was just after six. "They gave me the rest of the day off and—"

"And you figured you'd just get out of this town, right?"

"Yeah. I'm in Bellingham."

"Well, I could use a visit with my dad anyway, so how about I take you out to dinner there first?"

I thought that was a nice idea and we agreed on a pizza place that was close to the laundromat where we met before. Brandy texted me that she wasn't going to be able to make it this evening so I had time. The restaurant looked busy so after I parked I went inside and put my name down for a table. By the time Noah arrived, they were able to seat us.

"Before we go ahead I have a very serious question," he began, looking at me from over the top of his menu.

My stomach dropped. "Okay. What is it?"

"Pineapple on pizza. Yes, or no?"

"Yes." I giggled. "Ham and pineapple is my go-to pizza."

"Damn, I was afraid you were one of those…" He put the menu down and got up from his chair as if he was leaving, then quickly sat back down as a chuckle rattled in his throat.

When the waitress appeared, he ordered a large ham and pineapple for us to share.

"Oh, so you're on the pineapple side too, huh?" I laughed. "I thought you were going to be a straight-up pepperoni kind of guy."

Conversation was smooth and easy with not a single mention of murder or Hope Harbor. We talked about our favorite out-of-the-way camping locations and the movies we loved the most. I could tell he was making a concerted effort to distract me, and I'd be lying if I didn't admit I found it sexy as hell.

When he insisted that I take the leftover pizza for myself even though he paid the bill, I began to realize how much I could fall for Noah Adams. His easy kindness and sexy body were locking down my heart. And it scared the hell out of me.

He walked me to Bubbles, pressed my back against the van, then kissed me long and slow. My insides were warm and liquid when we broke apart.

He brushed my forehead with his lips and whispered, "Drive safe."

"Do you want to—" I nodded behind me "—come inside for some dessert?"

"Not tonight. You said you had plans, remember? And I'm going to stop in and visit my dad."

He never asked what my plans were, which meant I didn't have to lie that they involved fire scrying. Still, if he'd kissed me a second or two longer I probably would've blown off gazing into a fire for some skin-on-skin time.

The thought that he knew the gun was a thirty-eight special still left an unsettling feeling in the back of my head but even the marshal had admitted that Noah probably overheard that at the bakery. No doubt while he was choosing my birthday cake. I felt guilty for even thinking such a thing when Noah had been nothing but kind to me.

The sunset was a spectacular parade of red and amber that cast Noah in ethereal gold as he drove away. That glow around Noah left me feeling unsettled.

The more I enjoyed Noah's company, the more my brain was putting on the brakes and sending up warning signs not to get involved. I needed Murray's killer behind bars and then I needed to drive far away from Hope Harbor. I definitely did not need a complicated romantic involvement with the town's most eligible bachelor. A tumble in the sheets? Sure. But nothing more than that.

When I'd gone inside the restaurant I hadn't bothered to put Muffin in her crate because she was fast asleep on the bed. Apparently, I also hadn't properly closed my bathroom door and when she woke up the kitty had decided to stalk and slaughter an entire roll of toilet paper.

"Not funny." I waggled a finger at her while she tossed a piece of tissue in the air and batted it with her paws. I laughed anyway. "I guess it's a *little* funny but, hey, if you're going to live with me there's some things you should know." I picked up Muffin and held her nose to mine. "I'm not rolling in cashola so that means we must conserve stuff like toilet paper and not use it for entertainment purposes, okay?"

I kissed her nose quickly before she could dig her razors into my face and then plopped her into her crate while I tidied up the rest of the mess.

"I know what you're thinking…" My finger tapped Nan's picture as I stuffed the last of the tissue in the trash. "You always said don't give your heart away too soon. Make a man work for it." I chuckled as I put the small box of pizza in my barely cool refrigerator. "He's definitely trying, I'll give him that. But you never said anything about at which point do I inform any guy that I'm a psychic. How about that, Nan? Would've been nice to have that convo with you before you died."

It was dark by the time my headlights illuminated the dirt road that brought me back to Farmer Miller's property. I let Muffin out of her crate, and as I lay spread out on my bed, she climbed up the rear drapes and then jumped up and down with tiny meows. I laughed at her antics and the laugh turned into a yawn. It was early but I was tired. Before I got too comfortable, I'd better close up. As I pulled my drapes shut around the front windows Muffin used the litterbox. The unpleasant smell immediately filled the entire van.

I scooped out her box and placed the offending clumps in a trash bag. The smell was still bad so I dug into my glove box for one of those cardboard air fresheners, ripped open the plastic wrap, and dangled it from the mirror. The saccharin scent of phony vanilla filled my nostrils and I frowned.

My visions earlier...

Long dirt road—just took that to my parking spot.

Golden sunset—like the one that surrounded Noah's truck after the pizza.

Smell of vanilla—filling the van at the moment from the air freshener.

A quick peek between the shades told me the sky was clear with a multitude of stars like brilliant diamonds set in the dark sky. Slim chance of a sudden hailstorm on a night when there wasn't a cloud in the sky. At least that was reassuring.

The air freshener only added vanilla to poop, and the noxious mix was making me queasy.

"There is no way I want to sleep with a bag of your smelly business in the room with me," I told Muffin.

I decided to stick the bag of cat poop outside for the night and deposit it in the dumpster behind Pincher's in the morning. As I slid the door open, Muffin squeezed past me and leaped out the door.

"Muffin!" I cried, jumping out after her.

She made her way under the van and I got down on my belly to reach for her. At that moment, a fast-moving vehicle came tearing down the road, lights out and kicking up clouds of dust.

"Stop, Muffin!" I cried out, terrified she'd go run-

ning onto the road and get flattened by the fiend bar-
reling down near us.

Luckily, Muffin was playing with a small stick behind the tire, oblivious to the danger. I could almost
reach her. I concentrated so hard on trying to wrap my
hands around the cat that it took me a moment to realize the vehicle going past had slowed its approach to
a near stop.

Suddenly...

PING! CRASH! THUMP! POP!

Someone was shooting up Bubbles!

NINE

At least a half dozen shots rang out as I lay pressed to the ground, my body half underneath the van, the gravel stones imprinting the length of my body. I was able to snatch Muffin and press her to my side, and the kitten, as if knowing this was life or death, remained still and didn't even chomp or scratch my hand.

The vehicle where the shots came from never came to a complete stop, and after the assault sped off, spraying a cloud of dust behind it in the dark. Muffin and I lay frozen to the ground. I was too terrified to move.

After a long while of hearing only mosquitos as they buzzed my ears, I inched out from beneath the van and scrambled to my feet. I peeked out beyond the side of the van to ensure the assailant wasn't lying in wait. When it appeared clear, I jumped into the van to survey the damage. As I studied the shattered windows I dropped to my knees and sobbed before, finally, I reached for my phone and called 9-1-1 first and then Brandy second.

In case the shooter decided to make a return trip, I stuffed Muffin into her carrier and then made my way across the street. I sat hunkered down in the dark behind a scrub of brush listening to the crickets, whose chorus was loud in the stillness.

Marshal Cobb arrived first on the scene, looking disheveled, his face pulled into a look of simultaneous annoyance and concern. He walked circles around Bubbles, using a flashlight to check the area, and stuck his head inside and surveyed the damage while I explained between sobs what happened.

"You didn't see the make or model of the car?" he asked, for the tenth time.

"No." I hiccuped as I tried to control my tears. "Like I said, I was on the ground under the van trying to get Muffin when the vehicle rolled by and the shots started."

He glanced down at the animal carrier at my feet. "Guess that furball saved your life."

"I—I told you!" I yelled, my voice shaky with shock and rage. "I told you the threats were real!"

"We don't know the messages and the shooter are connected." Cobb dragged his hand across his short-cropped hair and placed a fresh toothpick in his mouth. When I began to protest he held up his hand. "I'm looking into it. I swear I am looking into it all."

Brandy arrived on the scene shortly after, followed by Sheriff Duthroyd. Cobb had just finished telling me I needed to pack up all my personal effects because Bubbles would be towed in as evidence.

"But—but it's my home…" I spoke in a whisper that was half pleading.

"I'll help," Brandy said.

We took a duffel bag out from my back storage area and I stuffed it with my clothes while Brandy grabbed my toiletries.

I paused at Muffin's belongings. "There is no way the litterbox, cat carrier and all my stuff is going to fit in your Corvette."

"I brought my boyfriend's SUV," she said.

I glanced to the road and saw a large dark vehicle and then blinked at her. "You have a boyfriend?" I frowned. "You never told me that."

"You never asked." She shrugged and snagged Muffin's carrier and my duffel and walked them over to her vehicle, then she returned with an oversized empty tote and handed it to me with a whisper in my ear, "Pack Nan's stuff."

When I winced, she added, "Who knows how long they'll have Bubbles? Do you want them going through her things?"

"Okay. Good idea."

She lowered her voice even further. "And don't forget your gun."

I shrank back and blinked at her. "How did you know I have a—" Then I shook my head. "Never mind."

My feet crunched on the broken glass as I carried the large tote over to my mattress. I got on my knees, opened Nan's cabinet and scooped out her belongings without even looking at them, but still a waft of her lavender hand cream reached me, and fresh tears stung my eyes. I glanced furtively around before sticking my hand down the cubby next to my bed and retrieving my gun. I stuffed it into the tote beneath Nan's other items.

Cobb was on the roadside with other marshals, marking the location of shell casings with small yellow plastic numbers.

"I'm leaving," I told him.

He mumbled something under his breath about where I'd be staying and it occurred to me that I didn't know.

"I guess at a hotel in Bellingham."

He glanced up at me briefly. The glow of his flashlight highlighted the dark blueish half-moons beneath his eyes as he simply nodded and turned away. Sheriff Duthroyd walked over and asked me to check in with either him or Cobb to give my new location once I was settled.

I climbed into Brandy's vehicle. "The cheapest motel you can think of," I told Brandy with a sigh. "My insurance deductible on Bubbles is going to wipe me out."

She was looking in the rearview mirror and applying lipstick. Then she started to drive, pulled a U-turn just up the road and drove back past Bubbles. She eased her vehicle slowly between the police cars parked on either side.

"No hotel," she said, accelerating now that we were away from the chaotic scene.

"What?" I turned to her. "I still have to work at Pincher's tomorrow so going to your place in Seattle is too far for me to commute."

"First of all, you're off work for the time being. Probably permanently. Someone is trying to kill you, or haven't you noticed?"

"I get that but…" My voice trailed off as a shudder traveled through my body. It was just now truly sinking in. "Oh my God, someone really tried to kill me. And Muffin." My voice broke.

"I'm taking you somewhere safe and that's all you need to know." She held out her hand. "Give me your phone."

I handed it over and she drove with her knees a bit while she pressed a few digits on my phone, then tossed it out the window and into a nearby ditch.

"What the hell, Brandy!"

"You don't know if someone's tracking you on that

thing." She reached into the car console, took out an-other cell phone and tossed it onto my lap.

"Okay, it's definitely an upgrade, but throwing out my phone seems a little excessive."

"Maybe. Maybe not. Do you really want to roll that dice?"

I blew out a slow breath and nodded. "Thank you."

"The phone is a spare I use for work. Sometimes I don't want clients to have my personal number."

"I guess that makes sense."

"If anyone besides me calls that number, just let it go to voicemail."

"Okay." I blew out a breath. "But I lost all my con-tacts and all my pictures."

"Trust me when I say it's a small price to pay." She exhaled loudly. "I've forwarded your old phone to mine. Anyone tries to text or call you, it comes to me. So if it's important then I'll let you know, got it?"

"Okay."

She drove north but avoided the highway, and for a while it felt like we were driving in circles. When I asked about it, she said she wanted to be sure we weren't being followed.

Over an hour later we turned up a long rutted and narrow driveway surrounded by thick bush on either side. When the private road angled to the right, the headlights illuminated a tiny bungalow with a screen porch.

"Ta-da! Home sweet home." Brandy turned off the ignition, climbed out and started grabbing my stuff.

With Muffin in her carrier in one hand, I slipped my purse over my shoulder and grabbed the other bags.

I followed Brandy up the path, the tote bag bumping against my thigh on the rocky trail.

She pushed spiderwebs aside and slipped a key into the lock. Once we were inside, she cautioned, "No lights yet."

My eyes squinted in the darkness. Using her cell phone as the only light, she closed blinds and tugged black-out drapes tight over the shades before she finally flicked the light switch.

The room was small but cozy. There was an over-stuffed couch, a television in the corner and a coffee table. A stone fireplace took up one wall and a stack of firewood was in a basket. I put down the animal carrier and bags and then we walked into the kitchen, which was basic but still more than I had in the van.

Brandy flung open the cupboards to reveal some canned goods and then opened the fridge to show there were condiments, and when she opened the freezer it was jammed. "There's enough here to keep you fed for a bit."

"Whose place is this? Is it yours?"

"It's my boyfriend's cottage." She left the kitchen and I followed her down a short hall. She showed me a small bathroom and pointed to a closet across. "Linens are there." We walked to the next door, which she opened. "There's only one bedroom."

The queen-sized bed had a thick duvet and it looked soft and inviting. "You can have the bed, I'll take the couch," I told her.

"I'm not staying."

"What?" I frowned. "But where are you going?"

"Back to Seattle. I have to testify in court tomorrow." She shrugged. "A case from last year. Sorry, but it can't be helped."

"Oh. Thanks for coming all this way to rescue me." I dragged my fingers through my hair. "I honestly don't know where I'd be without you."

"Probably dead." At the look of horror on my face, she laughed. "But you're pretty resourceful on your own so maybe not."

"Gee. Thanks."

She took out her phone and sent a text. The phone she gave me vibrated in my back pocket with a message that said: ME

"Call or text me anytime but, like I said, I'm in court tomorrow so it might take me a bit to get back to you."

"I'll be fine. Don't worry about me."

"Here are the rules."

"Rules?"

"Number one, you don't leave here under any circumstances. You're in lockdown. There's enough food in the pantry and freezer to keep you for at least a few days and I'll be back before then." She held up two fingers. "Second rule, you call nobody from that phone except me."

"What if the marshal or sheriff need to reach me about what happened and have more questions?" I frowned. "And Penny will need to know I'm not coming in and…".

And Noah. What about Noah?

"I'll call your boss and tell her you won't be in. Chances are word of what happened will have spread all over town by morning anyway. Anyone tries to reach you, it comes to me, remember? I'll let you know if you need to call anyone." She pointed to the phone in my hand. "That phone should be safe from tracking, but we need to use an abundance of caution at the moment, okay?"

"Okay. Sure."

I followed Brandy to the door, and she hugged me awkwardly before she left.

"As soon as I'm gone, you make sure this door is locked and then double-check all the windows and the back door are also locked."

I promised her I would and I listened to her car wheels crunch on the driveway and then all around me was complete silence until a loud meow.

I unlocked the cat carrier, introduced Muffin to the location of her litterbox and put out her water and food bowls. As Brandy suggested, I double-checked that everything was locked up tight and then I fell onto the bed.

My mind was racing. Every moment of the evening ran on a loop in my head. I could hear the sound of exploding glass, could feel the vibration of the shots as they rang out around me, and could taste the fear in my mouth as I relived the horror. Although the shooting only lasted seconds, in my mind it was a slow-motion film reel. I stared at the stucco ceiling retelling myself what happened and searching for clues as to who could be the shooter. I don't know how, but eventually I drifted off and probably would've slept longer but Muffin began attacking my hair on the pillow.

For a millisecond I had no idea where I was. I bolted upright, my heart pounding. Then it all crashed down on me again. Poor Bubbles! In my shock last night I hadn't really taken a good look at the amount of damage the van had sustained. I knew there were broken windows, but beyond that I wasn't sure. A painful knot of emotion formed in the center of my chest, but I was distracted by Muffin, who took a chomp on my toes through the blankets.

"Come on. I'll get you breakfast."

Muffin purred and wound her way between my feet and I nearly tripped over her a number of times between the bedroom and the kitchen. I tore apart my duffel bag and a sack of incidentals until I found her cat food. One single can. I opened three drawers before I found a can opener.

"Enjoy," I told Muffin as I put down her bowl. "If Auntie Brandy doesn't bring you more food, that might be your last meal for a while."

Brandy had only stated that I had enough food to last a few days and that she'd be back before then. That didn't mean today. Or tomorrow. I frowned.

"Just great." I dragged my fingers through my hair. "I don't even know where I am."

But if I had to walk to a store for cat food, I would.

The cabin had a well-stocked cupboard and I didn't realize how much I missed a basic drip coffeepot until I'd made half a pot just for myself.

I took a loaf of bread out of the freezer and made myself some toast. While I ate, I checked the phone that Brandy gave me. There were two missed calls from someone I didn't recognize and the voicemail icon said there were messages to listen to but since they were probably from ex-clients of Brandy's, I wasn't about to touch them. No messages from Brandy but I sent her a text.

Good luck in court today. When you come back here please bring canned cat food. Muffin prefers the seafood flavor. Thanks for everything.

I knew it was unlikely I'd hear from Brandy until later in the day.

Sipping my coffee, I went to the living room and peeked between the blackout drapes for my first clear look of the property in the light of day. The yard was overgrown and surrounded by thick bush and tall trees. I glimpsed through the bedroom and kitchen window coverings and saw pretty much the same thing. A perfect hideaway but I had no idea where I was, which was a bit unnerving.

Both the front and back entrances had screened-in porches. I promised Brandy I'd stay in the house, but the porch was part of the house, right? After Muffin had devoured her food, I brought her onto the screened-in back deck. I sat on a padded lawn chair that smelled faintly of mildew and campfire, I drank my coffee and watched kitty climb the screen enclosure like Spider-Man.

Abruptly, I got the idea to use the cell phone map function to figure out my location. I zoomed in and then out to get a clear picture. The cottage was a bit outside the community of Birch Bay. A stone's throw from the Canadian border. The town was considerably larger than Hope Harbor, but I was at least a mile from another house and three from the closest store. That was going to be a bit of a jaunt if I had to run out to buy cat food.

Perusing news sites gave me zero information about the Bubbles shoot-out. I guess it wasn't big news to anyone but me, or else the information was being withheld from the press. There hadn't been much reporting on Murray's death since that first day either, except in the local rag, which had blown it up to be the murder of the century.

I had so many questions burning inside my head.

I was itching to find out where they'd taken Bubbles and dying to know if Marshal Cobb was able to find any other clues around the shooting other than the shell casings. Maybe there were clear tire impressions that would help them find the culprit. The loaner phone took the same charger as my old one. I plugged in the phone to charge on the kitchen counter and then wandered the small cabin.

For all I knew Brandy might show up and tell me I was being moved to another location, but out of boredom I emptied my duffel bag anyway and put clothes into drawers and my toiletries on the bathroom counter. On the edge of the tub was a large bottle of bubble bath. It had been over a year since I'd soaked in a bath and suddenly it was the most important thing in the world.

Soon I was surrounded by bubbles that smelled of sweet peas, and my fingers pruned like pale raisins. I didn't want to ever leave the confines of the tub. For a while Muffin sat on the edge and pawed at the fluffy bubbles and looked at me quizzically as if amazed I'd choose to be immersed in water. When my phone rang, I jumped out of the tub and ran to the kitchen without so much as a towel.

"Brandy?" I breathed.

"You didn't even check the call display?" She sounded annoyed.

"Oops. Sorry." Water was pooling at my feet and I shivered in the cool air. "How is court going?"

"It's long and drawn-out boring stuff. I'm on a break. Wanted to tell you that you had a call from Marshal Cobb and also practically everyone in that piss-pot town has also texted."

"Everyone?" My heart squeezed.

"Yes, that Noah guy because I know that's who you're really wanting to hear from." Her tone was an eye roll.

"Well, what did everyone say?"

"I replied to all your messages with exactly the same thing. I texted: I'm safe but I'll be away for a few days."

"Okaaay." I didn't like the idea that I couldn't even reply to my own messages. "But I don't see the harm in—"

"I know you don't, Scarlet, and that's why I'm taking charge here. I had a vision that the person who killed that Murray guy is someone you know. Someone you're close to and that someone now wants you dead." She paused a beat, and I could hear my heart pounding in my ears. She sighed. "Look, until we can figure out exactly who the bad guy is, you aren't talking to anyone, get it?"

"Yes." My throat thickened with emotion and my head began to pound. "What about Marshal Cobb?"

She seemed to hesitate there. "I guess you'll need to be reachable by the law. I'll send you his number. Answer any questions he has about last night but don't tell him where you are."

"What if he wants to see me?"

"You tell him that you're scared and you're staying with me for a while."

I frowned. "I don't like the idea of lying to the police."

"It's not exactly a lie. You *are* staying at a place I arranged for you and you are scared," she explained impatiently. "If he insists on seeing you just tell him that your sister will drive you to his station to talk but that can't happen today because I don't know when I'll be wrapped up here. Hopefully today but it could run over into tomorrow. Also, I'm going to notify my lawyer that you may be in need of his services."

"Okay." My heart pounded at that idea. "You really think I need a lawyer?"

"The longer this goes without being solved, the greater the possibility they'll continue to look at you and, no, I don't think the shoot-up of your van puts you in the clear. They could just assume you did it yourself as a distraction or paid someone else to do it."

I hadn't thought about that. With a hand to my forehead to stem a headache I moaned.

"Anything else you need?" she asked.

I paused. "Did you get my text about the cat food?"

"Yes. I'm sure she won't die if you feed her some meat or tuna instead of canned slop for a day." Then she quickly added, "I've gotta go, my break is over. I'll check in later."

"Hold on, how long am I going to be here?"

"I can't say for sure, Scarlet. Until it's safe, obviously. Maybe a week. Maybe more."

A week? I frowned. "Well, can I make a fire here so I can, you know, practice my thing?"

"Sure, but not until it's dark. Smoke from the chimney might make neighbors curious."

With that she ended the call and I was left quivering in a pool of bath water in the kitchen. I jumped when Muffin began licking bath water off my feet. Seconds later the phone beeped with a screenshot of Marshal Cobb's phone number.

I took a few minutes to mop the wet floor, drain the tub and then pull on sweatpants and a T-shirt before I called him back.

"I've been trying to reach you."

"Where is my van? When do you think I'll get it back?"

"It's evidence at the moment so it'll be a while. Check with your insurance. Maybe they'll pay for you to have a rental car in the meantime."

"Not a rental I can live in," I pointed out. "Were you able to find clues about who shot at me?"

"Not much," he admitted. "The shell casings were from a common gun and that road is used so much there weren't any tire tread marks we could identify."

"Oh. What about DNA?"

"On what?" he laughed. "Sounds like you've been watching too many crime shows."

"I don't even own a TV," I said impatiently. "Obviously, the same guy who took shots at me also killed Murray."

"Obviously? Nothing is clear at this point."

"Really? What reason would someone have to shoot at me? They must think I know something about Murray's murder."

"Do you?"

"How would I know anything?" I shouted. "I'm only the one who found the body! What about the gun found in the store? Who was it registered to?"

"Red, I'm not going to discuss details of a case with a prime suspect, okay?"

He asked for a rundown of my evening and I told him everything from pizza with Noah in Bellingham to Muffin escaping the van when I was putting trash outside. I described, as best I could, everything that had happened while my face was pressed into the dirt underneath the van while I tried not to get shot.

"From your location under the van could you see the make and model of the vehicle? Tires even?"

"No. You asked me this last night and I'll tell you the same thing. It was dark and they had their headlights off."

"Okay. Tell me where you're staying in case I have further questions."

"I'm...well, I'm staying with Brandy. If you need me, you have my number." With that I hung up and drew in a deep jagged breath. Brandy was right about one thing. I was truly terrified.

I turned on the television and realized after flipping channels forever I hadn't missed a lot living without a TV. Still, I settled on an old romantic comedy because I needed something predictable and easy in my life. Muffin explored the house from the top of every piece of furniture to the bottom and then curled up on my lap to sleep. It was adorable and now I didn't want to move so I sat through a lot more television than I liked.

Eventually Muffin moved on and so did I, searching the small cottage and deciding what to make for dinner. I opened a can of tuna and made a sandwich, sharing some with Muffin. After eating I found a bottle of wine and had a glass. I'd felt on edge ever since the shooting and now I was pacing the floor waiting for the sun to go down so I could at least light a fire and see if I could glean any more clues, but dark was still a couple hours away.

I found a puzzle on a shelf in the living room and began assembling it on the coffee table while Muffin explored a bag near the front door. The sack toppled onto its side and the cat crawled inside.

"Hey, leave that alone."

I got up to shoo her away and remembered the tote was filled with all of Nan's stuff. Although I'd been quick to rid the van of the majority of her clothing and personal effects, this was the cupboard I'd left untouched. Even now, my fingers trembled at her memory as my hands hovered over the bag.

"No time like the present," I announced with far more bravado than I felt.

I tugged the tote toward me and began pulling each item out slowly and reverently placing them on the floor nearby.

The first item was a photo box, which I knew from experience had pictures of Brandy and me when we were just babies. Wrapped in one of Nan's scarves was a heavy pewter-framed picture of my mom, taken when she was about my age now. Her hair was long and dark like Brandy's, her eyes green like mine, and we shared the same small bump on the bridge of our noses.

I looked long and hard at the picture and felt an ache and longing coated in a ton of regret. We were never close but I always thought we'd have time to bridge the gap between us. Even though we were different and our main form of communication growing up was screaming matches, I thought we'd get there eventually. Turned out there wasn't enough time. When I thought about what Brandy said earlier about Mom taking me to the fire exhibit at the museum to broach the topic of fire-seeing, it made me feel so much remorse and sorrow. If only she'd found a way to bring it up before that night but Mom had always been quick to distract from anything that might come close to either a meaningful conversation or something that, heaven forbid, brought about conflict.

My feelings toward Nan were different. She seemed
to understand me in a way Mom never did and though it
felt like a betrayal to my mother, I missed Nan more. I
put the framed picture and the photo box aside. I wasn't
feeling strong enough to go down that road today. To
look at pictures that would dig up deep feelings of grief,
regret and loss.

There was a notebook that contained mileage we'd
done on our few trips before Nan got sick. I flipped
through a few pages and then saw notes Nan had written in the margins about medications and doctor ap-
pointments. I snapped the book shut.

When I reached back inside the tote, my fingers
grabbed something soft. It was a black wool shawl Nan
wore often at the end of her life and it was wrapped
around a fragile Christmas ornament. The small red-
and-green glass bauble had belonged to her own mother,
and when we'd celebrated Christmas in the van, we'd
hung if from the fan and draped tinsel from it, quite
content to have that one bauble be the only seasonal
decoration in the camper.

I went to the kitchen and grabbed a handful of paper
towels and wrapped the ornament carefully, then draped
the shawl across my shoulders and pulled it close. I shut
my eyes tight and breathed deep to take in the faint lilac
scent of Nan. It caused my heart to hurt. I made myself a cup of herbal tea then brought it out to the living
room. The cup sat on the floor next to me while I took
out the rest of the items.

First was the keepsake urn with Nan's ashes. Her
wish had been to have her ashes scattered in Redwood
National Park, which had been our first van trip, but
after she was gone, I asked to have a small amount

of her ashes placed in a brass heart-shaped urn small enough to hold in the palm of my hand so that I could keep part of her with me. I'd made the trip to Redwood Park and scattered her remaining ashes under a giant tree and my tears had mixed with her remains as they fell.

Momentarily, I clutched the brass heart to my chest. My entire body filled with a dizzying emotional heat so I quickly set the urn aside while I got out the rest of her items: slippers, a paperback novel and, finally, a small jewelry box. The only jewelry Nan had in the box was a class ring that belonged to my mom, a silver charm bracelet that she never wore, and a few pairs of cheap earrings. Until nearly the end of her life she'd worn the ruby ring that now adorned Brandy's finger and I still felt a pang of hurt that it wasn't mine.

"I thought there'd be more things." I frowned into the now empty tote bag and wondered why it had taken me this long to go through those few items.

With the shawl still snug around my shoulders, I placed the stuff back in the bag. The last item to go inside was the photo box. Toward the end of Nan's life, she'd made me promise to go through the photo box and give some pictures to Brandy.

"Promise me you'll do it right away," Nan had said, squeezing my hand.

"Sure," I'd said dismissively. "If she ever shows up again, I'll give her some pictures."

"Even if you don't hear from her, go through the box," she'd insisted.

At the time it had seemed an almost ridiculous request because Brandy hadn't been sober in years and certainly wouldn't give a damn about a few pictures, but Nan had been adamant.

"Go through the box once I'm gone so you're ready to give her pictures," Nan had said, grabbing my hand. "Promise me."

I thought it was the cancer and the pain making her act a little odd, so although I'd made the promise, it wasn't until this moment that I'd held that photo box. And suddenly I felt overwhelming guilt for not doing it sooner.

"I'll do it now and when Brandy comes back, I'll give her the pictures."

I took a deep breath and opened the box, surprised to find a pale pink envelope resting on top of the photographs. My fingers trembled as I picked it up. My name was written neatly in Nan's flowery script and she'd drawn tiny hearts all over the front and back. I clutched the note to my chest and a sob escaped my lips. My hands shook as I unfolded the flap and lifted out the sheet of paper and began to read.

My dearest Red, if you are reading this then I guess I've gone to be with your mom. I would say don't be sad, but grief is natural. Just don't live inside that dark place for long.

I have failed you and I am truly sorry. So many times I wanted to tell you the truth about your psychic abilities but, in the end, I was afraid that you'd blame me and your mother for handing this burden down to you. Please know that this is a calling that you do not have to accept! My own mother tucked her psychic abilities away. I only did water scrying when absolutely necessary.

Your mom rarely chose to read tea leaves. This is your choice. If I could choose for you, I'd hope that you would sell the van, meet a nice man and have a family. But I sense you are not built to live a quiet life. If you choose to take on this talent, there are things you should know.

Your abilities come from all the women in our family before you but yours are stronger than any I've heard of in our ancestry. Your mom and I tried to keep fire from you—no birthday candles, not even a gas stove at home or in the van. You were a toddler when you first screamed out a prediction at a barbecue. The women in our family had abilities that grew over time, but you seemed to be born with extraordinary sight.

We never meant to keep the truth from you permanently. We just wanted to protect you from this load as long as possible.

I remember when we were on the beach and someone was having a fire. You had a vision that I was dying. You thought the removal of your brain tumor was causing you to hallucinate. At that time, I made up my mind to tell you the truth, but then I became ill and it never felt like the right time.

If you choose this path, you need to know that scrying is not a science but a skill that improves with practice. Make notes of what you see. If you want information about a person, it is helpful to have something of theirs with you. A personal object is best. Do not be afraid to call on your own angels for guidance. Your mom and, now, also me.

I caution you to use your skill only when it

can help. If you try to use scrying in a negative way, it will almost always backfire. Your sister has found this out the hard way. You should know that Brandy's drug use has brought her abilities down a dark path. I have promised her my ring with the hope it will help her out of the darkness. It's okay to love your sister, but I caution you not to trust her.

What you have may feel like a heavy weight, but it might be a gift that can empower you. It is always your choice whether or not to heed this calling.

I am so sorry to tell you in this way. No matter what you choose, I know you will have a life full of purpose and promise.

Love forever, Nan

TEN

My HEAD SWAM with thoughts as I took in Nan's words. I read the letter again, hearing every syllable in Nan's strong voice. The second time it felt no less of a betrayal. Angrily I stuffed the page back in the envelope and dropped it back into the box.

Everything Nan, Mom and even Brandy had kept from me. All the times I experienced headaches, sounds and smells of burning whenever I was around fires big and small. Of course, they'd tried to protect me from even the slightest flame, but many times I caught glimpses out in the world. The few times I mentioned my experience to Mom she played it down and made me feel like I was imagining things. Eventually, I stopped mentioning it at all.

Muffin came out from exploring under the sofa to pounce on me as I remained cross-legged on the floor.

"What should we do?" I asked the cat, stroking her from head to tail.

Muffin's only response was to let me know she'd had enough patting by chomping my fingers. When I shooed her away, she promptly batted my teacup and knocked it over.

"Ugh!"

Quickly, I gathered Nan's things back into the tote before the tea could soak everything. Then I dumped the satchel in the bedroom with the rest of my things. After

I mopped up the tea, I began to dust, sweep and wash up the small cottage. Furiously, I scrubbed every corner while my thoughts raced. Once I was done, the place was immaculate, and I'd formulated a plan. I called Brandy's number and, as expected, it went to voicemail.

"I want to get a personal item from Murray," I told her. "It's time I stopped hiding and began figuring this thing out. Call me." I paused. "Also, this is a reminder that you need to bring cat food when you come."

The sun sank behind the tall trees and the mosquitos buzzed the screen windows late into the evening but there was still no word from Brandy. As I crawled into bed that night, I remembered Nan's words that I should love my sister but not trust her. Although Nan hadn't lived to see Brandy get clean, that warning still rang true. As much as I loved my sister, she could relapse at any moment. Sure, she'd been clean a couple years this time, or so she claimed. But how many times had I seen her get clean for a few weeks or months only to watch her flush it all away?

I wanted this time to be different and it was; Brandy had come to my rescue and put me up in this safe house. She remembered my birthday and bought me a fridge for Bubbles and, yes, she even took the time to try and tell me about my abilities. All of these sat on the plus side of my inner pros and cons list. Still, I knew from a lifetime of bad experiences, I couldn't one hundred percent count on her just because of one week of kindness. But I sure wanted to. I wanted her to be the sister I always needed. I knew addiction was a sickness and I loved Brandy. I just couldn't trust her.

Even with so much on my mind, I fell asleep with determination and a plan in my head and was woken up by the ring of the cell phone. I snatched it up and took the call without checking.

"Hello?" I said groggily, sitting up. "Brandy?"

There was nothing but breathing on the other end of the line, and my skin prickled with nerves.

"Hey, whoever this is, you've got the wrong number." When there was no response I added, "Who is this?"

The answer was a click followed by dead air. It was only five in the morning but there was no going back to sleep now. I knew Brandy would be pissed if I told her I took a call that wasn't her, but I was going to have to tell her about some weirdo.

A couple hours later there was a curt text from Brandy:

Got your message. Tied up again today but I'll call later. Don't do ANYTHING until we talk.

"Whatever," I grumped as I headed to the shower.

A shower, coffee and toast later I was putting my plan into action despite Brandy's message. As soon as they were open, I called a car rental company in the closest town and within the hour they'd dropped off a black compact car to the cottage. My credit card was going to take a hit, but that mattered less than finding out who killed Murray.

I gave Muffin some tuna and promised I'd be back with proper cat food.

My first stop was the closest store. It was a small mom-and-pop operation in a building that was a home at one time. The owners probably still lived in the upper half of the building. It was right off the highway outside town.

Even though nobody around here should know me, and I wasn't driving Bubbles, I was still being cautious. There was ample street parking right out front, but I drove around back and parked in the small lot. When I entered the store an older woman was watching a tiny television behind the counter and hardly looked at me when I went to the counter to pay for the thick black beanie hat, dark-framed reading glasses and some cat food.

With the sack of my purchases in hand, I rounded the corner to the rear parking lot and noticed, to my shock and surprise, a pay phone attached to the building. Certainly not a common sight these days with everyone having a phone in their back pocket. I climbed into the car and tossed my bag onto the passenger seat. Staring at the pay phone in my rearview mirror my fingers played with the strap of my purse until finally I couldn't stand it any longer.

"I just gotta do it." I dug coins out of my wallet and walked purposely toward the back wall. I needed to use the cell phone to search for the phone number first. Brandy's dire warning that there was a possibility someone could still trace my call on this new phone made the pay phone seem like a safe idea. I placed coins in the slot and punched in the number.

"Adams Hardware." When I couldn't bring myself to immediately reply, Noah's clear baritone repeated, "Adams Hardware. Hello?"

My mouth opened and closed a couple times before a small "Hi" squeaked out of my mouth.

"Red, is that you?" Noah's voice was laced with concern. "Where are you? *How* are you?"

"I'm good. I'm safe."

"Jeez, I've been worried sick. It scared me half to death when I heard someone shot up your van."

The emotion behind his words caused a lump to form in my throat. I know Brandy didn't think I should trust anyone, but Noah wasn't just anyone. I connected with him. Hell, I'd slept with him. That had to count for something.

I heard him blow out a long breath before he added, "I've been trying to call you but it keeps going to your sister's voicemail. I guess your phone got shot up or something? Are you staying close by?"

When I didn't reply he rushed on.

"What do you need? Tell me where you are, and I can get my nephew to watch the shop and come to you."

At his third question asking about my location I felt uneasiness twist in my gut.

"Brandy is taking care of me. I'm with her…um… I just…" My voice trailed off. I'd called just to hear his voice and I realized that this was a dangerous and dumb idea. "I just wanted you to know that I'm laying low but I'm okay."

"Good. That's really good." I could picture his eyes knitted together in concentration. He waited a beat then said quietly, "I'd like to see you. Is there anything I can do for you? Can I come to wherever you are?"

My hand felt sweaty on the phone's receiver. "Thanks, but no. I should go." I hung up quickly and with more force than was necessary, then wiped my sweaty palms on my jeans as I returned to the car.

"That was stupid, Scarlet," I mumbled to myself. "Stupid. Stupid. Stupid."

Back at the cottage I spent time getting ready. I piled my hair onto my head in a tight bun and covered it with the thick beanie. I'd found an oversized denim jacket in the bedroom closet that probably belonged to Brandy's boyfriend and I slipped it on over my black hoodie. After cleaning Muffin's litterbox, I left her with fresh food and water but she still offered me a ferocious glare as I left the house without her.

As a precaution, I took back roads into Hope Harbor and eventually wound my way toward Main Street. It was raining hard, but I figured that would only work in my favor. First, I did a slow roll down a lane behind Main Street. I paused between two buildings so I could check out Pincher's Dollarama across the way. I could clearly make out both Penny's and Tess's vehicles parked out front. Next, I made my way toward Penny's street. Doing this next part undetected might be tough. I was counting on two things: First, that nobody in Hope Harbor locked their doors like everyone claimed. Second, that the nosy neighbor that lived above Murray's apartment went off to meet other neighbors for coffee at the diner each and every morning like Penny told me that time I was at her place for coffee.

I pulled the hood of my sweatshirt over my hair, tugged the beanie over the top of the hood and popped the collar of the denim jacket after buttoning it to the top. Shoving the reading glasses onto my nose I looked at my reflection in the mirror. From close up you could definitely recognize me but, from a distance, I hoped nobody would have a clue who it was. I parked a block away and stepped out into the heavy rain. Running might attract attention so I quick walked as I cut through two yards and came up behind Penny's neighbor.

Pausing in the bushes, I listened for any sounds in the upper part of the house. Cold drops of rain dripped off the frame of the glasses and into my eyes as I waited. Once I was sure things were clear, I pulled on gloves as I walked toward the rear entrance of what must be Murray's apartment. My hand went to the knob and found it locked.

"Dammit!" I muttered. It made sense that the police would've locked his place after they were finished investigating, and I cursed myself for not thinking of that detail. This definitely messed with my plans.

I looked furtively around. As luck would have it, the house had older slide windows and I'd had experience as a teen wiggling those open to sneak out at night to go and hang with my friends after curfew. I was too short to hoist myself up to Murray's window but after a moment of searching I spied one of those old-style lawn chairs with woven plastic webbing. Using the lawn chair as a stepping stool I heaved on the window, encouraging it to slide. The window was rigid with disuse, but after a minute of constant pressure it finally creaked open. With forearms on the sill, I hoisted myself upward and managed to drag my rain-soaked body through the window and onto Murray's kitchen counter.

The small apartment was surprisingly tidy for a perverted bachelor. Guess I'd been expecting centerfold posters taped to the wall at the very least. Things that were obviously missing were any kind of computer or chargers and I surmised those would've been brought into evidence. Luckily, what I was looking for was something that had a more intimate and personal connection to Murray.

Taking a grocery bag from my pocket I began to search. There was fingerprint dust everywhere and, even though I was wearing gloves, I was careful not to touch anything if I could help it. First stop was the bathroom where I snagged both Murray's toothbrush and comb. After I dropped those into the bag, I made my way into his bedroom. I opened his laundry hamper and took out a mustard-stained T-shirt that was on top of the pile of other dirty clothes. From what I remembered, he'd worn it to work for at least two full days before he was killed.

After dropping that in the sack I made my way to his bedside table. Curiously, there was a small loose school picture resting on top. The girl was pixie cute and maybe first grade. As far as I knew, Murray had no relatives so who could this child be? I picked up the picture and looked at the cherub face with the curls with curiosity then placed it back on the table. I opened the drawer of the bedside table to find a stack of revolting porn magazines.

Ugh. Guess he kept things old school instead of watching porn online. I wasn't going to touch those with a ten-foot pole. I cringed and shut the drawer. I was heading to his closet when I heard a door slam upstairs. I froze.

"Shit!"

I hustled back over to the kitchen window with the grocery bag clutched in my hands. Quick as I could, I climbed back through the window and landed on the lawn chair below, but the plastic webbing gave way and I went right through the chair. As I wriggled out of the chair, it landed with the aluminum frame making a loud crash against the side of the house. It took me a split second to silently slide the window shut and then I bolted toward the back of the yard.

I was just diving behind the back shrubs when I

heard the door open and the neighbor woman shout, "Hey!"

My feet pounded through puddles until I reached the car. Once inside I wasted no time getting out of town. I zoomed down side roads and farm lanes as fast as I dared. I kept glancing in the rearview mirror, expecting the marshal to be hot on my heels, but I didn't encounter another vehicle until I was well away from Hope Harbor.

Winding my way back to the safe house, I somehow got turned around and had to take another route. The advantage of taking the side roads back was that I learned a lot about the area where I was staying. I wasn't far from a small park that sat right on the ocean. The next time I got cabin fever, I'd walk over. If I was going to be here for a week, maybe I'd bring Muffin so she could practice her stealth leaf pouncing. I removed the denim jacket, beanie and glasses and then made one more stop to pick up fresh produce and milk before I showed up at the car rental lot. The same young guy who'd delivered the car in the morning drove me back to the cottage.

"This is a nice place but it needs work," he mused as he drove up the driveway. When he came to a stop, he handed me a business card that said he was a handyman. "I'll give you a good price on yardwork and painting."

"Thanks." No need to tell him I wouldn't be here very long. I stuffed his card into the sack of groceries and then climbed out. As I closed the door behind me, I caught his last sentence.

"After that guy died inside this place, I didn't think anyone would want to live here again."

"Excuse me? What did you say?" I called out but he

was already backing down the driveway, leaving me standing with my mouth hanging open.

Balancing my sacks in one hand I managed to get the porch door open and then the door to the house. As I stepped inside Muffin attacked my feet and then I heard, "Well, look what your cat is dragging in."

With a squeak of surprise I dropped the bags I was carrying, narrowly missing Muffin, who proceeded to attack the parcels in revenge.

Brandy was sitting on the sofa wearing a scowl and a dark sundress so tight I wondered how she could sit at all.

"I had to go out." I scooped up the bags and headed for the kitchen.

"What could possibly be so urgent that you risked being found?"

She followed and watched me dump the two bags on the counter then reach in one, grab a can of cat food, and plunk it noisily onto the counter.

"I seriously was going to get the damn cat food, like you asked. I was just dropping in first to see what else you needed only to find you'd left. I had no idea if you were abducted, dead or just being ridiculous." She walked over and pulled the wool beanie and jean jacket out of the sack on the counter. "Apparently being ridiculous was the right assumption."

I ignored her remark.

"I didn't see another vehicle in the driveway. How did you get here?"

"Well, once I knew you weren't here, I parked behind the cottage in the grass."

"So that you could jump out and scare the hell out

of me?" I took the jean jacket and hoodie and put them both on the back of a chair.

"No, so that I could plan out what I needed to do in case you were taken. I was just about to get out my mirror to see if I could get a bead on you—" her voice raised to screaming level "—and here you were just out getting groceries!"

"That wasn't *all* I needed." I took the sack containing Murray's belongings and dumped them onto the kitchen table.

Brandy slowly shook her head. "What have you done?"

"I'm tired of running. I need to find out who killed Murray or I'm a prisoner. The best chance I have is to get a good fire going and use some of Murray's personal effects to try to encourage a vision."

Brandy tilted her head and smiled with appreciation. "Well, look at you getting all professionally psychic on me." She laughed as she lowered herself into a chair at the table. "Did anyone see you breaking into this guy's place?"

"Of course not." I cleared my throat. "Besides, I was in disguise."

"I have news for you, Scarlet. Hiding your hair under a wool cap and wearing an ugly jacket doesn't exactly hide your identity."

"I also wore glasses."

I pulled out the glassless black frames and slid them onto my face, and Brandy sighed from the depth of her soul.

"You know, if you really wanted some of this guy's stuff, I could've sent someone to get it."

"You were busy. I couldn't reach you." I tossed the

glasses in a drawer in case I needed them again and took out some cheese, bread and butter. "I'm making grilled cheese for dinner. Do you want one?"

"Grilled cheese?" She smiled. "That was Mom's go-to dinner so many nights I remember thinking she didn't know how to make anything else."

"Is that a yes?"

"Damn straight."

As I fried up the sandwiches Brandy did her best to keep Muffin from climbing into her lap but by the time our dinner was done she'd given up.

"Now you're going to be covered in cat hair." I smiled as I slid her plate in front of her.

"That's one hundred percent your fault." She picked up the cat and placed her on the floor along with a corner of her sandwich. "You were always begging Mom for a dog or a cat, so I guess you finally got what you wanted." She pointed to a cupboard in the corner. "There are a few bottles of wine in there. Feel free to choose one for yourself that you think will go good with this fancy dinner."

I took down a bottle of merlot and when I brought two glasses to the table Brandy shook her head.

"None for me. When I said I'm clean, I meant from everything."

"Okay."

I put her glass away and filled my own, then took a seat across from my sister and began to eat. Halfway through my sandwich I reached the bottom of my glass of wine, frowned and refilled it.

"I went through Nan's stuff. There was a letter to me that she wrote before she died. She admitted she felt bad for not telling me about my psychic ability." I refilled my glass. "Tell me the truth, Brandy…why did you, Nan and Mom keep this scrying thing from me?" I took a gulp of wine. "When I think of all the effort it took to avoid campfires, birthday candles and barbecues… Hell, I remember Mom even replacing our gas stove with electric when we moved in. Why not just be honest with me? I don't remember anyone hiding mirrors from you."

"I wanted to." Her face grew hard. "I told Mom and Nan it wasn't fair, and I argued that you'd find out eventually but nobody would listen to me." She shrugged. "I wasn't exactly the favorite."

"Bullshit. Mom and Nan loved you just as much as they loved me."

"Really?" She got up and filled a glass of water from the sink, then placed the glass down on the table harder than necessary. "Everyone was always so worried about poor, delicate Scarlet. Scarlet gets headaches. Scarlet can't handle knowing about fire until she's older." She released a derisive puff of air. "That got pretty old from my side of things."

We ate the rest of our sandwiches in silence and then she got up, grabbed our plates and took them to the sink.

"All Mom and Nan would do is tell me to not be a showboat. Not to use my talent for bad things and to protect you at all costs. No teenager wants their kid sister hanging around." She smirked. "No offense but you were such a pain."

"Is that why you ran away?" I asked quietly. "You were sick of protecting me?"

She sat back down and shook her head. "I didn't run away. I moved out instead of going to college like Mom wanted. Got a job and took care of myself."

Took care of herself by sticking a needle in her arm.

"You never came to visit until you were so screwed up on drugs that you needed money," I countered.

She didn't deny it.

"I have a lot of regrets." Brandy sighed and dug out her favorite coral lipstick from her purse and applied it. "Mom thought if you knew about your fire scrying talent too early it would crush you. Apparently, out of all the family psychic skills of fire, tea leaves, mirrors and water, the spiritualist talent of fire is the strongest. Nan said that our great-grandmother was a fire seer and her abilities were so powerful that she couldn't handle it." Brandy twirled Nan's ring as she added, "Apparently, she took her own life."

Once again, I was thrown by a family fact that was kept from me. "Wow. Our family seems to have more skeletons than a cemetery." I blew out a puff of air. "If this is true, and I am so powerful, then why haven't I been able to see Murray's murderer when I've tried?"

"Like I said before, you just need practice." She pointed to the bag containing Murray's personal stuff. "And maybe that's your edge. Just like I sometimes need something personal when gazing into a mirror. Do you want to get a fire going and give this a shot?" She glanced at her phone. "I don't have much time. I'm meeting Nick."

"Nick? That's your boyfriend?"

"Yup. We've both been pretty busy lately so I promised I'd drive back to Seattle tonight."

"Oh, that reminds me, someone called for you this morning." I held up my hand to stop her protest. "I know, I shouldn't answer unless it's you. It was five in the morning and I answered because I was half asleep. Some heavy breather who just hung up."

She waved it away with a flutter of her hand.

"Drawbacks of the industry. Lots of sketchy perverts." She pointed a finger at me. "Or someone trying to track you down. That's why I told you not to answer."

"Fine. Another question. Who died here?"

"Here?" She rolled her eyes. "I think the previous owner died in his sleep. Why?" When I didn't reply she hurriedly said, "Are we going to do this fire thing, or what?"

"I want to try this on my own. I can make a fire and give it a go. You've got a long drive back." I got to my feet to walk her out.

Muffin was playing with the strap of Brandy's purse.

"Hey!" Brandy shooed the cat away from her bag. "That's designer leather you're chomping on, you little rat."

"How did you meet Nick?" I asked at the back door.

"We met in rehab, actually." Brandy slipped her handbag onto her shoulder.

"Oh. He's an addict."

"*Recovered* addict. Like me." Brandy leaned in and kissed me on the cheek. "He's a good man. Far better than I deserve and we have a ton in common. Don't be worrying about me. I've got my life under control. Focus on yourself." She poked me in the chest with a manicured finger. "No more sneaking off. You stay put until you hear from me. Got it?"

"Yes."

"And I expect you to text me if you uncover anything good while fire scrying. If you get a clear vision about who killed this guy, you don't go off on your own trying to make a citizen's arrest, okay?"

"Of course." I laughed at the idea. "I'm not stupid."

"After what you did today, I'm not so sure about that." Brandy opened the door and then closed it again. She walked over and pulled me into a tight hug. "I need you to stay safe," she breathed into my hair.

"I will." I hugged her back, blinking back tears.

After she closed the door behind her, I watched through the back window as Brandy carefully backed out of the tall grass and then disappeared down the driveway. Quickly I washed up the few dishes while Muffin chased something around the floor at my feet. It was when I was giving the table a wipe that I realized what Muffin was batting around was Brandy's lipstick.

"Oh no." I snagged the lipstick from the floor, and Muffin scurried up my pant leg to try and retrieve it. "Brandy's going to make cat stew out of you," I warned with a laugh as I stuffed the tube into the pocket of my jeans.

I took a look at the stack of wood next to the fireplace and realized there weren't any smaller pieces for kindling. Since Muffin was literally climbing the screens trying to get out, I strapped her into her harness and we made our way outside. Using my phone as a flashlight I searched the edges of the bushes for small sticks while Muffin leaped, rolled and pounced on anything and everything. She scrambled a few feet up a tree and probably would've gone a hundred feet up if I didn't have her on a leash. When she realized she was being restrained, she leaped to the ground and chomped on a tall weed.

From where I stood tucked up against the hedge, I could just make out the bottom of the cabin's private road where it met the street. A dark pickup truck approached. It slowed and then stopped at the end of the

driveway. I held my breath as it turned up the lane leading to the cottage. Grabbing Muffin off the ground and
holding her to my chest, I stepped deeper into the hedge,
waiting for the driver to approach the house, but he just
sat there not moving.

I glanced toward the cottage and winced. I'd opened
the blinds earlier in the day and now, with the lights
on, you could see clearly inside. Squinting toward the
truck, I leaned forward trying to make out the driver
but the headlights prevented me from seeing anything
inside the truck besides a shadow.

Muffin squirmed and scratched my arms to be set
free but I held her firm. I was prepared to take off running into the dense brush if that truck came any closer.
Suddenly, he backed down the driveway and zoomed
away. I let out a loud relieved breath and bolted for the
house.

Once inside, I shut the blinds and black-out curtains
and double-checked that all the windows and doors were
locked tight. Lastly, I pushed the kitchen table against
the back door and moved the coffee table to block the
front door. My barricades wouldn't stop someone from
entering if they were really determined but it could
slow them down long enough for me to draw my gun.

I went into the bedroom and opened the drawer
where I'd placed my shirts. In the corner, wrapped in
a scarf, was Nan's old 9 mm Glock. It felt foreign and
weighty in my trembling hand, but Nan had taught me
how to use the weapon and, if it came down to it, I was a
pretty good shot. With the firearm tucked into the waistband of my jeans at the small of my back, I returned
to the living room and went to work building the fire.

I could only find two wooden matches in the box

next to the woodpile so that would mean no multiple chances at getting this fire going. I remembered what Noah had said about his trick using dryer lint. Snagging an empty paper towel roll from the recycling bin, I stuffed it with lint from the dryer screen, then I took the driest of the twigs I'd gathered, broke them into smaller pieces and jammed them into the roll as well. In the fireplace I placed the rest of the kindling pyramid style around the roll and larger logs around those.

The fireplace flue creaked loudly when I cranked it open but when I struck the match to the paper towel roll, the flames caught immediately. I leaned forward and fanned the small blaze with my hands and soon the fire was raging. It was much bigger than I actually needed. It was going to get very hot in this small cottage especially considering I couldn't open the doors or windows to get a breeze going.

I stripped out of my jeans and replaced them with shorts. When my denim hit the floor the sound it made reminded me that Brandy's lipstick was still in my front pocket. I dug the tube out and brought it into the living room with me along with the Glock in my waistband. I needed to put the lipstick somewhere Brandy would see it next time she came but also keep it out of Muffin's paws.

The flames were red and gold dancing ribbons stretching up the chimney as I settled onto the sofa, well aware of the gun in my waistband pressing into the small of my back. I placed the lipstick on the end table at my elbow and emptied the bag of Murray's belongings onto the couch cushion next to me. The dirty T-shirt, comb and toothbrush sat waiting to be called to service. A ping of nervous energy traveled up my spine as I closed my eyes and prepared myself for visions to come.

As I'd observed with Brandy, I closed my eyes and drew in a long slow breath up my nose and then released it from my mouth. I repeated the meditative breathing again and again, trying to relax my body and will my mind to be open to receive whatever truths were available. I could feel Muffin claw her way up my bare leg and then up my T-shirt to settle on my shoulder. The kitten decided to groom me, licking my neck with her sandpapery tongue. Trying to ignore the cat, I repeated my breathing exercises until I felt my body relax. Before I even opened my eyes, I reached next to me for one of Murray's items. My fingers wrapped around his comb and I held it tightly in my hand until I could feel the teeth digging into my palm.

"Who killed you, Murray?" I asked the room and slowly opened my eyes to peer deep into the fire.

A wave of dizziness and nausea swept through my body. A slideshow of images flew through my mind like a movie on fast-forward and I couldn't seem to slow it down. Abruptly, Muffin leaped from my shoulder onto the sofa then over to the end table next to me, landing on Brandy's lipstick. I dropped Murray's comb and my vision and concentration evaporated.

"Oh come on!" I shouted at Muffin as she batted the lip color onto the floor and then played hockey with it until she scored a goal of swatting it under the sofa.

"That's it." I picked up the fluffball and carried her across the room. "You're just going to have to go into your crate until I'm done."

Muffin protested with a slash of her murder mittens

and clawed the back of my hand as I shoved her inside and slid the latch. Then she howled like she was in pain.

"Oh stop being a drama queen. It won't be long."

I crossed the room back over to the sofa and stopped to fan myself in the hot space before getting on my knees and looking under the sofa. The lipstick was nestled just within reach between a couple of dust bunnies. I pulled it out, then dropped down onto the sofa and glanced up at the flames.

The fire felt as though it stabbed my eyes. My fingers sharply clenched the lipstick, forcing it to cut grooves into my palm. A vision raged through my head showing Brandy slumped across the steering wheel of her Corvette, her eyes wide and unseeing, her face pale as death.

ELEVEN

WITH A SHRIEK anybody within earshot could hear, I was on my feet and fumbling with my phone. I called Brandy's number and it went straight to voicemail. I called half a dozen more times with the same result and I sent just as many texts telling her she needed to call me as soon as possible.

I put the vision on a loop in my head to see if I was missing anything. The only thing that was off was that she wasn't wearing Nan's ring in the vision, but that felt inconsequential. She was in danger. Everything in my gut told me that and here I was out at some cottage without a car or any way to get to her. Frantically, I looked through the phone she'd given me and found the yellow app and the contact section. Brandy told me she lived across the street from her office. The vision I had showed me she was in her car so she could be anywhere but at least I could start at her office. If I could get there. My credit card was maxed out renting the car earlier to go to Murray's and, besides, the rental place was closed.

After a few more seconds of pacing the floor I decided I had no choice. I put a phone number into my phone.

"Hello?" Noah's gruff voice answered.

"I need you."

Flying in the face of every warning Brandy had

given me, I gave Noah the address of where I was staying. I put out the fire, let Muffin out of her carrier and gave her a few treats to make up for me leaving. Within half an hour Noah's truck was pulling up the driveway and I ran out the door to meet him.

I hopped into the passenger seat and he reversed away from the cottage.

"You said we're headed to Seattle?" he asked.

"Yes."

"And you're still not going to tell me why?"

I hesitated because I didn't know how to tell him how I knew Brandy was in danger. "Brandy's in trouble."

"Okaaay." He slid a glance my way as we accelerated down the road and headed toward the interstate. "Are we talking she's feeling sick kind of trouble and we got to stop for chicken soup and aspirin, or is this the kind of trouble that means I should be packing a shotgun for protection."

"I don't know." I pulled my purse close to my side and I could feel the metal outline of my gun through the leather of my bag. "I'm sorry for dragging you into this."

"It's okay. Let's just call this a welfare check."

"Yes." My hands were fisted at my sides. Noah took one hand off the steering wheel and reached over to cover my fist with his palm. "It's going to be okay."

"Thanks." *But you don't know that. You didn't see what I saw.*

The image of Brandy slumped over her steering wheel looking pale and lifeless caused me to shudder.

"Sorry for the mess." He pointed to the floor at my feet, which was littered with a half dozen empty paper coffee cups.

"Maybe you have a coffee problem," I remarked, half joking.

"Nah, my problem is more about not taking the time to clean my truck."

I offered him a tight smile and he attempted small talk a bit more, but I didn't have it in me to keep up a conversation. We rode in silence toward Seattle with Noah's face set in a frown of concentration and my fingernails cutting half-moons into the palms of my hands. Every so often I pulled out my phone as if I'd somehow missed a call or text from Brandy but there were no replies to my umpteen texts or calls.

"Sorry, gotta stop for gas," Noah said, steering his truck toward an off-ramp.

We were about halfway to Seattle now and with every passing mile my uneasiness grew. While Noah stood outside and pumped gas, I sat stiff with fear. Then my phone rang and I dropped it onto the floor in my haste to answer it.

"Hello?" I shouted.

"Oh my God, it's good to hear your voice! What happened? Was there another shooting? Are you okay?" Brandy asked.

"Yes, I'm okay but are *you* all right? I've been worried to death."

"What? I'm fine." Brandy blew out a raspberry and added, "What is this about, Scarlet? I'm trying to have a romantic evening with my guy and you've called me like a million times!"

"I, um, I had a vision." My gaze tripped over to Noah who had just removed the nozzle from his gas tank. "I saw you were half dead in your car..." I gulped.

"Never mind half dead. You looked really, really and completely dead."

Brandy let out a long sigh. "Well, Scarlet, I'm fine. I don't know what to tell you. I haven't been in my car and I don't plan on driving anywhere at the moment." There was some rustling to the side and a low mumbled voice in the background followed by Brandy's giggle. "As a matter of fact, I don't plan on leaving my bed."

"Oh." My shoulders dropped with relief and confusion. "I guess my vision was wrong." But even as I said that, it was hard to shake the realism of it. "Tell me, are you still wearing Nan's ring?"

"Of course," she bit back with annoyance. "I never take it off. I'm telling you, it's *my* ring, Scarlet, so don't even go there, okay?"

"No, it's just that in my vision you weren't wearing it."

"Well, there you go." She chuckled mirthlessly. "Remember what I said about practicing? This is why. Your skills are weak." She paused a beat. "Or maybe you're seeing something from the past. I was rear-ended in the Corvette last year but it was a minor accident. I bit my lip and there was a little blood from that but, other than that, I wasn't hurt. You probably jumped to conclusions before seeing the whole thing."

"Maybe..." I chewed my thumb nail thoughtfully.

"Besides, I thought you were going to try and get a reading on that Murray guy?" Brandy said, her voice laced with impatience. "Why don't you put your energy there. I'm fine other than some boyfriend trouble which I'm hoping to resolve tonight with some sexy time if my kid sister leaves me alone. If you can't handle your visions just wait until I can help you with that Murray guy's stuff. Sounds like you need some serious mentorship."

"Okay." But it felt wrong and not okay at all. "By the way, you forgot your lipstick at the cottage."

"Thanks for letting me know." Her voice sounded distracted as she whispered something to Nick. At that moment a loud truck pulled into the gas station and Brandy picked up on the noise. "Where are you? You better not have left the house!"

"Just in the yard with Muffin and a truck went by on the road," I lied then hurriedly added, "Look, just promise you'll be safe. Maybe have Nick drive you if you need to go out."

"Yeah, yeah. I'll chat with you tomorrow…" She giggled off to the side then the call ended.

Noah climbed back inside the truck and stuck his keys in the ignition.

"Change of plans," I told him. "Brandy just called. She's fine. There was just, um, a miscommunication."

"Oh. That's good news, right? Why do you look like you're not happy about that?"

"Oh I am." I nodded vigorously. "I'm just real sorry that I dragged you out for nothing."

"Are you kidding?" He laughed as he started up the truck. "You gave me the chance to rescue a damsel in distress. It made my week that you trusted me that much."

"Really?" I offered him a lopsided grin. "You're not ticked off that I hauled you out of your warm bed to waste your time?"

"Tell you what, if you give me a kiss goodnight, I'm willing to call it even." He wriggled his eyebrows comically and I laughed.

When we pulled up to the cottage, I gathered the coffee cups on the passenger side floor of his truck and tossed them into the recycle bin inside the front porch.

"Thanks for that," he said as he climbed out of his truck.

"The very least I could do. Seriously."

Then he turned and bent his head toward me. The goodnight kiss was long and deep. My arms wrapped around his neck and drew him close, our bodies melded together perfectly.

"If I don't leave now," he breathed against my mouth, "then I'm going to have you naked in the next thirty seconds."

"I'm okay with that," I whispered against his neck.

Before you could say "mosquito" we were making frantic and passionate love against the cold metal of the pickup. Even in the cool night air I was covered in a sheen of sweat.

Afterward Noah released me and stepped back with his hands slowly lowering me to the ground on shaky legs. He bent to the ground to retrieve our clothing.

"A comfortable bed probably would've been a better idea," he said, still trying to catch his breath while he yanked his jeans over his hips. "I hope you don't have bruising on your backside from my truck."

"Totally worth it," I drawled, leaning in to playfully nibble his lower lip as I buttoned my jeans.

Noah untangled himself from my grip and took a step back. "A proper date." He shook his finger in my face and then hooked his arm in mine as we walked toward the cottage door. "That's what we need. A good and proper go-out-to-dinner date and a get-to-know-each-other over dinner kind of date."

"Well, we had pizza out and we also went to the diner so that counts. Seems like we already skipped past any other formalities when we first gave my van a shake, Mr. Adams." I leaned a hip against the doorway and watched him back away.

"True, but I like you, Red." He almost lost his footing going down the steps of the cottage backward as he kept his eyes on me. "I like you a lot and, as awesome as this was, I don't want to just have sex with you. I want to know you. All of you."

His words made my heart squeeze in my chest. I stood outside until I could no longer hear the sound of his truck going down the road.

I let out a low whistle. "You say you want to know me, but I don't think you could handle what that means," I murmured as I stepped inside the cottage.

Even though the fire had been out for a couple hours, it was still extremely hot inside. I found Muffin fast asleep on top of Murray's nasty T-shirt on the sofa. I was suddenly completely exhausted and had no desire to build another fire tonight. Murray's stuff would have to wait.

I barricaded the door again then climbed into bed. A few seconds later a ball of fluff joined me. Soon Muffin began kneading the center of my chest.

"I think you missed me," I yawned and gave her back a rub. "Sorry for just running out like that."

Muffin began to purr and soon we were both fast asleep.

When my cat alarm went off at the butt crack of dawn I wasn't ready but there was no snooze button on a kitten that wanted breakfast.

Muffin got her food and fresh water before I even

filled the coffee maker. I now understood mothers always putting their kids first. Even if that child had razor paws and liked to bite your toes through the sheets.

I shoved the kitchen table aside from the door and took my coffee cup out onto the back porch. The furniture barricade felt silly this morning. The truck that I'd seen yesterday must've just been someone who'd driven up the cottage drive, realized they were at the wrong location and then headed back on the road. If it had been someone here to hurt me, they certainly wouldn't have just left without even approaching the house. Whoever had shot up Bubbles didn't waste time just driving up to say hello.

"Some psychic you are," I told myself. "Besides some fuzzy gold hair that showed the murder weapon, you've never hit the mark on this thing. Even the shooting at the van you only saw as a hailstorm. Not to mention the Brandy disaster." I frowned as I remembered my vision about Brandy being hurt but my lips soon turned up at the corners as I recalled how the evening ended with Noah.

Thoughts of other murder situations like when I was in Seattle and Aberdeen had me confused. There I had visions that helped law enforcement. Clear clues and visions of the murder, and when I had those images in those circumstances it didn't involve me having a personal item belonging to the person. Why was this time so different? Was it because I was too involved and close to the situation?

I sighed and realized that Brandy was right. My skills were weak and I was too inexperienced to do this myself. It felt like it could be time to turn over Murray's belongings to Brandy and ask her to give it a go. Maybe it was an ego thing, but that just irked the hell out of me. It was my life on the line here and before I turned the power over to Brandy, maybe I could give one hundred percent to getting this thing done myself.

Brandy called and asked a few more questions about the vision I had regarding her. "Do you think your vision was me in a car wreck in the Corvette? The one that happened a year ago?"

"Maybe," I admitted. But it didn't feel like that. It felt like she'd been attacked but it was hard for me to separate the vision from my emotions.

"Okay, well, I'm going to be driving Nick's SUV the next while anyway. Getting some new rubber on the Vette. You get anything off Murray's stuff that you stole?"

"Borrowed," I corrected. "And I haven't really tried. But it's on my list for later."

"Okay, today's my last day in court but tomorrow I'll come out and help you with this thing."

"Thanks."

"Don't sound so sad. I have a little news that will brighten your day."

"What?" I felt myself get excited.

"Well, Cobb called yesterday and said your van was ready for release and I pulled some strings and had it brought into the shop to get the windows replaced and body repaired. You'll never even know that it was shot up."

"Really? Oh my God, that's awesome!"

"Not only did I get the windows fixed, I had them replace your fridge while it was in the garage. Your birthday gift has been redeemed."

"Oh man..." I closed my eyes and a happy tear slid

down my face. "That means a lot, Brandy. Thank you. I'll be so-o-o glad to get Bubbles back."

"Yeah, but it's a little hard to be in hiding in a van with neon bubbles all over it. The garage will just keep Bubbles on their lot until we're ready. You need to sit tight at the cottage until they catch Murray's killer."

"That could take weeks, or even months." I frowned. "What if they never catch this guy?"

"Once you and I put our heads together, that killer doesn't stand a chance."

"Sure," I replied, but I didn't feel that positivity in my gut.

Hiding out was not helping me find Murray's killer. Regardless of what Brandy said, I had a hard time believing anyone in Hope Harbor was capable of tracking me using the cell phone she gave me.

I sent a text off to Noah: Thanks again for driving me last night. It means a lot.

He replied: My pleasure. Seriously. With a heart emoji followed by a kiss emoji that caused my palms to get sweaty.

I texted back: I don't have anyone's phone numbers on my new phone. Could you send me Penny's and anyone else's you can think of?

He replied with a thumbs-up and I waited.

A few minutes later I received a screenshot of a slew of phone numbers, which included just about everyone in town. I sent him a thank-you text and then I went to work firing off texts.

The first person I called was Penny.

"It's so great to hear your voice!" she gushed. "I thought for sure you'd been shot and they were keeping it hush-hush."

Who was "they" and why would they keep me being injured a secret? When I asked Penny she just brushed it off. She assured me she and Tess were fine running the shop together and that I should just stay away and keep safe.

"Your job will be waiting for you once all this is over," Penny promised. "Oh, and you'll never guess what happened at Murray's apartment!"

"What?" A feeling of unease skipped up my spine.

"My neighbor, Barb, said she came home from her coffee klatch and saw someone running across her backyard. She called Marshal Cobb and he said that it looked like someone broke in through the window but nothing seemed to be missing."

"That's weird." I cleared my throat. "I mean, why would someone break in if they weren't taking anything?"

"Exactly!" Penny continued, "One of my other neighbors suggested it might be you, but I told her that was impossible since everyone knows your van was brought in for evidence and you're staying with your sister in Seattle."

"Yeah. That's right." My nerves itched at the lie. "Why would anyone think it was me?"

"Oh people just like to talk," Penny said dismissively. "Besides, Barb said it looked like a teenage boy. Chances are it was just some kid wanting to break into a murder victim's house for kicks."

I could hear Tess's voice in the background say something that sounded like "That's why I moved out of this town. People are always talking!"

And Penny replied, "Not everyone is a gossip, but of course we know it wasn't you, Red. You're in Seattle with your sister and you sure don't look like a teenage boy with glasses!"

"Of course, it wasn't me," I lied weakly. "I'm sure your neighbor is right, and it was some teen breaking in for kicks or bragging rights."

"Yes. She only saw the person from the back wearing a hat and a jean jacket. Certainly not a pretty redhead like yourself." Penny let out an exasperated breath.

"Have you heard anything about Murray's investigation? Do they have any suspects at all?"

"Gosh, I don't think so, but don't you worry, Marshal Cobb is all over it," she said sweetly. "Before you know it, you'll be back at work here and this will all be behind us."

"Thanks," I said and meant it. Penny was so sweet and I was grateful to have her on my side.

There was some tussle of movement and Tess got on the line, "Don't worry your pretty little head about anything. Marshal Cobb and Sheriff Duthroyd are doing their investigative rounds and I'm sure they'll uncover some transient who happened to be blowing through town that day."

"A transient? Is that what they think?"

"It can't be anyone who lives here, could it? If any of us wanted to kill Murray we would've done it years ago." She laughed pretty loud at that idea.

I thought about the balance in my bank account and realized this better get resolved sooner rather than later. The money I'd stashed away for a new battery wasn't going to last long. After promising Penny I'd keep in touch, I moved on to the next call.

"Oh my God, Red, I've been thinking about you night and day!" Melody exclaimed. "How are you? Were you shot? Everyone's saying you weren't hurt but I was thinking maybe you were and they just weren't telling anyone since you haven't been around at all and your phone number is going to someone else's voicemail and—"

I interrupted her excited roll. "I wasn't hurt."

"Good. That's good. And Muffin? How is she?"

"She's great." I glanced over at my kitten. "At this very moment she's terrorizing some drapes."

Talking with Melody and keeping her on one topic was a lot like herding cats. I allowed her to ramble about all the gossip in town. I hoped that some of it might be about who the killer could possibly be but, unfortunately, the only person people were talking about was me.

"Have you heard anyone offer a hint as to who could've wanted to shoot at me?" I asked with exasperation. "I mean surely everyone knows that if someone is coming after *me*, I'm not the one who killed Murray."

"Wellll…" She chuckled nervously. "Some people said that shooting up your van was staged by your witchy sister so you could make it look like you're innocent and also get a new paint job from the insurance company."

I rolled my eyes and smacked my forehead with my palm. "But you don't believe that, right?"

"Of course not!" Melody said sweetly then aside she shouted at one of her cats to leave another alone before she returned to our conversation. "I keep telling everyone that nobody who would rescue a kitten the way you did could possibly hurt another person."

Oh great. The local strange cat lady's defense for me is to turn me into another weirdo cat lady.

"Could you do me a favor and let me know if you hear *anything* about Murray's killing? Even if you don't think it's a big deal, it might be to me."

"Oh sure, I can do that." Again, she screamed at one of her cats and this time she didn't bother to move the phone and nearly deafened me. "Sorry, Arthur keeps trying to hump Coco and I'm just not going to tolerate that kind of sexual harassment in my house."

"Right. I'll let you go and defend Coco's honor. Call me at this number if you hear anything."

I was getting nowhere, and it was getting depressing. My next call was to Marshal Cobb but he had more questions than answers.

"Somebody broke into Murray's apartment and that somebody looked a lot like you," he said.

"That's absurd," I protested. "Besides, I heard that Barb said it was a teen boy in a jean jacket, hat and wearing glasses. I don't own a jean jacket and don't wear glasses. Besides, you realize I don't have a vehicle and I'm still out of town." The lies rolled effortlessly off my lips even as my stomach clenched. "What could someone possibly want to take from Murray's apartment anyway?"

"Didn't look like anything was taken, which makes it even stranger. Look, I know your sister does her spooky psychic readings and, for all I know, maybe you two want to have some kind of séance with Murray and needed a lock of his hair," he snarled.

"You can't be serious." I blew out an indignant puff of air while I simultaneously cringed at how close his guess was. "I sure hope you're actually spending time looking for whoever killed Murray and who shot up my van instead of worrying about imaginary rituals!"

"Oh I've been doing my research all right." His voice held an angry sneer. "Care to tell me about the time you were using a stepladder to dust the higher shelves in the toy section of Penny's?"

"I don't know what you're talking about." I chewed a hangnail on my finger.

"Let me refresh your memory. Liz Smith, who runs the diner, told me one time she walked into Penny's to buy some printer paper and when she walked in she heard you telling Murray and I quote, 'Don't make me hurt you.'"

Ugh. It's not that I'd forgotten about that, I'd just forgotten that there'd been a witness. "It wasn't a big deal. Murray grabbed my butt while I was on the stepladder and thought it was a joke. That was my way of telling him not to do that again."

"So you lied when we asked you if Murray had ever grabbed you. So did he do it again? Did you have to hurt him permanently to make it stop?"

"No and no!" I shouted and then lowered my voice. "Look, Marshal Cobb, you and I and every single person in Hope Harbor know that Murray was a lecherous pervert who liked to grab women. If that's the only motive you've got, then half the town could've killed him."

"But half the town was used to him already and maybe a new girl wouldn't be able to handle a little innocent ass pat and would fly off the handle."

"Innocent ass pat!" I roared and then I drew in a deep breath, released it slowly and calmed my tone. "Just because I didn't appreciate Murray's attention does not mean that I killed him. Please, just do your damn job."

And with that I ended the call and tossed the phone onto the couch cushions for good measure.

Probably losing my temper with Marshal Cobb wasn't my best move but it had the benefit of proving to me that if this thing was going to be solved without my ass ending up behind bars, then I would have to do something to help it along. It was unusually warm for mid-September and the prospect of any kind of a fire in the small cottage was unappealing. A quick search online showed me that the small ocean-side park had barbecue pits for the public to use. I'd bring along some wieners and buns and have myself a little barbecue.

If the fire I made happened to be a little bigger than most, at least nobody would suspect that what I was really doing was trying to find a killer.

TWELVE

MY ORIGINAL PLAN was to bring Muffin along on her harness, but after I'd filled my small backpack with some wood, the hot dog supplies and Murray's belongings I decided to leave kitty behind. Since she'd curled up to sleep on the back of the sofa, I figured she wouldn't mind anyway.

On my way out the front door I paused at the recycle bin and gathered a few of the paper coffee cups from Noah's truck as well as an empty cereal box for kindling.

Across the road I easily found the path in the trees that wound its way toward the ocean. It was the kind of day where the breeze off the water kissed you, leaving salt on your lips and caressing you with just enough refreshing air that you didn't mind. This would be the kind of day Nan and I would've found somewhere to sit on the sand and eat peanut butter sandwiches for dinner. Those months traveling together were a special kind of magic. Thinking of her now made my chest ache with longing.

I gathered a few dry twigs and by the time the path opened onto the seaside park my arms were filled and my expectations high. The beach itself was more large boulders than sand because the tide was in. This worked to my advantage because the area wasn't very busy. One mom with a couple of young kids had claimed a picnic table near the water and I chose the one farthest from the parking lot and just outside the tree line.

I went to work building a small fire in the cast iron barbecue pit. I'd brought a towel to sit on so that I could be in front of the fire at eye level but not on a seat where I could fall should I get dizzy like I had at Noah's. While the kindling caught, I lined up my items next to me on the towel. Murray's toothbrush, comb and T-shirt as well as Brandy's lipstick. At the last second, I also set aside one of the coffee cups from Noah's truck.

As the heat of the fire warmed me, I cracked my knuckles in anticipation, closed my eyes and drew in slow, even breaths. I felt both nervous and impatient for results, but I decided today would be all about patience.

I repeated thoughts in my head.

Breathe in: *Don't rush.*

Breathe out: *Take your time.*

Breathe in: *Let the answers come.*

Breathe out: *Be open to all information.*

Slowly my heart stopped pounding against my ribs, my shoulders relaxed, and my hands were able to unclench from fists to lay palms down against my thighs.

When I opened my eyes, I did so gradually with almost a sleepy, trancelike gaze into the orange streamers of light that blackened the wood. Instantly, I felt lightheaded and put my left hand down to steady myself, but I kept my breathing even while I looked at the fire, into its heat and even beyond the charred splinters. Remembering what Nan's note had suggested, I whispered a plea to Nan and my mom for help. As if in reply, a gust of wind caused sparks to fly in my small fire.

My right hand reached next to me for Murray's belongings. I'd folded the comb and toothbrush inside of the T-shirt and now I drew all the items onto my lap. Without lifting my eyes from the fire, I unwrapped the shirt and took the comb and toothbrush in my right hand while holding the T-shirt in my left.

Instantly the embers in the fire swirled before me and began to show me snippets like a movie: There was Murray at the store, stocking shelves with his smarmy grin. As if it were happening to me, there was a noise behind in the stockroom but I wasn't startled or afraid. I could feel him turn toward the sound, as if he was expecting someone. He reached into his pocket for a paper but before he could face his assailant, a blow like a hammer hit the back of his head and brought him down, face-first onto the storeroom floor.

I gasped, dropped the items and squeezed my eyes shut. My head swam and a smell of burning swirled in my sinuses. After a moment I composed myself and tried again. And again. Each time that story replayed and the killer's identity remained obscured. I repeated the process with each of Murray's objects individually. Other scenarios played out: Murray sneaking a few dollars from Penny's cash register when her back was turned. Him stealthily walking up behind a young woman and then grabbing her butt. After twenty minutes of trying with Murray's objects, the fire was mere embers. Everything I was seeing was from Murray's point of view. If he had his back to his killer, reaching into his subconscious wouldn't reveal his murderer.

Disappointed, I got to my feet, raised my hands above my head and stretched. My head throbbed and I stroked the long scar on my scalp as I wondered if Brandy would have more luck with Murray's things. She seemed much more skilled. I glanced at her lipstick on the towel next to where I'd been sitting. A shiver traveled up my spine at my last vision of her crumpled over her steering wheel. Perhaps she was right. What I'd seen could very well have been something from the past and not the present or future.

I had a small amount of wood remaining, so I added that to the dying cinders and fanned the air until they caught. Lowering myself back onto the towel and folding my legs crisscrossed, I repeated my breathing exercises, lifted the lip color in my hands and squeezed it gently while I opened my eyes.

Again, a vivid picture of Brandy slumped over the steering wheel of her car jumped into my head. Clearly, she was not wearing Nan's ring. Her eyes were unseeing and all life was drained from her face. Sucking air in between my teeth, I forced myself to remain seated and encouraged the scenario before me to play out.

"Show me," I whispered to the fire.

No sooner had those words left my lips than the car vision faded and was replaced by an equally disturbing one. She was still in the car, slumped over the wheel, but now the vision was from the passenger seat. From the bend in her elbow dangled a syringe. I fought to tell myself this was the past, before she got clean, but as if to disprove that thought, the vision panned to the driver's window behind Brandy. It was dark and rainy, but I could plainly make out a neon dancing cupcake sign in the window of a shop next to Brandy's office.

Unlike some of my other visions, this one was not dreamlike or vague. It was as clear-cut and evident as the mother and her children at the picnic table not far from me.

That first evening she visited me in Hope Harbor

she'd told me, "The butcher shop closed a couple weeks ago. It's been replaced by a bakery with an annoying dancing cupcake sign."

If she'd been clean a couple years, there was no way what I was seeing was more than a year ago. A burst of emotion exploded from my lips and the vision left. If that bakery had only existed for a few weeks, that meant she'd been using recently. Sure, my vision could be wrong, but everything in my gut was screaming this was accurate. In fact, it felt more assured than any other vision I ever remembered having.

"Mom? Nan? Is this vision true?"

A piece of wood crackled and a random spark flew beside me, igniting a patch of dry grass. I grabbed a handful of dirt and smothered the small blaze.

Everything Brandy told me was a lie.

Extinguishing the fire in the pit with my water bottle, I gathered my things and stuffed them into the backpack. I paused when I picked up Noah's coffee cup, regretting I hadn't done a reading using his item, and after debating whether to just toss it in the trash, I stuffed it into the backpack with the rest.

I stopped at a concession stand at the end of the park for a chocolate bar and a barbecue lighter. Then I marched back in the direction of the cottage while munching my chocolate, my head swirling with reflections and fury.

My phone rang in my hand just as I was crossing the road to the cottage. It was Brandy. "Where the hell are you?"

"Outside." I stomped up the steps and flung open the door to find her sitting on the sofa, arms crossed and looking pissed.

"Where have you been?" she demanded. "And don't try to tell me you were just in the yard because I've been here for half an hour!"

"I went to the park to have myself a little fire. It was too warm to have it inside the cottage when I have to keep it closed up tight." I opened the backpack, retrieved her lipstick and tossed it to her. "How long have you been using, Brandy? Or have you *ever* been clean?"

"What are you talking about? I told you. It's been a couple years." She opened the lipstick and deftly applied the color.

"I used your lipstick for a reading. Again, I saw you in an accident and I also saw you with a needle sticking out of your arm." My voice was ice as I narrowed my eyes and waited for the lies that I knew would come.

"Like I told you before, you're probably seeing stuff from the past and—"

"The dancing cupcake was in my vision! You told me specifically that the bakery just opened a couple weeks ago so either you were lying about that, or you're lying about being clean."

"I am *not* using!" Brandy waved a hand over her body. "Look at me. Do I look strung out?"

"Not at the moment," I admitted. I walked toward her. "Show me your arms."

She rolled her eyes and then pushed up the sleeve of her left arm.

"You're left handed. Show me your *right* arm."

She did so reluctantly and quickly added, "I was just at the doc and had bloodwork done. It bruised a little."

Sure enough there was a red puncture mark surrounded by a deep purple bruise.

"I knew it! When will I ever learn not to trust you?"

I pointed a finger in Brandy's face. "Get out. I want you gone."

"Oh come on." She rolled her eyes. "You're being completely ridiculous."

"Get out or so help me I will throw you out," I snarled.

"Ha! You and what army, little sis?"

When I only stood defiantly glaring at her, she rolled her eyes so far in her head I swear she could read her own thoughts.

"Fine. Technically this isn't your place to throw me out of, but I'll leave because I don't have to prove myself to anyone." She got to her feet and yanked the strap of her purse up her shoulder. "Call me when you've changed your mind."

"That will *never* happen," I shouted to her back as she went down the steps toward her boyfriend's SUV.

When I could no longer hear the car in the driveway, I walked over to the sofa and pummeled the cushions with my fists until I was sweaty and exhausted. I slumped down and curled into the fetal position to have a good, hard cry.

Muffin jumped up on the sofa and began angrily biting my toes.

"Ow!" I sat up, grabbed the kitty and held her to my face. With a sad sniff I told her, "Guess we should get out of here."

There was no way I wanted anything to do with any place Brandy had arranged for me. I called up the garage where Bubbles was and told them I wanted to pick her up.

"We're closing in five minutes," the guy told me.

"So unless you can teleport here, it'll have to be in the morning. We open at nine."

Guess one more night wouldn't make that much of a difference. There was also the little matter of finding my way there. I could hop a bus to the Bellingham garage but not with Muffin and all my things. I could go on my own then drive Bubbles back here and gather my things but when I checked the bus schedule, I realized I wouldn't even be able to catch one until almost noon.

I dialed Noah's number. "I need another favor," I told him.

"Do I get another kiss in payment?" he drawled sexily.

"Definitely." I smiled and felt my heart heat in my chest. "I need a ride to Bellingham tomorrow to pick up the van. Feel free to say no because I know you have to open the store."

"I don't open until ten. If I pick you up at eight I can make it back in time. Does that work?"

"Yes. Thank you so much!"

With that all set, I made myself some pasta for dinner. After I was done eating, I packed up my things to get ready for the morning. I placed everything at the front door to make sure it was a quick escape once Noah arrived. When I placed Nan's tote at the door I couldn't resist unzipping it and then kissing a finger and placing that kiss on the heart-shaped urn. Then I removed the photo box where I'd found my letter.

With the box on my lap, I opened the lid and took out the envelope. I reread Nan's letter a half dozen times, and it still made me equally happy to hear from her and sad because of all of the unanswered questions it triggered. Placing the envelope to the side, I scooped up a handful of the photographs and began shuffling through them. They weren't in chronological order so one picture might be of Nan holding my mother as a baby and the next picture could be Brandy and me having a birthday cake without any candles. So many memories that now felt so wrong knowing how my family had conspired to keep me from fire.

I reached for a second handful of pictures and noticed there was another envelope beneath the photos. Eagerly, I snatched it up, hoping for more words from Nan, but my heart fell when I saw *Brandy* scrawled across the front in Nan's loopy cursive.

The flap of the envelope wasn't tucked inside like mine; it was sealed shut with even an extra piece of tape holding down the flap. I held it up to the light and then let it sit on the end table for a few minutes while I poured myself a glass of wine and debated opening it. After I finished that glass of wine, my courage was at its peak and I picked the envelope up again.

"If there's anything in here that Brandy *absolutely* needs to know, then I'll pass it on."

It was morally and ethically sketchy, but damn it, I was sick of my family keeping secrets from me! I tore open the envelope and began to read Nan's words:

Dear Brandy,
I have so many regrets that you and I weren't able to be closer. My wish was always that you'd get clean in my lifetime. I hope that when you get this letter you are well and sober. As you know, I have paid in advance for a treatment center. By now the center should have contacted you directly to let you know that it is there when you are ready.

I hope that if you get clean you will try to mend things with Scarlet. She's going to need you once I'm gone. But she's going to need a sober sister. Not an addict. I hope I make myself clear.

I know I promised you the ring and, yes, I left it in the storage unit in the coffee tin like I promised. Please use it for good. I know your mom wanted you to have it as the oldest girl. I am respecting her wishes on one condition. If the day comes when Scarlet decides she wants to explore her gift, it would only be fair that she have the opportunity to wear the ring. As you know, it carries the power of all the visionaries in the family before me. It promotes vision clarity, which will be so important with her when dealing with the innate dangers of fire.

May you find happiness in your life, Brandy, and know that I've always loved you.

Nan xo

"Oh my God!"

I dropped the notepaper into my lap and I sat back dumfounded. My palm went to my forehead in shock.

I thought about the simple ruby ring and how Nan never took it off until it became too loose after she became ill. When I asked about it, she told me she put it somewhere safe. Now to find out it offered some kind of power to the user and, of course, Brandy knew and left that out! I closed my eyes and allowed a wave of disappointment to flood through me. Once again, it felt like Brandy was trying to pull one over on me.

Well, Nan pointed out that it would be only fair that I

be able to wear the ring when I wanted to use my powers. Well, guess what? That time was now.

I took a picture of the letter and sent it to Brandy along with a text that said: I found this letter for you from Nan. I hope you'll honor her wishes and give me the ring.

She replied: How long have you had that letter? Why didn't you give it to me?

I replied: I just found it now. It was in Nan's stuff that I hadn't gone through since her death. You can have the original when you bring me the ring.

Minutes ticked by but she didn't reply. I poured myself a second glass of wine and finished it before sending another text: Nan wanted me to have a chance to wear it so please give it to me.

Brandy replied: I'm the one making a living using our talents. I need the ring.

I messaged: I need it too! I need to work on my fire-seeing and it sounds like it would be a big help.

Brandy texted back: When you grow up and realize you need me, I'll come help you try to find Murray's murderer.

"Argh!"

I looked up at the ceiling and screamed. Muffin glanced up at me with curiosity before returning to hunt dust bunnies under the sofa. Fury ate at my gut. It was frustrating to know that my sister held something that could help my psychic gift but she wouldn't share it with me. Once again she was proving to be her usual selfish self! True, the ring helped her be accurate in her business, but she was only thinking about herself.

The darkness of the evening settled over the cottage, and a warm buzz from the wine caused me to feel emotional. I shed a few tears over all that had happened in the last couple years and had myself a pity party with Muffin nearby. As grateful as I was to have a place to stay while Bubbles was being fixed, it was going to feel good to sleep in my own bed again.

"What do you think, Muffin, should I make one more fire and see if anything pops up?" I took a tissue from my pocket and scrubbed my eyes dry.

The cat's reply was to climb up the door screen and then leap off.

I took Muffin outside on her harness, leaving through the back door. While she leaped and pounced I gathered some dried twigs. My movements were dulled by alcohol and emotion, but the crisp air helped clear my head. We ventured a little farther into the tree line that was closer to the road and then I saw him. Parked on the shoulder was the same pickup truck that had pulled into the driveway. The driver was only a dark shape but they were clearly turned toward the cottage watching for me. Thankfully, this time I'd kept my blinds and drapes closed and the cottage looked dark. I debated calling the cops but abruptly the truck pulled onto the road and drove away.

"This safe house is no longer safe," I told Muffin.

Once back inside, the kitty curled up in the corner of the sofa and snored softly while I built a fire and drank another glass of wine.

This fire was made to burn quickly. No heaping stack of logs and kindling, just enough of each to have a few minutes of flame, which was just as well because I was feeling the wine and needed to get to bed.

As the smoldering smoke turned to liquid bands of orange licking its way up the chimney, I knew that my attempt to gather information on Murray probably wouldn't reveal much more than what I'd already seen.

True enough, I took each of his items in turn and held them while gazing into the fire and all that came to me were vignettes about his warped propensity for sexually harassing women. Finally, I received the same vision in Murray's point of view as he turned his head in slow motion in the direction of a sound made by his killer but then the vision went to black.

"Damn."

I sighed and it turned into a drunken yawn that caused me to think warmly of bed but then I remembered Noah's coffee cup still inside my backpack. I took the paper cup out of the bag and ran a fingertip along the rim where his lips would've touched as he drank. Then I gazed dreamily into the fire while I clutched the cup to my chest.

Short confusing videos began playing in my head. A lot of driving and walking in his point of view. Sometimes his breath was heavy with either anger or anxiety and I could feel a sense of fear in my own pounding heart. Abruptly, the vision slipped into another vignette. Still in Noah's point of view, a door was opened. Then I was looking at Melody's face and walking into her home. Cats everywhere with the new white cat, Arthur, in view. Melody seemed happy to see Noah and then, suddenly, her arms were around his neck and I could feel the sexual arousal as they stumbled from living room to bedroom.

A loud gasp escaped my mouth as my eyes flung open and I tossed Noah's coffee cup into the fire.

THIRTEEN

THE NEXT MORNING I felt ill from a wine hangover and the vision I'd seen between Noah and Melody. The intimate moment between Noah and Melody may have happened a while ago. Or maybe not at all. It felt real, but I didn't get the same assured feeling I did with the vision of Brandy having a needle in her arm.

Melody told me someone left her roses and that she and Noah had shared "moments." At the time I blew it off, and Noah certainly seemed surprised by the rose thing...but what if I was wrong?

If the vision of the two of them was real, it was also recent. The doughnut-thieving cat, Arthur, was a very new addition. If the vision was to be believed, Noah and Melody had been together romantically not long ago. Maybe even since Noah and I had tumbled into the sack. The thought made me want to throw up.

I shook off the ugly sensation as I made my way into the shower. Afterward I made some toast and coffee, then gathered up my groceries as well as a few of the nonperishables in the cupboard.

"I'm just borrowing these," I told Muffin as I bagged up rice, pasta and soup, as well as a few other things. "I'll pay Brandy back once she brings the ring to me."

Muffin meowed at my feet, but it was only a demand for breakfast.

I fed the cat and then sat on the front porch with her waiting for Noah.

"He's a grown-ass man," I told Muffin. "And it's not like we're in a relationship. What he does and who he sees is none of my business, right?"

Muffin meowed in agreement.

Just before eight I heard Noah's truck coming up the driveway. I'd cleaned out the litterbox and Muffin's dishes and placed them with the rest of my things at the door. Now I gathered up the squirmy kitten and placed her in her kennel together with a toy mouse.

My arms were full as I approached the truck.

"I have quite a bit of stuff," I told him as I loaded the cat carrier into the back seat.

"I'll help." He got out and assisted me with gathering belongings from the front porch and stuffing them into the back seat.

"Thanks," I told him as I buckled up in the passenger seat. "For driving me," I added.

"No problem." He offered me a bright smile, which I didn't return. I gave him the address for the garage where Bubbles was located and then turned my head to look out the side window.

Noah attempted small talk but my answers were short and monotone until we were getting close to our destination.

"So," I began, trying to sound casual. "How have things been around town lately? How is everyone? Have you seen Penny? Tess?" I looked pointedly at him. "Melody?"

"Fine." He nodded. "Everyone's good. Concerned about you, of course, and worried that Murray's killer and whoever shot at you hasn't been caught. Everyone is on edge."

"Yeah." I cleared my throat as he turned into the driveway of the garage. "And you? How have you been?"

"Worried." He parked, turned off the ignition and turned to me with warm eyes crinkled in a frown. "Really upset about what's happened to you and wishing there was something I could do."

"Can I ask you something?"

"Of course." He put a hand on my knee and I just stared at it.

"What do you think of Melody?"

He shrugged. "She's nice. Too many cats."

Nice.

"Have you and she ever…"

He chuckled loudly and then unbuckled his seat belt and leaned over to put his hand on my cheek. "I like you, Red. Really like you. Once all of this is behind us, I'm hoping you won't take off in your van and leave me in the dust."

Tears pricked my eyes at his sincerity, but I was aware that he didn't exactly deny he and Melody had slept together either.

After I got the keys to Bubbles from the garage, I drove it from the back lot and parked it alongside Noah's pickup to make it easier to transfer my things. He had to go and open his store but he hesitated outside the van even after all my stuff was inside Bubbles.

"Where will you be parking?" He shifted uneasily from one foot to another. "I know you probably don't want to go back to Farmer Miller's field."

"Definitely not," I agreed with a nervous laugh. "I'll find somewhere."

He nodded and then pulled me into a quick hug. "If you need a place, my house is available." His words were hot against my neck and then he pulled away and lifted my chin to look me in the eyes. "I'm serious. And if you'd rather sleep in your van, my driveway is also available."

"Thanks for the offer but I'll figure something out." I shrugged and then gave him a quick kiss. "Thanks so much for the ride and for...for being my friend."

"Okay." He nodded and gave me a brief kiss, whispering in my ear, "I don't want to be just friends, Red."

Then he climbed in his truck and drove off.

After he was gone, I climbed into Bubbles and breathed in the scent of her.

"I missed you," I said to the van in general and then I walked over to the picture of Nan on the wall and touched it with my fingers. "Love you, but I'm a little pissed too. I have so many questions and you aren't here to answer them."

All my things needed to be properly stowed before I could head out on the road, so I went to work. The few perishable items went into the new fridge, which was already cold.

"I'm still pissed at you, Brandy," I grumped. "But taking care of Bubbles was a great gift."

I was still super angry with my sister but I owed her at least a thank-you text: I've got Bubbles & I'm out of the cottage. Thanks for taking care of repairs and the fridge. I'll stay safe. Hope you do too.

She replied with: Let me know when you need my help.

Not *if*, but *when*. That irked me.

Being new, Bubbles's windows were almost impossibly clean and clear. A startling reminder that if it hadn't been for a naughty kitten trying to escape under the van, I would be in a grave right now.

As if on cue, Muffin let out an angry hiss along with a paw poking through the bars of her crate.

"Sorry, but you're going to have to stay put until I find somewhere safe for us to hang."

I did a quick search for where to boondock. Turned out there was a casino between here and Hope Harbor located on Lummi Nation land that allowed free parking for recreational vehicles.

Although I usually preferred to camp somewhere more private, being in a busy casino parking lot had a lot of advantages. Security cameras were definitely one of those benefits when you were worried you could be a target for a gun-toting serial killer. Also, I could use the casino's free Wi-Fi.

Once I was parked on the lot I went through social media for everyone I could think of in town to see if there were any clues. There was another anonymous direct message that was all threatening emojis: a skull and crossbones, knife and gun.

Again, I took a screenshot and sent it to Cobb. I followed it with a text: Do something about this!

While I scrolled through social media I also looked for evidence if Melody or Noah had ever posted any pictures of the two of them that might suggest they actually were or had been a couple. Melody's social media was all cats. Big surprise. Noah's was practically nonexistent except for a few posts when the hardware store was having sales. Tess's privacy settings made it difficult to see anything. Penny mostly reposted about causes she believed in with the occasional badly lit selfie.

There was one picture of Penny and Tess together that caused me to pause. They were standing shoulder to shoulder behind the counter at Pincher's. I was under the impression that Tess had arrived not long before Murray's killing due to her separation and had stayed to offer comfort and support after Murray's death. Although the picture was posted by Penny in the last couple of days, I knew that it was taken before Murray was killed.

I clicked the photo to enlarge it and took a closer look. On the shelf behind the counter was a parcel with a fluorescent sticky note with my name on it. I'd ordered an item online for the van and Penny had told me I could use the store address for mail. When the parcel arrived, she stuck it behind the counter on that shelf. It came in on a Friday and I'd forgotten to take it with me at the end of my shift and the following day was my day off. That meant that Saturday was most likely the day Penny and Tess had taken the selfie that she recently posted. That was a full nine days before Murray was killed.

"Big deal," I mumbled to myself.

But it felt like I was missing something.

I was getting nowhere with my research and then I remembered Tanya Smith, the dental hygienist who'd been caught doing the tongue tango with Murray. The phone number for the office where she worked was in my old phone and I couldn't remember the name of it, so I sent a text off to Melody and she replied with the number and with a follow-up text: Let's do a coffee date!

I replied, Hope we can do that soon!

But I didn't hope that at all. What I really wanted

was Murray's killer locked up and me on the road to a campsite in a forest somewhere.

When I called the dentist office, I was told Tanya was busy with a patient. I left my name and number and hoped she'd call me back. Surprisingly, my phone rang a few minutes later.

"My name is Scarlet, people call me Red and—"

"I know who you are. You live in a bubble van and everyone thinks you killed Murray." Tanya had a nasally voice. "Nobody in Hope Harbor can keep a secret worth shit." She laughed. "I'm actually surprised I didn't hear from you days ago."

"I tried but you were on vacation," I admitted. "Did you go somewhere fun?"

Or did you take a few days off to recover from killing Murray?

"My bestie got married and I was in the wedding party. Look, I've gotta get to my next patient. If you wanna talk, I get off at five. There's a burger joint across from me and I can meet you there."

I agreed and she told me the name and address of the restaurant where we'd be meeting.

When Tanya walked into the burger place, I was sipping a soda in a back booth. Since I'd looked her up online and she was wearing scrubs I had no problem picking her out and gave a wave. She pointed to the counter and headed to order her food. When she arrived at the booth, she sat down with a sigh.

"Hi. How ya doing?" she asked, pulling a compact mirror from her purse and powdering her nose. She had thick black eyeliner and a mass of pitch-black hair with light roots just beginning to show.

"I've been better. Been shot at, had to go into hiding so can't work." I shrugged. "At least it hasn't been boring."

"That town is a crap magnet." Tanya shook a finger in my face and then ate a couple fries. "If I was you, I'd blow that place. Like I did." She spoke around a mouthful of burger. "You think I wanna look inside people's mouths all day?" She shook her head and swallowed. "Nope, but guess what? It's better than working in Mom and Dad's greasy spoon diner or spending one more second in that shithole town."

"So-o-o…" I put my soda down. "Talk to me about Murray."

She held up a finger while she took another huge bite of her hamburger, chewed and swallowed. "Murray was a complete waste of skin." Then she crossed herself. "God bless his soul."

"I heard you and he had, um, issues…" I didn't know how else to word it.

"Ha!" She rolled her eyes. "I orchestrated that whole thing." At my confused look, she continued, "Mom and Dad wanted me to finish high school and stay in that godforsaken town my entire life running the diner with them." She shook her head violently. "There was no way I was up for that, but they wouldn't listen. At least not until I got caught sucking face with Murray. He was over at the diner doing some repair work in the back and I convinced him to go in the freezer with me at the exact time I knew my dad would be coming in to get the frozen food he'd need for the dinner rush. Murray knew my plan and he was all in."

"Why would Murray go for it if he knew it would just make him look bad?"

"Well, I told him I was playing a prank on my dad,

and you know Murray." She smiled slyly. "He had that sick kind of humor, thinking every ass and boob grab was all in good fun. Anyway, after that happened, Dad held a meeting with a bunch of people in town and they were going to take matters into their own hands and just run Murray out of town, but Penny begged to have him stay. She said he was helping her out with money. I said I wanted to go to finish school out of town because I was so traumatized." She smirked. "I finished high school in Bellingham and got a scholarship to become a dental hygienist. Rest is history."

My eyes grew huge. "Did Murray know you set him up?"

"He told everyone we pulled a prank on my dad and he was right, but of course because of his history nobody believed him." She shrugged. "But he deserved it. Especially after what he did to Jane."

"Jane?" I frowned. "Noah's dead wife?"

"Yeah, didn't you hear? When Jane was first sick, her boyfriend moved out and she was living on her own. She called up Murray to fix something in her apartment. He tried crawling in bed with her while she was literally sick in bed with cancer."

"Oh my God!"

"Well, that's what the rumor was anyway." She looked suddenly doubtful. "Some people say Jane only said that because immediately Noah asked her to move back home so he could take care of her."

"Oh." That was messed up. "Do you think she made it up?"

"Anything's possible. Jane was known for stretching the truth, and Murray had a reputation for putting his hands where they don't belong."

"And Jane wanted Noah back?"

"Oh definitely. He told her to move out when he found out she was playing hide the salami with a car salesman in Burlington, but I think she never wanted the marriage to end. I'm sure if she knew cancer was in her future she would never have screwed around on Noah." Tanya stuffed more fries into her mouth and tucked a strand of hair behind her ear. "But Noah being Noah, of course when he heard what happened he took her in and cared for her. But everyone knew there was no romance there. He was done with her once he found out about the cheating. One of my mom's friends cared for Jane at Noah's house whenever he had to work and she said by the time Jane moved back, she was too sick to rekindle anything anyway, but even if she wasn't, he had her set up in the spare bedroom."

"Okay." I let that sink in before I asked, "What about Melody?"

"Kooky cat girl?" Tanya snorted. "What about her?"

"Why do you call her kooky? Besides the fact that she has far too many cats."

"Have you met her? She can flip her mood on a dime. One minute you're in her good books and the next she's gone all batshit crazy on your ass."

I thought about her screaming at her elderly father. "You've seen it?"

"Oh yeah. Everyone in town knows she's got a quick trigger and most of us have been on the receiving end." She laughed. "One time I walked into the grocery store to pick up a couple things and she overcharged me for something. She was all sweetness and light until I pointed out her error. Her face turned purple and the veins in her neck stood out as she screamed her fool head off. But I stood my ground and her manager threatened to fire her unless she got her shit together." She smiled. "One day that volcano is really gonna blow."

"Do you think *she* could've killed Murray?"

"Nah." Tanya pushed her tray away, got out the compact from her purse and checked her teeth in the mirror. "I mean, she'd have no motive, right? And I doubt she'd even own a gun. Could she lose her mind and scream in his face? Absolutely. But sneak up on him in a storeroom and shoot him in the back of the head? I can't see it."

"Okay. How about Melody and Noah. Are they a thing?"

Tanya tossed her compact back in her purse and eyed me curiously. "I thought *you* and Noah were a thing?"

"Who told you that?"

"Hon, your business is everyone's business in Dope Harbor."

"But Melody and Noah…"

"I think Mel has always had a thing for Noah. Did he ever give in? Who knows?" She shrugged. "I mean, men can be weak, and knowing someone has the hots for you can be a powerful aphrodisiac. Add to that the fact that Noah is never leaving that town, I guess anything is possible."

My throat tightened at that prospect, and then she added, "But I'm not around there much anymore so I'm out of the loop. Gossip gets to me late these days."

"So where was the wedding?" I asked, sipping the last of my soda.

"The what?" She frowned and blinked at me.

"You mentioned that when you were off work you were at your best friend's wedding."

"Oh that." She waved it away with a flick of her hand and I got the immediate feeling she might be lying about the wedding as she fiddled with the empty food containers on her tray.

"Wedding was in Ferndale. A fun time," she added distractedly as she got up from the booth and pointed to the ladies' room.

Ferndale was only about ten miles from Hope Harbor. Easily doable to kill a man the morning after. It wouldn't even have made her late to work.

As soon as she was out of sight, I reached across the booth to her open purse sitting on the bench. I snagged her compact and swiftly tucked it into my own bag. Maybe Tanya was lying about Murray being in on the prank. If he really did assault her, she had a great motive to get some revenge. I had a feeling that Tanya wasn't being completely honest and maybe a little fire and her makeup would tell me why.

Once Tanya was back she told me she needed to get going but offered me her cell number in case I had any more questions. We paused to throw our stuff in the trash and as we made our way out the door together I asked a few more questions.

"How well do you know Tess?"

"Penny's daughter?" She pressed the fob on her keychain as we walked toward her car. "As well as anyone, I suppose. She babysat me growing up."

"She seems a little…"

"Uptight?" Tanya finished, opening her car door.

"Yes," I agreed.

"You gotta respect someone like that in Hope Harbor. When everyone is busy putting on a fake smile and pretending everything is perfect when it's not, it's a relief to have someone who calls people out on their bullshit."

"Do you think she'd have any reason to kill Murray?"

"Well, she hated Murray more than most. Didn't like how he treated her mom and probably would've stepped on the accelerator if she saw him lying in the street." She climbed into her car and looked up at me. "But do I think she shot him in her mom's storeroom? Nah."

"If you had to guess, who would you think had the most reason to kill him?"

"The person with the biggest reason would be Penny, of course, but I don't think she has it in her. She doesn't have a mean bone in her whole body, does she?"

I startled at the idea of Penny having a reason to kill him, but agreed the sweet old lady I knew couldn't possibly be a murderer.

"By the way, did the marshal or sheriff come and ask you questions about Murray?"

"Nope."

Considering her history with Murray, you'd think Cobb would've at least called Tanya for an interview or asked her where she was that morning. She was about to close her door and I put a hand on the door to stop it. "One more thing, I like your hair. Do you do it yourself or get it done somewhere local?"

"Oh, the color?" She put a hand to her Goth-black head. "I do it myself. Just did it a few days ago. Being a blonde gets a little old, you know?"

I watched her drive away and let her comments settle over me. Two things I knew when Tanya pulled away. That girl had had blond and possibly wavy hair at the time Murray was shot. So the blond hair I originally saw may not have just been about the wig and the gun.

The second thing I knew was that it was time to return to Hope Harbor.

When I pulled onto Main Street, every person I passed stopped in their tracks and stared at Bubbles with wonder and outright curiosity. Some let their mouths drop open. I guessed that nobody expected I'd be stupid enough to return after someone tried to take me out. Or else they believed that I'd shot up the van myself as some kind of ploy to make it seem like I was the victim and now they thought I had some nerve returning. But I was sick of hiding and even more tired of taking a back seat to the turtle speed of detective work in this town.

I drove right up to Pincher's and went inside.

Penny was behind the counter, looking a tad frantic at the line of customers. "Red!" She placed a hand over her heart. "Come here…" She waved me over. "You're a lifesaver."

"What's going on?" I made my way behind the counter.

"Tess thought it would be brilliant to have a big sale to clear out some of the old stock."

"Oh." I began to ring up orders at double the pace that Penny had managed on her own. She bagged items next to me. "Where is Tess?" I finished one order and moved on to the next person.

"We had a big fight," Penny muttered under her breath. "And then she just abandoned me."

It took less than ten minutes until the line of customers was dealt with and we were left with only a few people wandering the aisles.

"I was actually going to call you and see if you could come in today and then you showed up to rescue me." Penny smiled.

Probably not the best time to tell her I was just here hoping she'd cut me a final paycheck. She could obviously use the help. "I wanted to see how you were doing. Do you want to talk about your fight with Tess?"

Penny frowned and rubbed the back of her neck. "She thinks the store is too much and I should consider selling it."

"But you love Pincher's," I protested.

"Yes, but it's not exactly making as much money as it used to." She blew out a breath and admitted, "That damn Murray…stuck it to me even after he was gone." She laughed without humor. "I've made some bad investments over the years and, well, it's taken a drain on my finances."

"Was Murray responsible for some of those bad investments?"

"All of them in fact." She took out a rag and began to dust the counter. "To add insult to injury we took out life insurance policies when we were together, and he let his policy lapse. It wasn't a big amount, but it would've taken care of some of my debts at least. Tess was super ticked off about that."

"I'm sorry to hear that. I guess you were counting on that money?"

"I didn't know he was going to die so, no, I wasn't counting on it. But when he invested my retirement money in stocks, he told Tess that my money was safe because he had savings in his life insurance policy. He assured her that if the investment went sideways, he'd pay me back using those savings. That put her mind at ease. I didn't even know she'd talked to him about it, but she's always looking out for me." She smiled and patted my arm. "Just like you."

I looked into Penny's gentle eyes and smiled at her. "I'm happy to help."

A woman with a basket of items approached the counter and while I rang up her purchases, Penny disappeared into the storeroom and didn't return. When it was time to close up, I went to the back to see if she was still around or if she'd simply left out the back door without saying goodbye.

I found Penny sitting at her desk with her back to me, engrossed in some paperwork. After all Tess's work to organize the area, Penny had quickly placed it in disarray with papers scattered and family pictures once again spread out along the back of the desk.

There was a framed picture of Murray sitting on a riverbank fishing as he looked over at the photographer with a mischievous smile. I'd seen the picture there before but only now did I realize its significance. Murray was younger in this picture. Certainly much younger than he would've been when Penny and Murray supposedly met at Tess's wedding. Tess would've been a baby when this was taken, if she was alive at all.

The next thing that caught my eye was a framed photo collage. It was one of those frames that held school pictures from kindergarten through graduation and, of course, the girl in the pictures was Tess. It was the picture in the first-grade spot that caused me to catch my breath.

At my gasp, Penny startled and turned to look up at me.

"I've closed up," I told her and then I approached and placed a hand on her shoulder. "Can I ask you a personal question?" I didn't wait for Penny to reply. I blurted out the question that sprang to my lips even though I was pretty sure I already knew the answer.

"Penny, who was Tess's father?"

FOURTEEN

PENNY TURNED AWAY from me with a flustered back-handed wave. "Red, you know I'm a widow. I told you about Ted dying and—"

"Yes, I know you were married to someone named Ted. Was he Tess's biological father?" I walked over to the desk and picked up the picture of Murray. "Because this picture of Murray must have been taken when he was in his late thirties or early forties, and Tess said that you two met at her wedding." I put the picture back on the desk and placed a gentle hand on Penny's arm. "You told me Tess was married for ten years and that you two met at her wedding. How do you have a picture of Murray twenty years earlier than that?"

"He gave it to me." Penny hastily got to her feet and looked at me with annoyance. "When we were dating, he gave me that picture of himself because he liked how he looked at that time." She smiled at the picture. "He looks handsome, don't you think?"

I didn't think so but, obviously, Penny found him attractive.

"I'm going home." She got hastily to her feet. "Thanks for your help today. I think it would be best if you took a few days off until this murder thing is resolved."

With that she walked out the back door, leaving it bouncing against the frame instead of locking it behind her. A gust of wind slammed it open and when I walked over to close it, I saw Penny climb into Murray's pickup.

As she drove around the corner, my thoughts raced. I used my phone to take a picture of all the photos on Penny's desk and then I locked up the store and returned to my van.

I called up Sheriff Duthroyd and asked him if he knew whether Murray knew Penny much earlier than she claimed. I suggested he might even be Tess's father.

"Look, Scarlet," the sheriff began with a sigh. "I appreciate the information, as insignificant as it could be. Sometimes even the smallest detail can help with a case. I know you're just trying to be helpful. However, I'm up to my eyeballs in a different case and that's why I have Marshal Cobb running your investigation. I assure you he has been busy gathering information on this case and reporting back to me daily. Perhaps you'd best pass on this information to him, okay?"

"I've been shot at and received online threats and, honestly, I get the impression that all of this is over the marshal's head."

"I'll follow up with him," the sheriff promised. "In the meantime, pass this latest information along, okay?"

I thought about calling Cobb's number and then decided against it. This was silly. I sure didn't believe Penny was guilty of anything. Lots of people have skeletons in their closet but that doesn't make them murderers. My own family was a prime example. I rested my head on the steering wheel and muttered some curse words when suddenly there was a rap on my window.

I let out a squeak of surprise and was glad to see it was Noah. I rolled down my window.

"What are you doing here? You okay?"

"I'm good. I'm just…" Tears sprang to my eyes and my throat tightened. "It's been a day and a half."

"You know what you need? A home-cooked meal by the best chef in town."

"Are you claiming to be the best chef?" I sniffed and offered him a small smile.

"The absolute best you're going to find standing on this side of the street and offering you a free meal."

I hesitated only a second before replying with a laugh, "That sounds absolutely perfect."

"Great! See you there."

I stopped by the grocery store to pick up a bottle of wine. To anyone who blatantly stared my way I offered a bright smile and a hello. If they didn't like me around, too bad.

"Just between you, me and the bread aisle…" Melody leaned in and whispered as she rang me up. "I heard the marshal is following up a hot lead."

"Is that so?" I closed my eyes and sighed with relief. "That would be so great."

"Yes." Melody nodded her curly blond head. "Unless, of course, it's someone you're close to. Then you might have mixed feelings about it."

"Someone *I'm* close to, or someone *you're* close to?"

Melody pursed her lips and made a locking motion with her fingers.

"Oh come on." I dragged my fingers through my hair in frustration. "Don't leave me hanging."

"I'm really not at liberty to say."

Another customer came up behind me and I stepped aside while Melody took care of his order and once he was gone, I came up to her again.

"Melody, if you know who the suspect is, please let

me know," I pleaded. "I'm the one who's been shot at. It would be nice to know who to avoid."

The door to the store opened at that moment and in walked Marshal Cobb.

"Did you get my earlier message?"

"Yes. Thank you for your information and I'll be looking into that. Along with a lot of other things."

He may have been speaking to me but his eyes were on Melody and he gave her a nod and smile as he chose a candy bar and then approached her counter. Melody actually giggled in reply.

I looked from one to the other and the sexy tension in the air was stifling. Melody was blushing as she twirled a lock of hair around a finger, and the marshal made some kind of remark about the chocolate not being nearly as sweet as her.

Well, well, well. I just might throw up right here.

I arrived at Noah's with Muffin on leash in one hand and the wine in the other. He greeted me with an arm around the shoulders, leading me into the kitchen. The home was older but well-crafted with high ceilings and exposed beams. The kitchen was massive and had obviously been recently upgraded.

"Your home is beautiful." I ran a hand along the granite countertop.

"Thanks. I did a lot of the work myself so I'm glad you like it." He clapped his hands. "Now, I can barbecue us some steaks or do pasta. Lady's choice."

"Steak, please." I put the wine on the counter and released Muffin from her leash. "What can I do to help?"

"You can do this…" He handed me two wineglasses and pointed to a counter stool. "And you can sit there."

"I can handle that."

Noah seasoned the steaks and threw together a salad. I tried to think back to a time when a man cooked for me and was coming up blank, unless you counted the time Jimmie shared his sandwich with me in third grade. This was a very nice feeling.

Noah went out onto the deck to put the steaks on the grill and set an egg timer on the counter before joining me. I told him about seeing Melody and Joel Cobb at the store and how there seemed to be something romantic happening between them.

"That would be great," Noah said, taking a drink from his wineglass. "I know Joel has had a thing for Melody forever. Sounds like he finally won her over."

"I hope the bloom of love doesn't distract him from finding Murray's killer."

"I'm sure the sheriff has his hand in the investigation too."

When I didn't reply he asked me what I was thinking about. I told him about my concerns around Penny having the picture of a younger Murray and driving away in his pickup truck.

"I can't see darling old Penny having anything to do with Murray's murder."

"But why would she drive his truck though?"

"I've seen her drive it before. Getting larger items from the post office or getting stuff from my store."

Huh. I guess that was easily explained. I took a sip of my wine. "Did you know Tess's father?"

"Everyone knows everyone around here. Of course I knew Ted. Went to his funeral along with the rest of the town. He was a good, decent man."

"So you don't think Murray could've been Tess's father?"

"Huh." He tilted his head at the question and seemed to give it serious consideration and then just shrugged. "Does it really matter?" The timer went off to flip the steaks so he added, "Hold that thought."

He went out on the deck for a few minutes and when he returned, he placed the meat on the counter with a grand, theatrical "Ta-da!" that made me laugh.

I waited until we finished dinner before I returned to the topic of Murray being Tess's father.

"All I know is what the rest of the town knows, and that's that Penny was born and raised in Hope Harbor. She moved to Seattle for a time, which is where she met and married Ted. They returned to Hope Harbor with Tess in tow as an infant, and Penny bought the old five-and-dime and called it Pincher's Dollarama. When Ted passed away, I was just a kid and so was Tess. Was it possible Penny married Ted while pregnant with another man's child? Sure. It wouldn't be the first time that happened, right?"

We cleared the table and loaded the dirty dishes into the dishwasher.

"You can understand why that might make her a suspect, right? Or even Tess?"

"It's a bit of a stretch to say it was worth killing him over," Noah argued. "I mean, he'd obviously kept the secret and Tess is a grown woman now. I doubt either of their reputations would be hurt much by that kind of revelation."

Maybe he was right. I frowned into my wineglass and put it down before drinking any more. "Tell me about Jane," I said, gently changing the topic. "I heard the reason why you despised Murray so much was that he tried to climb in bed with her when she was sick."

"Well…" He blew out a long breath and dragged his hands through his hair. "Jane later admitted to me that she exaggerated Murray's attention because she was trying to get a response out of me." He smirked. "And it worked."

"Oh. That's…um…" I didn't know what to say.

"Not to speak ill of the dead but Jane had a way of manipulating people and getting what she wanted. Unfortunately, that didn't work when it came to cancer."

I nodded. "Even though you weren't a couple, it must've been really hard on you to watch her die."

"It was and you're right that I really hated Murray. It wasn't because of the Jane situation, it was because he seemed to be making his way through the entire town, groping one woman at a time, and the only thing Marshal Cobb would do was tell him to knock it off." He folded his hands on the counter in front of him. "So I took matters into my own hands."

I grew very still, half expecting a murder confession, but then Noah added, "I told him if he didn't stop grabbing the women of Hope Harbor I was going to personally run him out of town."

"When was that?"

"Couple weeks ago." Noah shrugged. "Walked into the market and saw he'd cornered Melody in the back of the shop, and I grabbed him by the neck and dragged his ass out of there." He held up his hands then and quickly said, "I didn't kill him."

"Funny thing that Melody told me Murray never laid a hand on her."

"Probably because I got there beforehand."

"I'll never understand how Murray was allowed to

pester and assault the women of this town and not be held accountable by the law." I shook my head. "And—"

Just then Noah's phone rang and he apologized before answering. The look on his face as he listened to the caller was shock and he was on his feet before he even disconnected.

"Pincher's is on fire." Noah took me by the arm and led me toward the door.

"What? How?" I snagged Muffin and we hurried outside without his answer. "I'll see you there." I unlocked Bubbles and climbed inside.

My heart pounded and mind raced as I drove into town.

Pincher's was fully engulfed. The wooden structure was licked with red-and-orange flames reaching skyward. Abruptly, the large front window shattered, and sparks shot onto the street where dozens of onlookers gasped. I'd taken a parking spot directly across the street next to Noah's truck. He was standing in the middle of the road trying to keep people back.

At one point Noah stood with one arm around Penny's shoulder and the other around Melody's. The three of them stood close together with their stiff backs to me. I was definitely the outsider in this equation, and I was eternally grateful I had Noah as my alibi if the fire turned out to be arson. Where the hell was the fire department? Where was the marshal?

Finally, two ladder trucks arrived on scene. The firefighters valiantly raced to hook up their hoses to the hydrant, but anyone could see it was going to be too little too late.

I'd never seen a fire this massive in person. I couldn't look away, and the blaze coaxed me in and hypnotized me. Distant wind chimes sounded a familiar melody, and the smoldering odor engulfed my sinuses from deep within. I was aware of Muffin mewing from inside her crate and then I was aware of nothing at all except the swirl of ghosted figures in my head.

Faces showed in my vision on a speedy slideshow: Murray, Penny, Tess, Melody, the marshal and Noah. The same faces over and over picking up speed with their images twisted together and ending with Murray's dead body and the gun in the wig box. Suddenly the vision shifted to Brandy sitting in her Corvette. She sat in her car, the dancing cupcake neon light throbbing in the background but there was no needle in her arm and she appeared to be fine. Unexpectedly she turned in her seat and looked directly into my soul.

"Get out of there, Scarlet. You're in danger." Her voice was a distant whisper that sounded like it was being carried off on a breeze, but her hands reached up and she clapped them in my face. "You have to leave now!" The last part of her warning felt like a slap in the face. It was as real as if she was sitting next to me.

Without any explanation to Noah or any other towns-folk, I turned the key in my ignition and pulled slowly away from the scene. The pain in my head from the trance-induced headache caused my hands to shake. I drove Bubbles at a leisurely creep out of the center of town and once I hit the outskirts, I put the pedal to the metal and rocketed out of the area.

When I reached I-5, I drove south toward Seattle and my phone pinged to notify me that I had a voicemail message from Brandy on my phone. It must've come in when I was with Noah since there was no cell range at his home. As I picked up speed on the highway I played the message and Brandy's voice filled the van:

"Scarlet, I had a clear vision that you are in danger. I don't know how or who, but you need to get out of that town right now!"

Her message was clear, but her syllables ran together quickly in either panic or a drug-induced fury.

"You sound stoned as hell." But her message, no matter how jumbled, reinforced what I'd seen in my vision.

I called Brandy's number repeatedly on the two-hour drive into the city and it just kept going to voicemail.

The closer I got, the more frantic I became. When I pulled up to the street where Brandy lived, it was torrentially raining and dark. I spied the Corvette sitting under a streetlight and pulled up behind it. From the back, the sports car appeared empty, the sheets of rain sloshing off the gleaming yellow paint in torrents. Glancing up, I could see lights on inside an apartment that I assumed was hers.

Hopping out of the van was like walking into a waterfall. I held my hand over my eyes to shield my vision from the shower. I decided to take a loop around Brandy's car before heading up to her apartment. As I approached the driver's side I saw her. Brandy was slumped sideways onto the passenger seat and appeared unconscious.

I shouted and tried the door but it was locked. As I ran back to Bubbles, I called 9-1-1 and stayed on the line with the operator as I took a hammer from my utility drawer and ran up to the passenger side of the Corvette and smashed the window open. Bits of glass fell onto Brandy and her car alarm sounded, but still she didn't move. I reached to unlock the door and then I grabbed

Brandy under her arms and pulled her half onto the passenger seat. She wasn't breathing. As I moved her a syringe that dangled from the crook of her arm tumbled onto the floor mat. With my phone on speaker I told the 9-1-1 operator I was going to start CPR. Brandy was completely limp and impossibly pale as I pumped her chest.

"Come on," I begged. After thirty compressions on her chest, I pinched her nose and breathed into her lungs. Without a response to my breaths, I continued with chest compressions. I pleaded and screamed through tears, "Fight, Brandy! Don't give up!"

It felt like forever before paramedics arrived, but it was probably only a few minutes.

I was tugged aside and the professionals took over.

"Narcan!" I shouted as I watched them check for vitals. On a cry I added, "I think she's overdosed."

She was pulled onto a stretcher and loaded onto the ambulance.

"Where will you take her?"

They shouted the name of the hospital. I took the Corvette keys from the ignition, grabbed Brandy's purse from the floor of her car, then I ran to Bubbles.

I was completely drenched, and the rain that ran off my hair mixed with tears as I followed the ambulance that carried Brandy's lifeless body.

FIFTEEN

BRANDY WAS CREMATED on a Saturday morning. The day was sunny and looked full of false promises.

When I carried her box of ashes into Bubbles, I buckled them into the passenger seat.

"Yeah, I know camper van life is beneath you," I told her as I pulled away from the curb. "But until I find a place to scatter your ashes, you're stuck with it."

A call came in from Sheriff Duthroyd, which I ignored along with the countless calls and messages from everyone in Hope Harbor that I'd received over the last number of days. Even Noah.

Life had been a blur of grief and activity. After the hospital gave me the horrible news, I'd gone through Brandy's phone contacts and reached her boyfriend, Nick. Turned out Brandy had broken up with him a few days before her passing. He sounded shocked to hear she'd overdosed.

"She was doing so well," he said over the phone as he choked back tears. "We split because she wanted only to focus on business for a while, and I've been wanting her to settle down with me and consider having a family. It was amicable. I—I—" He struggled to compose himself. "I loved her."

I found a will in a lockbox in her apartment and Brandy left everything, except Nan's ring, to Nick. He insisted that she probably would've changed that given their breakup, but there was nothing I wanted. Nan's ring was now stashed inside my purse, waiting for me to get up the nerve to slip it on a finger. The regret of our fight weighed heavy on my heart and the ring felt like a blistering reminder. Adding to my misery was that her last phone call had been to me. Her last words may have been to save my life when she should've been trying to save herself.

The shame and guilt were chains around my already heavy heart.

She'd taken a few calls from another number I didn't recognize on that fateful night but, otherwise, her phone had been silent.

I made arrangements with Nick a few days later to get together and discuss the will. We met at a café and when he saw me, he hugged me long and tight. His face was drawn and tired as we took our seats and ordered coffee.

As we talked, Nick filled in some blanks about my sister's life. He told me that Brandy had made a lot of enemies doing her psychic work, and he sometimes worried about her safety. It was something they fought about constantly. He wanted her to put the psychic stuff aside for a while until things cooled but that wasn't her style.

"You were okay with her being psychic?" I asked him.

"Of course, Scarlet. It was part of her, and it's something we had in common." When I'd opened my mouth to pursue that comment he held up his hand and finished, "Yes, I have visions but I didn't have her talent. We started the app together and I wanted it to be all about helping people in need. Finding lost children or helping people who truly required our assistance but, well, Brandy loved the idea of making a buck."

I nodded in agreement because I could see how their two visions would not be something easily mixed.

I thought back to the angry caller who'd reached me on her phone at the cottage. When I asked Nick if he thought it was possible Brandy met with foul play he shook his head.

"Don't go there, Scarlet." He placed a hand on my shoulder. "Recovery is a day-to-day process and we're all just a moment away from a relapse. She was doing awesome and attended meetings often to keep her on the straight and narrow, but she admitted to me she struggled. I do too. It looks like she had a weak moment and, unfortunately, that's all it took."

Before I left, Nick pressed a few thousand dollars cash into my hand.

"It's going to take a while to sell all the stuff in Brandy's estate." He shook his head when I protested. "I know you said you didn't want anything and her will left everything to me, but she worried about you and she would've wanted you to have some money." He told me to stay in touch so he could forward me more money as it became available. Apparently, Brandy owned the condo where she was living and the money from that alone would help me tremendously.

There was also the matter of Brandy's business. Nick said he would keep the app going in a more low-key fashion in the meantime, but he wanted me to give serious thought to working with him. I told him I'd keep in touch but I couldn't see myself stepping into Brandy's shoes. Even when he offered to change the app to be all about helping victims, I still told him no. At least for now.

Muffin and I pointed Bubbles northward and then east toward Ross Lake. The place where Brandy, Mom and I had spent a summer eating peanut butter sandwiches and getting sunburns and mosquito bites. Paradise.

The weather had turned crisp and frosty and the Cascades were expecting snow. Bubbles didn't have tires for that kind of weather, but still I hung around the beautiful lake a couple of days to think back on childhood memories and talk to Brandy of happier times. I scattered some of my sister's ashes into the lake at sunset. I'd decided a small amount of her was coming with me on my travels. She would've hated that idea.

After scattering those ashes, I gave myself a day of grace before slipping back into the hard reality of Hope Harbor. I spent a day and night cuddling with Muffin and boondocking in the woods, where the only sounds were the birds and the wind through the trees. But when my phone rang at nine the next morning and it was the sheriff, I finally took his call.

"Before you start, my sister died and that's why I haven't returned your calls."

"I'm aware and I'm sorry for your loss." He sounded exhausted but his tone was firm. "Have you been in touch with Marshal Cobb since you left town?"

"He left me messages along with everyone else."

"There have been some further developments in Murray's case and it's important that you and I meet immediately. Are you able to come to my office? If not, I can come to you."

I told him I was hours away basically camping in the middle of nowhere, but he was insistent that it could not wait.

"I'll reach out to you tomorrow and come to your office. I've got some parking tickets I have to pay anyway." Might as well get those taken care of now that I had some cash.

Duthroyd agreed.

After that call I scrolled through my missed calls and dialed Noah.

"Aw, Red, I've been worried sick." I could hear the noise of the hardware store in the background.

"Sorry I haven't called."

"No need to be sorry. I'm the one sad to hear about Brandy. Hold on a second." He was working at the store and had me hold while he called his nephew over to man the register.

"How are you? Really?" he asked.

I took a second to think about it. "I'm good. Sad about Brandy, of course, but I'm holding up okay."

"Is it selfish of me to say that I've missed you like crazy?"

I smiled and felt my insides warm. "I've missed you too."

"When are you coming back? Come home to Hope Harbor."

I don't know that I'd ever consider Hope Harbor home and now that I'd been away from it a bit, I didn't feel like going back. But I did miss Noah far more than I liked.

"Well, I'm supposed to see the sheriff tomorrow sometime. How about I drop by the hardware store around closing?"

"The sheriff?" He sounded surprised. "What's that about?"

"No idea, just an update on the Murray thing I guess."

"I thought Sheriff Duthroyd had put it on Joel to handle all that," he mused. Then added, "I look forward to seeing you. You know our last dinner was interrupted and I never got a chance to serve you dessert. I think you need to give me the chance to make that up to you. Don't suppose I could talk you into coming into town tonight?"

I was tempted but I told him I was camping in the woods tonight and I'd see him tomorrow. He made loud kissy noises into the phone before we disconnected and that made me laugh, but I was still healing and Hope Harbor was salt on my wounds. As much as I wanted to see him, the entire town couldn't be a distant memory soon enough.

Muffin wanted to get out, so I took her to play in the fallen leaves. We wandered partway down a trail lined with cedars and aspen that seemed to touch the sky. A part of me desperately wanted to spend more time in Noah's arms, but an equally strong portion wanted to never return to Hope Harbor. While I played out scenarios in my head, Muffin rolled in leaves and stalked a squirrel. She was in kitty paradise. I'd missed just being able to roam wherever the wind blew, and only pulling into a town long enough to make a few dollars. Hopefully, the sheriff had some good news about the progress of the murder investigation.

When we returned I could hear my phone ringing inside the van. There were a half dozen missed calls from Penny in the span of a few minutes so I decided I'd better call her back.

"Oh, Red, it's awful!" Penny sobbed into the line. "I don't know what to do…or who to call!"

"What happened?"

"It's the insurance papers for Pincher's," she wailed. "I'm in such a mess. Tess was supposed to help me, and I can't figure out all these documents and I thought of you because you're always so helpful. I heard about your sister and I'm so sorry but do you think you could come?"

"Of course, I'm coming to town tomorrow so—"

Her sobs grew louder and I had to hold the phone away from my ear.

"I wish I wasn't such a stupid old bat," she cried. "I wish I could do these myself because I really wanted to submit them today. Honestly I need the money so badly and—"

"Okay, I can come today but I'm in a park over two hours away…"

"Are you sure you don't mind?" She sniffed.

I shrugged. What difference did a day make anyway? "Sure. I was going to come tomorrow anyway. I'll see you just after noon."

"You're an absolute lifesaver!"

I turned to Muffin. "So much for a quiet day in the woods, right?" I began securing items away in cupboards for the drive. I cleaned Muffin's litterbox and placed her into her crate with this promise: "There will be many days on forest trails in your future."

The scenic drive was made less peaceful by the idea of my destination. I thought about sending Noah a message but decided to wait and see how long I'd spend helping Penny. Half an hour outside of Hope Harbor I pulled into a gas station to fill up Bubbles's gas and propane tanks. I wanted to be sure as soon as I got the all-clear from Sheriff Duthroyd, I could roll out of town.

My heart felt a twinge about Noah but maybe, just

maybe, he wouldn't mind me leaving Hope Harbor and just visiting from time to time. And then perhaps he'd even consider the occasional forest vacation with me. It could work, right?

I made one more stop at Hope Harbor's bakery that tripled as a coffee shop and laundromat. I picked up a latte for myself and a variety of pastries for Penny. When I went into my wallet to pay, I saw Nan's ruby ring perched on top. I handed some bills to the cashier and, while she made change, I slipped the ancient ruby ring onto the ring finger of my left hand. It fit perfectly and tears filled my eyes as I stepped out of the bakery.

As I approached Bubbles I found Marshal Cobb leaning against my driver's door.

"Welcome back," he remarked with a smile that turned serious. "I am so very sorry to hear about your sister."

"Thank you." I put the box of pastries on the hood of the car and brushed away a tear with the heel of my hand before I fished the key fob out of my pocket and unlocked the van.

"Let me get that for you." The marshal held my door open as I climbed inside with the pastry box in one hand and the coffee in the other. "That's a lot of goodies. You've got quite the sweet tooth."

"I'm going to help Penny with some paperwork so didn't want to show up empty-handed."

"That's nice of you."

"You'll be happy to know I'm also going to pay all my parking tickets tomorrow." I opened my glove box and pointed to the yellow slips neatly stacked inside. "I have a meeting with the sheriff so thought I might as well take care of those while I'm there."

"Sheriff Duthroyd?" The marshal scratched the back of his neck. "What are you seeing him about?"

"No idea." I shrugged. "Guess I'll find out once I get there." I lifted my chin to indicate down the street to where I saw Melody waving. "Looks like your girlfriend is waiting for you."

Marshal turned to look. "Oh God she's not my girlfriend…a friend, sure…but not a girlfriend."

"Oh. I just thought—"

"You thought wrong."

"Okay. Sorry." I closed my door then and offered Melody a friendly wave as I backed up Bubbles and headed to Penny's.

Penny's driveway held her own car, a dark pickup and Tess's car. I parked Bubbles out front and left Muffin snoozing in her carrier in the back. Even though it was a cool day I opened a couple windows a crack to make sure she had airflow, and made my way to the door carrying the box of pastries.

Penny whipped the door open before I could even knock. "Come in!" She smiled brightly and I was glad to see she no longer looked upset. "You didn't have to bring treats." She took the pastry box, peeked inside and said, "Yummm. I'll put the coffee on."

"I just had a cup on the way over so I'm good." I kicked off my shoes and followed her through the living room, past the hundreds of dolls leering at us, and into the kitchen. The table was buried under stacks of paperwork and my heart fell. "Is that all insurance documents?"

"Oh no." She walked over and stacked some of the piles neatly so there was a clear space in front of both our chairs as we sat down. "But I thought now might be a good time to sort through a lot of the papers I'll need for filing taxes and also all the bills I've been ignoring."

The closest paper perched on a pile was a final notice for the electric bill on her house.

"Are you going to be okay?" I asked with a frown.

"Oh yes. Definitely." But her nod was overly enthusiastic and her eyes a little too bright. "As soon as I receive the payment from the insurance company, I'll be able to pay all my bills off."

Completely changing the subject, I pointed my finger toward the front of the house. "By the way, is that Murray's pickup? And I see Tess is back, have you made up?"

"Yes and yes!" She got up and went to the cupboard for a coffee mug. "I know you said you've already had coffee, but I must insist you try this new French vanilla mocha blend."

"Too much coffee makes me jittery," I said in protest.

"Good news! It's decaffeinated."

"In that case, sure."

She poured us each a cup and then brought little plates for the pastries.

"How about I take the insurance papers into the other room and get to work on those right away?" I offered.

"Nonsense." She waved a hand at me. "Let's enjoy each other's company for a few minutes first." She patted my hand across the table. "I am so very sorry to hear about your sister. I know everyone was saying how she was a witch doing black magic and may have cursed you and this town, but I never believed that."

"Oh. Um. Thanks." I took a big gulp of the coffee, which was bitter but also sickening sweet.

"Let's have a treat!" Penny opened the pastry box,

pulled out a lemon tart for herself and handed the box to me. I chose a cinnamon doughnut without icing to make up for the oversweet coffee.

After a minute of chitchat and local gossip about people I didn't know, Penny piped up, "Drink up, sweetie, so we can get to work on those papers."

I pushed the coffee cup away and took another bite of doughnut.

"I'm going to go grab some notepads and pens." Penny jumped up from the table and ran out of the room.

She was gone for a few minutes. I thought I heard voices in the other room and then I started to feel nauseated and woozy.

I got to my feet thinking I'd better race to the bathroom, but I'd only taken one step when I felt myself fall and the world turned dark.

SIXTEEN

I WOKE UP chained to a metal cot in a cold, dark, windowless room. Trying to bolt upright caused sharp pain in my ankles and wrists. As I strained to see around me, there was an explosion of agony in my head. I closed my eyes to stem the nausea that followed.

After a moment I calmed my breathing then slowly opened my eyes to take in my surroundings. In the dim light I could only make out vague outlines. I was in a square room with one chair in the corner and a floor-to-ceiling shelving unit stuffed with dolls. Their unseeing eyes seemed to gaze right through me. My instinct was to scream but I could hear distant voices and didn't want to alert my abductor. Memories flooded back.

It was Penny.

She drugged me.

"Oh God."

I shifted my weight and wriggled my wrists and feet but that only brought more discomfort. When I arched my back and twisted my body to see if it would be possible to somehow pull the chains hard enough to break them through the frame of the cot, there was not the slightest give or bend. The chains were heavy and the bedframe solid.

Fighting against panic I struggled instead to make out who was talking and what was being said but the voices were too far away and my head felt stuffed with cotton. If Penny had a random guest maybe I could scream and they'd hear me! Just as I considered that possibility I became aware of footsteps coming closer. The door to my room slowly creaked open and I shut my eyes and pretended to still be unconscious.

"She should be awake by now," Penny murmured. "Maybe I gave her too much. She didn't even drink it all though. Are you sure you researched the right amount?"

"What difference does it make. He's going to kill her anyway." Tess's voice sounded both annoyed and exhausted.

"Maybe he won't kill her," whispered another female voice. "He could just make it so that she never comes back."

It was Melody!

"That's not the plan," Tess said. "We gotta stick to the plan."

"Like you sticking the gun in the wig box and it getting found? That sure wasn't the plan," Melody snarled.

"It was only supposed to be temporary until I could toss it in the river," Tess protested. "She's the one that screwed that up."

Footsteps sounded on the floor near my cot, and then abruptly someone pinched my arm hard and my eyes flew open.

"Ha! I knew you were faking!" Tess declared with triumph.

Penny and Melody stepped back toward the door and looked uncomfortable.

"Why am I here?" My tongue was thick and dry from the drugs, and my voice came out shaking with fear.

"You don't need to worry your head about that," Penny said from the doorway.

"Should I give her a shot?" Tess asked, holding up a syringe.

"No." Melody shook her head. "He's going to need her awake, remember?"

"Just let me go," I pleaded. "I'll get in my van and drive away and you'll never see me again."

"Shut up," Tess hissed. "You had a chance to do that but here we are."

"I—I really have to pee," I said.

"Oh God." Tess rolled her eyes.

"Well, she did have that coffee I made her and one on the way over," Penny said sympathetically as she meekly nibbled her lower lip.

"If she's kept chained up we could bring her to the bathroom, and there's no way she could overpower all of us," Melody pointed out.

She might be right but I sure as hell planned to try.

"Don't you have to go pick him up?" Tess demanded. "Hurry or you'll be late."

Once Melody left, I pleaded with Penny and Tess. "Look, I don't know why you're doing this, but it doesn't matter. I swear I won't tell anyone anything. I'll leave Hope Harbor and I'll be on the other side of the country before anyone notices I'm gone."

They wordlessly backed out of the room and closed the door hard behind them. I heard their footsteps hurry away. My heart pounded against my ribs as I came to terms with the fact that I was being imprisoned by not just one, but three women. And apparently a man who planned to kill me.

Why were they holding me and who was the "he" who planned on taking me out? My head was so fuzzy from being drugged. Was it Noah? Oh God, please no.

I wriggled my wrists to see if I could squeeze them through their binds but I couldn't get free, and I wasn't able to scream without getting those women back down. In frustration, I yanked the chains hard repeatedly even as fiery pain shot up my arms and legs but the chains held fast. There was no way I could break free.

My only hope would be if I was being moved from here to another location. As I moved my index finger, I was able to rotate the ruby ring on my left hand and send up a plea to Nan, Brandy and Mom for help.

"Please," I murmured to the silent room. "Please don't let me die."

It wasn't long before the door flung open again. My heart soared as Marshal Cobb strode into the room. He wasn't in his standard uniform but was dressed all in black.

"Oh thank God you're here, Penny has—"

"Shut up," he growled.

Directly behind him, on the other side of the door, stood Penny and Tess. He reached into his pocket and pulled out a key. In his other hand he held a gun.

"Listen up, Red, because this is how things are going to go." He placed the muzzle of the gun to my forehead and I became completely still. "I'm going to get you out of these chains and then you and I are going to walk out of this house and get into your van. You're going to start it up and—"

"And I'll drive far away from Hope Harbor. I swear, you'll never see me again and—"

"Shut up!" he screamed. The side of the gun slammed against my cheekbone, and a flash of pain blinded me. "I'm coming with you in the van and you're going to drive *exactly* where I tell you." He paused and added, "Nod if you understand."

I gave a quick nod. He unlocked the chains from my hands first and I rubbed my sore wrists as he worked on my ankles. Then he yanked me to my feet.

"We're walking out the front door and I'll be right behind you," he stated and with the gun pressed between my shoulder blades he pushed me toward the door.

"Could I—could I please use the bathroom before we leave?"

He sighed dramatically, turned to Tess and said, "You go in with her."

There was a small half bath next to the room where I was held. Cobb shoved me in the door and Tess came with me. It was a tiny room with no window and the doll theme had continued in here. The counter was covered with makeup and hair ties.

"Hurry up," Tess ordered.

When she turned halfway I lowered my pants and as I relieved myself I frantically looked around the room for something to use as a weapon. I spied some metal tweezers on the counter at my elbow. As I pulled up my pants I pocketed them in a flash. They were small but sharp and while they wouldn't be a match against these three, maybe they'd come in handy when it was just me and the marshal. But as I left the bathroom Tess slammed me against the door frame, reached into my pocket and removed the tweezers.

"Your biggest problem has always been that you think you're smarter than the rest of us," she hissed.

My heart sank.

Wordlessly, they walked me through the basement

rec room and up the stairs into the main part of the house. When we reached the main floor I squinted in the light of the room but realized with dismay it was dark as pitch outside. That would definitely lower my chances of being seen leaving Penny's house.

At the front door Marshal Cobb ordered me to put on my shoes without any funny business. If I could figure out a way to be "funny" about disarming a corrupt law enforcement officer and take down these women, I'd try, but nothing occurred to me as I tied my laces.

Movement in my periphery caught my eye as I straightened. It was Melody standing off to the side cuddling Muffin. My heart twisted in misery.

"Please take good care of her." My words ended on a sob and Melody nodded sharply, then turned away.

"I have your van keys in my hand." Cobb held them in front of my face. "We're climbing in through the sliding door and then you'll get into the driver's seat and I'll sit in the seat behind you. Then you'll make your way out of town. You'll drive the speed limit and if you happen to see anyone you'll just nod politely and keep driving. If you do anything besides what I just told you, I will put a bullet in your back. Don't even think of trying to signal someone, got it?"

Before I could answer he pushed me out the front door and I nearly stumbled down the steps. He pressed the fob to unlock Bubbles and we made our way toward the van. There wasn't a soul on the street who could see what was going on, and as he opened the van door and shoved me inside, I felt overwhelmed by despair.

Once behind the wheel he tossed the keys into my lap and then pressed the gun to the back of my head.

"Drive."

The van roared to life and I did as I was told. Once off Penny's residential street I hesitated, and Cobb ordered, "Right through town. You're going to take Main Street and turn at the gas station, then head for the highway. Anyone hanging out in town will see you leaving."

"Okay."

My mind raced as I drove at exactly the speed limit through town. How could I draw attention or signal someone I needed help without getting a bullet through my head? A few curious townsfolk glanced my way as I drove down Main Street. They'd be witnesses that said they saw me driving my van and headed out of town. As I was told, I gave them quick nods.

"Keep your hands on the steering wheel and foot on the gas and maybe, just maybe, I'll let you live."

It was the first promising news that I might not be killed, and my heart clung to it even as my head knew it was a lie.

I took the turn at the service station, and one pickup truck was filling up. It was Noah! I desperately wanted to wave but needed to keep my hands on the wheel. I turned my head quickly, blinked frantically at Noah and flashed my high beams but I'd driven past before I could see his reaction.

Once past the gas station we were headed in the direction of the highway but when we neared the on-ramp, Cobb ordered me to pull over and put the van in Park. I slowly hit the shoulder and did as I was told. He got out of the back seat, then unbuckled my seat belt and yanked me out of the driver's seat. As he buckled me into the passenger seat, my cell phone began to ring in my purse. He reached into my bag, took out my phone and, as he did, I could see the caller was Noah. The marshal powered off my phone and tossed it back in my purse. Next, he got behind the wheel and his knuckles were pure white on the wheel as he pulled away from the shoulder. He got on the highway, but it was only a few minutes later that he took an exit and we disappeared down an unlit stretch of road where I'd never traveled before.

"Where are we going?"

Cobb didn't reply but after a few minutes of driving he seemed to completely relax. "This thing handles pretty easy. I might even consider getting myself one of these one day."

"Why are you doing this?" I asked quietly.

He kept on driving in silence as if he didn't hear. We'd come across hardly any other vehicles on our drive. At one point there'd been headlights behind us but even those disappeared as Marshal Cobb took a left onto a gravel forest service road. The route was overgrown and littered with deep potholes that jarred my teeth.

As Bubbles climbed then dipped and cornered, the occasional low-hanging branch would scrape across the roof. The farther he drove, the more nervous I became. In my head, I'd formulated the only plan I'd been able to come up with. When he stopped and ordered me out of the van to kill me, I'd run into the forest. He was taller and his legs were longer, but I'd always been pretty quick on my feet.

Eventually we reached a roadside pullout, and he turned into the curve and killed the ignition. He rolled down his window a couple of inches and I could hear water nearby.

"You weren't supposed to work that day."

I turned to him and just blinked before I said, "On the day Murray was killed?"

He nodded. "It was all arranged. I was meeting him in the storeroom under the pretext of fixing a parking ticket for him."

"The yellow slip of paper I saw under his hand. I thought it looked familiar." I pointed to the glove box of the van. "It was a parking ticket like all the ones you gave me."

"Right." Marshal Cobb dragged a hand through his hair. "You weren't supposed to work that day. It would've been a clean job. Kill Murray and we'd all live happily ever after." He snorted at that and shook his head. "Then I heard the door to the store open and just made it out the back door when you found him." He shook a finger in my direction. "You ruined everything."

"But why kill Murray? I mean, sure, he was a complete ass and everyone hated him, but the town had put up with him all these years…" I shrugged. "Why now?"

He turned away and looked out the window and I took that moment to twist my body in my seat to look at him. I placed a hand on my seat belt, ready to unbuckle and bolt if he reached for the gun in his waistband.

"He went after Melody," the marshal said, his voice softened to a whisper. "That was the last straw for me. Melody, she's… I am…"

"You love her."

"Yes."

I thought back. "So you *are* a couple. Why did you tell me you're not together? What difference does that make?"

"Melody thought it would be better if people thought

she had a thing for Noah and that she could care less about me. If people knew we were together, it might give me a motive if anyone heard Murray went after her."

"So you were defending her honor. Nothing wrong with that," I said quickly, trying to get on his good side. "I mean, I'm sure people would understand and—"

"It was still murder!" he roared and then quietly he added, "She's pregnant."

"I can see how that would make you even more angry about Murray assaulting her."

"Not just me," Cobb pointed out. "Penny was all in agreement because she wanted the insurance money. Murray's life insurance would help her regain what she lost in his investments, and Tess didn't want anyone to find out she was related to that piece of crap, but in the end I did it for Melody." He sighed. "Murray had no family besides Tess, and he'd been telling people for months he was thinking of leaving town for good. He bragged in the diner a few weeks ago that he'd almost saved enough to build himself a little shack near his favorite fishing hole and retire. That's the lake right there." He pointed to the front of the van. "That got back to Penny and made her furious. He'd taken all her money and lost it and now he planned to retire. With him bragging about leaving Hope Harbor, nobody would've thought anything of it if he disappeared one day. Everyone in town would've been relieved, and then when his body turned up in the bottom of his favorite fishing creek, Penny would've gotten his insurance and everyone would've still been happy."

"But Penny said he let his policy lapse."

"Well, obviously, she didn't know that at the time, now did she?" he said with exasperation.

"The threatening messages? The drive-by shooter?"

"Those messages and the shooting, well, just kids about town. Same ones who tossed beer cans at you. See? We weren't the only ones who had it in for you." He smirked. "If they'd shot you, that would've really screwed up our plan to pin Murray's murder on you."

"You had someone watching me. A person driving a dark pickup. How did you find me at the cabin?"

"Wasn't rocket science. I ran a search of properties and saw the cabin in your sister's boyfriend's name. Tess used Murray's truck to scope it out and see if you were there. She had all kinds of plans to take care of things there but I told her to hold off."

"What about the gunshot residue on my hands…"

"I submitted one of my own hands." He shrugged. "You're the new girl. A nomad. It would be the natural assumption that you killed Murray. But then your sister had to get her nose in the mix and—"

"What about Brandy?" My hand flew to my mouth. "Oh my God did you kill her too?"

"She called up the sheriff and told him she had a vision that I killed Murray and that you were in danger, so I had no choice! Shot her up with enough heroin to kill ten people." He slapped a hand on the dashboard, causing me to jump. "When I explained to the sheriff that she was a heroin addict and a nutcase, he shrugged it off, but then you made an appointment to talk to him and…" He waved his hand around. "Now here we are."

I started to cry. Why hadn't I believed her when she told me she was clean? Why had I doubted her when she showed up clean only wanting to help me? The guilt and shame tore through my heart. The harder I tried to control it, the louder my sobs became. Large, fat tears rolled down my cheeks as Marshal Cobb looked on horrified.

"Okay, let's just get this over with." He pulled the gun from his waistband and I swallowed my tears just as I spied something in his breast pocket.

"You smoke! I didn't know you smoked."

"Gave it up a year ago but lately I've been sneaking a few."

My hopes rose at the prospect. "You should have one. Hell, I'd love one too, if you don't mind."

"You smoke?" He looked skeptical.

"Like you, I gave it up a while ago but if I'm dying anyway," I said a little too brightly, "you can't deny someone a last cigarette, can you?"

He patted his pockets and shrugged. "Well, I don't have a lighter or matches so too bad."

"In the drawer next to my cutlery!" I quickly pointed behind us. "You'll find a barbecue lighter in there."

He hesitated but only briefly. With a gun pointed at me with one hand, he unbuckled his seat belt and walked over to where I'd pointed, opened a drawer and pulled out the lighter. He fished a smoke out of his pocket and put it between his lips.

"You can have one once I'm done."

I folded my hands in my lap with the fingers of my right hand embracing Nan's ring. If it was supposed to boost my powers, now would be the perfect time for that to happen.

Cobb took a seat at the table behind me, put his feet up on my table and pressed the button to engage the flame.

An orange ribbon of fire shot out from the lighter,

and I felt it engulf me in a spiral of heat that swirled around Nan's ring and shot up my arm and into my head. Pictures flew to my mind in a rapid shotgun-style slideshow. Murray in the storeroom turning toward his killer—the vision now included Marshal Cobb standing there, and when Murray turned away briefly, Cobb shot him in the back of the head.

Other slides included Melody looking stricken and terrified as Murray's hand creeped up her shirt and then Tess and Penny, their heads bent together conspiratorially.

From a distance I heard Marshal Cobb saying something and I knew I was running out of time.

"How do I escape?" I whispered and I hoped those words were in my mind and not said aloud.

Abruptly, the image twisted and showed me Nan's gun tucked into the cubbyhole next to the mattress but before the vision could show me more, my shoulders were grabbed and I was being shaken by Marshal Cobb.

"Sorry," I blurted.

"Thought you were going to pass out." Then he chuckled. "Not that it would've made a difference in the end result."

He walked over to my sink, poured water over the butt of his cigarette, then stuffed the damp butt back into the package. He was smart enough not to leave his DNA behind.

"Still want a smoke?"

"No." I shook my head. "How is this going to work? I assume you're going to make this look like a suicide?"

"You're despondent after the death of your sister and the fact that you're about to be arrested for murder, so you take your own life." He nodded his chin toward the ebony darkness outside. "We'll go walk down to the lake."

I nodded. "I expect you're going to leave the van here, so how are you getting home?"

"No need to worry about that." He glanced at his wrist. "I have a ride that should be here soon."

I closed my eyes and tried to figure out how I was going to get to Nan's gun at the very back of the van.

"Do you think," I began slowly, "that instead of shooting me outside, you could do it here?" I quickly added, "If I was going to kill myself for real, I would lie down in my bed—" I pointed to the mattress in the back "—close my eyes and pull the trigger." When he looked skeptical, I hurried on, "It makes sense because this van was my nan's and it's my happy place."

I saw him weighing his options and, to my relief, he shrugged. "Guess it doesn't matter." He pulled his weapon from his waistband. "Let's get it over with."

Please oh please oh please, I silently prayed to all the women who'd gone before me as I made my way to the back of the van.

I began to cry and that seemed to irritate the marshal.

"Hurry up, now!" He pressed the muzzle of the gun to my back and gave me a shove.

I climbed onto the bed slowly, trying to angle my body more to the left and hoping for the opportunity to reach for my gun, but Cobb stayed with me, his own weapon pressed to my spine.

Turning over onto my back, I moved slowly as he climbed in next to me, his gun trained on my head. I looked over at him and with pleading eyes said, "In that cupboard up and to your left is an eyeshade that says

Dreamer on it. Would you mind getting it down and letting me wear it so I don't see your gun?"

He rolled his eyes but with a harrumph he turned slightly to his right and reached up to open the cabinet. That was all the break I needed—I shoved my hand down between the mattress, pulled out my gun and pulled the trigger.

I'd aimed for his head, but he'd turned when he sensed my movement and I got him in the shoulder. He dropped his gun with a yelp of agony and then he frantically tried to retrieve it, but I was on my feet. As I squeezed off another round, I yanked the sliding door open. This shot caught him in the side but still he managed to get to his feet and stumble toward me, gun held in his outstretched hand.

We were parked up against the edge of the forest and as I lunged out the door and into the darkness, a shot whizzed past my ear and lodged in a tree. Pounding through the dense brush, I could hear Cobb's labored breathing behind me. Even injured, he was making better time than I ever expected but I tore through the forest as branches scratched my face and tore up my arms.

I realized my mistake when I ran out of cover and bolted right into a clearing. There was Marshal Cobb, one hand pressed to his oozing side and the other pointing a shaky gun at my head.

Remembering everything Nan had ever taught me, I jumped back into the brush, dropped to my knees, leveled my weapon and fired. I screamed, "That's for Brandy!" as the bullet lodged in the center of Cobb's forehead.

As if in slow motion, the marshal fell to his knees and then collapsed facedown in the weeds.

I sat down in the scrub and wept. My entire body shook from a combination of relief and sorrow. After allowing the emotions to wash over me for a few minutes, I gathered my strength to get to my feet.

"It's over," I said to the world. "Finally."

But the universe had other ideas.

At that moment I could just make out headlights approaching from down the road.

SEVENTEEN

THE MARSHAL HAD told me he had someone coming to pick him up but I'd hoped for enough time to drive out of the area. By the sound of the vehicle chewing gravel in my direction, I wouldn't even make it back to Bubbles before they arrived.

Since they wouldn't be able to hear my footsteps while they drove, now was the time to run like my ass was on fire and then find somewhere to hide when they stopped. The cloudy skies offered no moon or stars. It was black as Cobb's heart, and I had no light source with me. I had no idea if the person coming would have a flashlight and be able to follow my footprints and those of Marshal Cobb.

I took off in the direction of the water that I could hear nearby. It was a small creek that emptied into the nearby lake. The water was icy but I'd be leaving no footprints walking through the water. As fast as I could manage sloshing in the ankle-deep brook, I trudged upstream until I reached a culvert under the forest road. The vehicle was so close I ducked down inside the culvert until it passed by.

Once it had gone I peeked out and down the road to see if I could recognize the car. I was expecting maybe Penny's or Tess's car or even Melody's but the vehicle I saw didn't belong to any of the three guilty women.

It was Noah's truck and clearly it was him behind the wheel.

"Oh no-o-o!" My words were a defeated and heart-broken cry carried on the wind.

Noah was in on it too. If he was Cobb's ride, he was part of the plan. The crushing blow sucked the air right out of my lungs.

The truck took the corner up ahead. It was just past that corner where the pullout was located and where Bubbles was parked. As soon as the truck cleared the bend and could no longer see me in its mirrors, I jumped from my hiding place, bolted across the road and leaped back into the ditch on the other side.

I jumped blindly into the dark, hoping to land in the water on the other side. However, what I hit was a pile of rocks. The cracking noise when I landed, followed by excruciating pain, told me I'd just obliterated my ankle.

"Argh!" I bit down on my hand to stop the scream.

When I attempted to put weight on my left foot, light-ning rods of agony shot up my leg and nearly caused me to pass out. There was no way I was going to be able to outrun Noah. I glanced behind me at the culvert and realized I had no choice.

Dragging my dead leg behind me, I hobbled back into the dark culvert, grateful that the amount of running water at this time of year was light. However, tempera-tures were close to freezing and I was already soaking wet from the knees down. The only saving grace would be if Noah came across the empty van, panicked and left the area. Once he was gone, I'd have to drag my shattered ankle back to Bubbles and drive myself out of the area and to a hospital.

Shivering inside the dark wet culvert I held my breath as I heard my name being called.

"Red!" Then a second later, "Red, it's Noah!"

Yes, asshole, I know exactly who you are and why you're here.

A minute went by and he called out again, "Red, it's Noah!"

He was much closer this time. I forced myself to breathe slowly and evenly. He kept calling my name over and over and then I heard his footsteps on the road above me. He paused and I could make out the flicker of a flashlight. Immediately I realized my crucial mistake. I'd walked across the road and my footsteps in the dusty gravel would be clear as day. I curled my lips over my teeth so he wouldn't hear them chattering, and steadied the gun in my hand.

I could hear Noah climb down the ditch and pause at the entrance of the culvert.

"Jesus, please let her be okay," he murmured.

The plea caught me off guard. When he shone his light into the culvert and into my face I fired off a round but I was blinded by the light and it went wild.

"Red! It's me, Noah!" he cried out.

"I know! You're here to pick up the marshal! Well…" I laughed mirthlessly. "You're going to need a body bag for that, and they'll need to bring a second one for you too."

"I found Cobb's body," he said evenly. "I followed you guys out here and—"

"Nobody followed us!" I screamed back. "I was hoping and praying but I didn't see anyone after we left the main road and—"

"Red, I know this area. This is where Murray liked

to come fishing. I followed at a distance with my lights out when you left the highway. But when I saw your van take the corner into this area I could see you weren't the driver and I knew where the van was headed."

"I don't believe you!" I screamed back. My entire body was shaking from cold, fear and pain. "You're all in on this. All of you! Penny, Tess, Melody and Cobb. And the marshal told me he had a ride coming to get him after he killed me and made it look like a suicide, and here you are!"

The words were no sooner out of my mouth than we could hear the crunch of gravel and the sound of an approaching vehicle in the distance.

"I'm guessing that's his ride now. Stay quiet," Noah hissed.

I watched as he crouched low waiting for the vehicle to pass. I had a clear shot and could kill him easily now, but this new car changed everything. What if he was telling the truth?

The vehicle passed overhead and when the sound of the tires faded he said, "You wait here, I'm going to see who it is."

Once I heard his footsteps grow quieter, I dragged myself out of the ditch. Noah could be telling the truth, but I'd proven to have terrible judgment of just about everyone in Hope Harbor so I wasn't taking a chance. Dragging my leg and hopping along I followed the stream until it disappeared into a marshy area. I knew I'd get sucked into the mud, so I changed direction. The moon peeked through the overcast sky long enough to make out some large moss-covered boulders about a hundred yards away.

"That's my goal," I told myself.

As if in a distant memory I could hear Nan's voice cheering me on, "You've got this, Scarlet."

It felt like miles away as I limped awkwardly along, grateful for the occasional tree to lean on. I'd just reached the huge rocks when I heard a bloodcurdling scream.

It took all of my energy and strength to drag myself up and over the pile of rocks but, once on the other side, I tucked myself deep into a mossy crevice. There, protected from the breeze, I began to frantically rub my arms and chest until I could feel some warmth returning to my extremities. I wished I had my phone on me so I could at least try to get somewhere with cell range to call for help. I wondered whose scream I heard but I couldn't focus on that now. It felt like forever since Noah had cornered me in the culvert and now I could faintly hear footsteps behind me and his voice calling my name.

I pressed my back against the boulders. The structure of the rock formation was in a U shape making me feel confident nobody would see me unless they came directly in front of my location and, if they did, it would be the last steps they took. I bent my good leg and used it to steady my hand that held the gun and point it at the break in the rocks.

"Red, where are you?" Noah called out. Then a couple minutes later it was followed up by "It was Melody in the car. I've tied her up and put her in my truck."

I wavered because I really wanted to believe him. My heart gave a little squeeze of assurance, but I still couldn't bring myself to take the chance. The sound of Noah's feet crunching on branches and wading through leaves came closer and I held my breath but then he retreated. As he walked he never stopped shouting my name.

A few minutes later and from a great distance I heard him yell, "No cell service here. I'm going for help but I'll be back as quick as I can."

About fifteen minutes went by and then I heard the sound of Noah's truck ripping down the gravel road at a breakneck speed. Was this my chance to hightail it back to Bubbles and get out of here? I wanted desperately to believe that Noah had left and taken Melody (or whoever it really was) with him. I sat there debating what to do. My ankle was throbbing and had swollen massively, making the thought of moving unappealing. I decided I'd give it an hour. If Noah really did go to get help, it would be a reasonable amount of time to expect that to arrive.

My cell phone was in the van so I could only guesstimate the time. By the time it seemed an hour was up, the sky had cleared, offering me enough light to be able to move easier. But it also made me an easy target for a killer. I'd formulated a plan to scoot out of my enclosed rock cave and find a large stick to use as a cane and then find my way back to Bubbles around the back way.

I began to shift my weight onto my arms to push myself forward. Almost immediately I spotted a stick that would be good enough to use as a cane. The journey in the woods was arduous and excruciating. By the time I reached the van I spied Melody's vehicle alongside it and cautiously approached but there was no one around. I hefted myself inside the van but then realized to my dismay the keys were nowhere to be found. A sob broke from my throat as I realized they were probably on Cobb's dead body.

By the time I hobbled into the clearing where he lay, my entire body was soaked in sweat from the exertion of just getting there but I knew time was crucial. I felt queasiness nearly overwhelm me as I searched through the marshal's blood-soaked pockets. Finally I found the keys and then began the grueling journey back to the van.

I was still a couple hundred yards away when I heard the sound of a vehicle approaching fast. As the sound grew louder, I realized there was more than one car and then suddenly sirens began to howl. I could make out the burst and strobe of police lights through the trees as the vehicles advanced.

I gasped in relief. Driven now to be found, I worked my way forward. The stick I used as a cane snapped under my weight, and I fell forward onto the ground and lay there softly wailing in the dirt. But then I began to crawl toward the pulsing police lights that were in the direction of Bubbles. The trees were thicker here and I pulled myself up using one rough cedar and then was able to shuffle from one tree to the next to hold myself up. Deep in the shadows I made my way one painful step at a time and arrived in thick brush a few feet from the backside of Bubbles.

I could hear voices but I needed to be sure I wasn't stepping into another setup. Maybe there was more than one law enforcement professional on the same side as Marshal Cobb. Since Cobb's concern had been me talking to Sheriff Duthroyd, that was the only person I could truly trust.

Flashlights scanned the ground and numerous voices called my name as I approached. I was grateful once again that the moon and stars were covered in clouds so that I could stay unseen, but not so happy when the sky opened up and an icy rain soaked me to the skin. From within a thorny scrub I watched an officer I didn't recognize stand guard outside of Bubbles's open doors.

Suddenly a flashlight beam blinded me and Noah's voice cried with relief, "Red!" He scrambled through the thorny scrub to get to me and yelled over his shoulder, "Sheriff, I found her!"

And that's when I knew I was going to be okay. Noah really had gone to get help. When he reached me, I dropped my gun and fell, shivering and broken, into his arms. He tore off his heavy jacket and put it around my shoulders.

"God, Red, I thought you were…" He pressed lips to the top of my head and squeezed me tight. "You're shaking. Let's get you into a vehicle with some heat."

"My—my ankle is broken," I said, my voice cracking.

In a smooth sweep he lifted me off the ground as if I were no more than a child and walked me out of the brush. The sheriff came running too.

"Can I lay down in the van?" I pleaded.

"That's a crime scene now," Sheriff Duthroyd replied and to Noah he said, "We'll put her in the back of my car until we can get EMTs up here."

"I'm so glad you're okay," Noah said as he placed me in the back of the cop car. To the sheriff he said, "Do you have a blanket?"

Sheriff Duthroyd got out a heavy scratchy blanket from his trunk. It smelled of mildew and felt like heaven. Then he started up his car, cranked the heat and told Noah to leave so he could talk to me. Noah stood less than a couple feet from the car the entire time.

It took nearly an hour for paramedics to arrive and during that time I told the sheriff everything I knew and everything Marshal Cobb had told me. I sobbed when I got to the part about shooting Cobb, and he said they'd already found the body.

"I dropped my gun in the bushes where Noah found me," I told him.

"We'll fetch it for evidence."

"Did you suspect something about Marshal Cobb? Is that why you wanted to see me?"

"The bakery across the street from your sister's apartment reviewed their security camera footage from the night your sister died, and they reported seeing someone wrestling with her in her Corvette on the street. When they sent the footage to me, it was grainy and unclear but the man definitely reminded me of Joel Cobb." He scrubbed a hand over the stubble on his chin before he added, "I thought you were safe in the forest for now, and planned to bring him in for questioning last night before you came back to town. Unfortunately, all this happened before I could get him to come in."

The sheriff then let me know that Melody was Cobb's driver and was in custody thanks to Noah.

"What about Penny and Tess?"

"They've disappeared but we've issued a BOLO for them, and I'm sure it won't take long."

The heat blasting, the heavy blanket, and the shock settled over me and I wanted to close my eyes and sleep forever but I kept answering Sheriff Duthroyd's questions. The rest of the statement was going over minute details but eventually he had to stop questioning me when the EMTs arrived to take me to the closest hospital.

As they loaded me into the back Noah shouted that he'd see me at the hospital.

I don't remember the ride to the hospital. The next thing I remembered was when I woke up and the doctor told me about all the screws now holding my ankle together. I brought up my brain tumor and expressed concern about its return. A neurologist was called in and ordered an MRI but the doctor said the findings were inconclusive. He told me there might be something small but it looked like nothing to worry about at this point so I should just follow up with another check in a year.

Regardless of what the tests showed, a small part of me suspected that fire-seeing could cause that tumor to return. I'd have to start weighing the value of my abilities against the danger it might cause my health.

The painkillers caused me to mostly sleep. I had a vague recollection of Noah being bedside at one point but thought I'd dreamed it until a couple days later when it came time to be discharged and he was there.

"Your chariot awaits, madam." He bowed.

"Thanks for the ride." I paused as he pushed me in a wheelchair to the exit of the building. "But where are we going? I'm guessing Bubbles is still in evidence?" I asked sadly.

"I thought you should stay with me. Doc said you should be off your feet for a few weeks. Are you okay with that?" He hoisted me into the passenger seat of his pickup and I noticed he had crutches in the back seat.

After Noah returned the wheelchair to the hospital entrance, I thanked him and then said, "You don't have to do this. I can get comfortable at a motel with my foot propped up under some pillows and—"

"Look, I know you're Ms. Independent but I'd like to do this for you. I want to take care of you. Is it so hard for you to accept help?"

"Actually, yes, it is." I laughed and he chuckled too.

There was something on my mind that was causing me distress, but I put it aside for the moment. Once we were at Noah's house, he set me up on the sofa with a footstool with stacked pillows under my foot. Then he covered me with a soft blanket and set up a side table that held snacks, water and my pain pills. After he handed me the remote for the television he took a step back and tapped his chin thoughtfully.

"There's something missing."

"I can't think of one more possible thing I could use." I chuckled.

"Oh, I've got it." He pointed a finger at me. "Don't run off anywhere."

I rolled my eyes at the prospect.

Seconds later Noah reappeared and ordered me to close my eyes.

"Really? Is this necessary?"

"Yup. Close your eyes."

I did as I was told and a squirmy, furry bundle was placed into my arms.

"Muffin!" I cried. Burying my face in her fur, I held her up to my face and was promptly swatted for the trouble. She flew from my arms and walked away, twitching her tail furiously in the air. "She's angry with me."

"Do you blame her?" Noah took a seat on the sofa next to me. "By the time we found her at Melody's, she'd hidden herself in a corner to stop the unwanted attention of a half dozen other cats."

"Ha! She must be completely traumatized." My hand reached for his. "Thank you so much, Noah. Not just for Muffin. But for everything."

"And I should thank you too." He squeezed my hand. "For not blowing my head off when you thought I was part of the bad-guy crew."

DAYS WENT BY with Noah waiting on me like a nurse but when Bubbles was released from evidence, I knew it was time to go.

"How are you going to even drive?" Noah protested.

"It's an automatic, and the injury is on my left foot, not my right," I reminded him. "Besides, don't you have to return to work? How is the hardware store surviving without you?"

"First vacation in years," he said, watching me place Muffin into her carrier with a frown.

"Vacation?" I giggled. "Waiting on me hand and foot has been a holiday for you?"

"Yes." He wrapped me in his arms and buried his face in my neck. "It's been wonderful having you with me. I don't want you to go."

He kissed me then, and it was long and slow and caused my insides to turn to warm liquid.

"I—I can't," I told him simply. "I can't live here. In Hope Harbor." I shook my head. "I need to get on the road and just…" I shrugged. "Be free."

He nodded but I could tell he didn't get it.

"It's not like we can't see each other," I added quickly. "You can come visit me. Have a real vacation in a forest, near a lake, with nobody around except the birds, and maybe the occasional bear."

He smiled. "I'd like that."

But even as he said it, I had my doubts it would ever happen. Noah was a small-town man. He'd built his entire life in Hope Harbor. My heart ached as I watched him waving goodbye from my rearview mirror.

IT WAS AWKWARD getting comfortable behind the wheel with the massive boot on my left ankle, but I felt wonderfully at ease heading away from this corner of the state. I found a place to boondock in my van in the Olympic National Forest, which was two hours south of Seattle and more than four hours away from Hope Harbor. My kitchen pantry and fridge were stocked with everything I'd need, and I was happy to settle into the rainy winter months and do nothing but relax at this location. I sent a text to Noah giving him a vague idea of my location but never got a reply. It hurt more than I wanted to admit.

Cell phone range was limited in the forest, but down a certain trail I could get a couple bars. I was there with Muffin on her leash pouncing on a windswept weed when I got a call from Sheriff Duthroyd.

"They've been found," he said.

"Penny and Tess?"

"Yes. They were found just outside of Spokane."

I exhaled loudly and had to lower myself onto my haunches as I drew air into my lungs. I thanked him profusely for letting me know.

When Muffin and I got back to the van, I took a new gun that replaced the one now held in evidence, and tucked it into the cubby next to my mattress. Part of me had still jumped at every sound thinking maybe, just maybe, the two of them had somehow traced me to my location in the middle of the forest. It was a massive relief knowing they'd been captured.

A few days later I heard from the sheriff again. He told me that Penny, Tess and Melody had all confessed and were willing to plead guilty. That was huge. It meant I would not have to be returning to that area for weeks or months of court cases in the future. Finally, I felt I could exhale and truly say that Hope Harbor was behind me. My heart ached a little at the thought, but I did my best to put thoughts of Noah out of my head.

It didn't take more than a few weeks for me to be relieved of the boot on my ankle. Every day it felt stronger and, as I combed the nearby trails, I could explore pretty far before it began to ache.

One particular day the November sun shone bright in the sky and the temperature was an unseasonable sixty degrees. I left Muffin behind and took a trail I'd grown to love. It wound its way for a half mile and ended at a rocky beach in a sheltered cove. I'd brought some of Brandy with me and I talked to her as I walked, sharing my hopes and fears, just like I'd always wanted to do when she was alive. When the sun began to set and it became an impossible red ball lowering into the green Pacific, I sprinkled a little of her ashes into the surf and watched them disappear out to sea.

I'd talked to Brandy's boyfriend a few times. Nick said Brandy's condo had sold and he'd deposited a hefty sum into my account. He'd also pestered me about going to work with him using the app and my psychic abilities. I told him I needed more time to make that decision and he promised to wait.

Although I knew the trail quite well by now, I didn't want to be wandering in the dark, so I hurried to return to the van before the last of the sun disappeared in the sea and the forest went to ebony.

When I burst out of the trail I stopped short and gasped. There, leaning against Bubbles's hood, stood Noah.

EIGHTEEN

"YOU TOLD ME you were camping in the Olympic National Park," he said, removing his ball cap and rubbing the back of his neck. "You didn't say where in the nine hundred thousand acres you'd be."

"Guess I didn't." I dug the dirt with the toe of my shoe and smiled sheepishly at him. "But you didn't ask."

"True. So, I stopped at the visitor center in Port Angeles and the gal that worked there told me there was a rumor about some strange bubble-covered van in a deep, secluded site." He smirked. "Since I figured it could only be you, she gave me the general vicinity."

"I got one thing to say to that." I folded my arms and frowned. "What took you so long?"

He tossed his cap to the ground and closed the gap between us in just a few long strides. I screamed in laughter and joy as he grabbed me by the waist and swung me around until we were both dizzy. Then we fell together, his lips on mine, and soon even the thin layer of clothes between us was too much of a barrier. We made frantic love against the rough bark of a western red cedar that was at least a hundred fifty feet tall. Afterward we made more leisurely love inside the snug confines of the camper van.

Nestled in the crook of his arm with my hand resting on his heart, I felt a longing to never have this end.

"Don't you get lonely?" Noah planted a tender kiss on the top of my head.

"Sometimes," I admitted. "But then I've always been lonelier in a crowd of strangers than in the forest by myself." Just then Muffin decided to pounce on Noah's fingers. "Besides, I have my attack cat."

The days were simple magic with long stretches in bed together with Muffin often purring and kneading the blankets around us. We jostled in the van's tight space to make our meals and then we'd walk the trails, find waterfalls to hike and spend lazy evenings watching movies downloaded on my laptop. Noah had his nephew covering the hardware store for a week and we made the best of those seven days. Even though it wasn't forever, it was still amazing.

As we took a stroll one day, there was something I needed to have cleared up and I asked him about the cups that littered the passenger side of his truck. But I didn't mention that one had given me a vision of him kissing Melody. He said he'd been talking to the marshal throughout the investigation to make sure he was on top of things, and the abandoned coffee cups belonged to the marshal, who'd leave them on the floor after they'd meet up in Noah's truck.

"That's a strange thing to bring up," Noah remarked with a playful punch in my shoulder. "You've been concerned all this time that I'm a slob?"

I laughed and then grew serious. "There are some things you don't know about me…" I began but was unable to finish.

He lifted my chin and looked me in the eyes. "I look forward to learning everything in time. When you're ready."

"You're settled in Hope Harbor. Your business, your home…" I shrugged and took a step back. "Your life is there." My gaze settled on my feet. "As much as I'd like us to have a future, I just don't see how…"

Noah gathered me in a snug embrace, kissing the top of my head and breathing into my hair. "Maybe it's time I got more help at the store so I can take vacations and long weekends. I don't mind driving to see you, as long as you don't mind making room for me in your life."

"I'd like that." I squeezed my eyes shut to prevent the tears of relief from escaping down my face.

On the day he was to leave, I tried to keep upbeat. I cooked a huge pancake breakfast and we lingered over coffee and then leisurely made love. He packed up his few belongings and gave Muffin a goodbye snuggle before I walked him to his truck.

I told Noah I was thinking of making my way down to Oregon for a bit.

"Keep in touch so I know where you are," he said.

I reminded him cell phone range wasn't great in forests but promised that when I moved locations I'd let him know where I'd be as soon as that was possible.

"Guess that'll have to be good enough." He kissed me goodbye in a way that made me want to beg him to stay.

But I didn't.

The next day I secured everything inside the van and drove south. I found a fairly busy campground to stay in for the first night so that I could use their laundry facility and refill my water tank. A young couple stopped by Bubbles to chat. We talked about life living out of a van. They said they'd been on the road in their camper for a few months and had settled here but now felt it was time to move on because they didn't feel safe.

"A woman was killed just down the road last night," the man said to me.

"So tomorrow we're out of here," the wife added. "Because they still haven't caught whoever killed her." Then she pointed in the direction of the firepit between our two camper vans. "Do you want to sit around the fire with us later?"

I thought about the local murder and instinctively I twirled Nan's ring around my finger. I felt a warm tingle inside my head as I slowly nodded.

"I love a good fire."

* * * * *

ACKNOWLEDGMENTS

My heartfelt praise goes to editor extraordinaire, Deborah Nemeth, and the Carina Team for their hard work. As always, I am grateful to my agent, Melissa Jeglinski, who always has my back.

ABOUT THE AUTHOR

Wendy Roberts is a mystery and supernatural writer living a supernormal life. Cloak and dagger are her bread and butter. She is the author of four novels in the Bodies of Evidence series, five Ghost Dusters mysteries, as well as *Dating Can Be Deadly* and *Grounds to Kill*. She is an armchair sleuth and a fan of all things mysterious. Wendy resides in Vancouver, Canada, where she happily tends to feral cats and rogue raccoons and writes about murder. When not tethered to her desk, you may find her, and her skull muse, Chewy, in a forest writing inside her camper van. She is always working on her next novel.

Website: www.WendyRoberts.com
Twitter: www.Twitter.com/AuthorWendy
Instagram: @WendyRoberts_Author
Facebook: www.Facebook.com/WendyRobertsAuthor
TikTok: @WendyRoberts_Author

HARLEQUIN
PLUS

Try the best multimedia subscription service for romance readers like you!

Read, Watch and Play.

Experience the easiest way to get the romance content you crave.

Start your **FREE TRIAL** at
<u>www.harlequinplus.com/freetrial</u>.